NEVER SHAKE A FAMILY TREE

And Other Heart-Stopping Tales
of Murder in New England

NEVER
SHAKE A
FAMILY TREE

And Other Heart-Stopping Tales
of Murder in New England

Edited by

Billie Sue Mosiman
and Martin H. Greenberg

RUTLEDGE HILL PRESS®
Nashville, Tennessee

Published in Nashville, Tennessee, by Rutledge Hill Press®, Inc., 211 Seventh Avenue North, Nashville, Tennessee 37219. Distributed in Canada by H. B. Fenn & Company, Ltd., 34 Nixon Road, Bolton, Ontario, L7E 1W2. Distributed in Australia by The Five Mile Press Pty. Ltd., 22 Summit Road, Noble Park, Victoria 3174. Distributed in New Zealand by Tandem Press, 2 Rugby Road, Birkenhead, Auckland 10. Distributed in the United Kingdom by Verulam Publishing, Ltd., 152a Park Street Lane, Park Street, St. Albans, Hertfordshire AL2 2AU.

Cover and book design by Harriette Bateman.
Typography by E. T. Lowe, Nashville, Tennessee.

Library of Congress Cataloging-in-Publication Data

Never shake a family tree, and other heart-stopping tales of murder in
    New England / edited by Billie Sue Mosiman and Martin H.
    Greenberg.
        p.   cm.
    ISBN 1–55853–577–2
    1. Detective and mystery stories, American—New England.
2. Murder—New England—Fiction.   I. Mosiman, Billie Sue.
II. Greenberg, Martin Harry.
PS648.D4N46   1998
813'.0872083274—dc21   98–4799
                                                          CIP

Printed in the United States of America

1 2 3 4 5 6 7 8 9 — 03 02 01 00 99 98

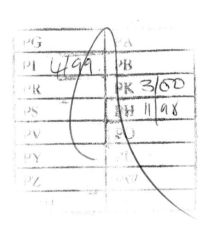

CONTENTS

INTRODUCTION

John Updike said, "There is no pleasing New Englanders, my dear, their soil is all rocks and their hearts are bloodless absolutes."

Updike might have been a little harsh, but it is true that the weather, the geography, and the people of New England are rugged.

In the following stories, that rugged nature is nicely illustrated. You'll find an inhospitable New England countryside in "The Old Barn on the Pond," by Ursula Curtiss. Someone wants to drain that pond. But it's much too early. "Not yet," the narrator says. "Not after only six months."

Linda Barnes, in "Lucky Penny," will take you along with her tough-talking, cab-driving female P.I. in Boston, Massachusetts. "Rugged" is exactly the adjective to describe her and the characters she runs into during her cab driving stints.

Taking us back into the past, S. S. Rafferty, in "The Rhode Island Lights," drops us into the autumn of 1736 and the struggling colonies where a man handily solves crimes that would puzzle a less imaginative detective.

Despite, not because of, ice storms and snow drifts, short summers and brilliant autumns, New England has its share of the crime of murder. From the time of the early colonists until today, the terrain has taken its toll on the population. It made them rugged, brave, and hardy. But sometimes, locked into the icy cold, unable to seek company or release for many months, those same strong individuals turned into themselves and nursed injustices, slights, and rebukes until there was nothing to do but strike out.

In this volume you will find the heroes and villains of New England—the great detectives, the amateur sleuths, and the slippery killers they track down. If you hear a north wind, it's just that, not an intruder at the door. If you feel a stray icy finger of breeze along the floor, it's simply a draft, and surely not coming from an open window where malevolence lurks.

Wrap up tight, get a warm drink, and enjoy the tales herein, written by some of the best in the field. It is our hope that even New Englanders, who Updike claims there is "no pleasing," will nevertheless be pleased by this collection of sinister doings in New England.

Billie Sue Mosiman
1997

NEVER SHAKE A FAMILY TREE

And Other Heart-Stopping Tales of Murder in New England

Ursula Curtiss wrote over twenty novels that successfully combined gothic elements with the detective story to create a surprising new type of mystery. Featuring everyday characters drawn into danger through seemingly mundane errands or events, her novels are swiftly paced, intriguing examples of the well-plotted mystery. Her stint as a columnist for the Fairfield, Connecticut, newspaper gave her a keen insight into the foibles of human life, which is reflected in her stories.

The Old Barn on the Pond

Ursula Curtiss

He came back on a raw, darkly glistening day in March, but it was not at all the triumphant return he had planned. It was a hasty, off-balance thing, like being pushed rudely onto a stage before the raised trumpets had blown a single note.

Conlon's letter—the letter that had brought him tumbling up from New York to this inhospitable part of the New England countryside—was still in his pocket. He had never liked Conlon, but the architect was Marian's cousin and it would have looked odd, when he had the old barn remodeled, to have given the job to someone else. And now here was Conlon writing " . . . have been approached by friends about the possibility of renting your property here for the summer, with an option to buy. As they have a young child, they would like to drain the pond, and although I told them I was certain you would not permit this—"

For a moment the typed lines had blurred before Howard Hildreth's eyes—except for that one staring phrase.

Drain the pond.

"Not yet," he thought lucidly—"not after only six months." Anonymous in the Forty-second Street Library, he had read up on the subject, and learned that under certain conditions—depth of water, amount of rainfall, and other climatic factors—this kind of soil might have sucked its secret under at the end of a year, provided there was no extensive digging.

But not yet. He had sat down at once to write a brief note of refusal, but another phrase struck up at him from Conlon's letter. " . . . I was certain you would not permit this—"

A deliberate challenge? Bill Conlon was Marian's cousin, remember, and had been away at the time. Better go up there, stay a week or two, establish the impression of keeping the place as a country retreat upon which he might descend at any time. It was only necessary for Conlon; the townspeople, he was sure, accepted his remodeling of the barn as proof of his faith that his missing wife would some day return.

At that thought, alone in his comfortable apartment, Howard Hildreth shuddered. . . .

On the station platform there were gratifying little whispers and stirs of recognition—"Isn't that Howard Hildreth, the playwright? I'm sure it is"—and a turning of heads which he pretended not to see. He could hardly pretend not to see Conlon, striding across the platform toward him with his fair head a little cocked. Conlon had Marian's eyes, light gray with a peculiar curl of lid; but that was the only physical resemblance between them.

Hildreth put out a hand and said with an air of geniality. "Well, this is kind. I hope you haven't been meeting trains all day?"

Conlon sent one of his roving glances around the platform. "Matter of fact, a fellow in our office was supposed to catch this one but he seems to have missed it. Come on, I'll give you a lift."

After his first annoyance at Conlon's balloon-pricking, Hildreth was pleased; this would give him a chance to demonstrate his calm. He said as they got into the car, "I can see how you thought I wouldn't be using the place this summer. I'd have been in touch with you sooner about coming up but we've had a little trouble in the cast."

He waited for Conlon to show interest, but the other man only said, "Too bad. Play still going well?"

"Very, thanks."

"I particularly liked"—Conlon turned a sharp corner with care—"the third act. It packs quite a wallop. Are you working on a new play?"

"I am, as a matter of fact, and I thought a little peace and quiet . . . You know New York," said Hildreth resignedly. In his tone were autograph hunters, sheaves of fan mail, a telephone carrying an invitation with each ring.

And part of it was true. *The Far Cry* was the rarest of things, a hit first play, and the playbill's revelation that it had been eight years in the writing had given an additional fillip. Eight years—what constancy! No wonder that superb third act expertly shivered like a diamond. Here was no glib young creature with a gift for bubbling out dialogue but a major talent who cut his work like a precious stone.

So the critics said, and the important hostesses, and Howard Hildreth, who had been laughed at in this little town, and had his credit refused and his electric light turned off, found his champagne all the winier and forgot those few hours of frantic typing. . . .

" . . . not a word," Conlon was saying, and Hildreth wrenched his attention from his play, his other self. They were out of the town now, rising into little hills and woodland, puddled and glinted yellowly by a sky which, having rained earlier, was now gloating over it.

Hildreth's mind spun back and recaptured the sense of his companion's words. He said, "Nor I. But I refuse to believe . . . you knew Marian—"

"I think she's dead," said Conlon bluntly without turning his head. "I think she was dead all the time the police were out looking for her."

"But . . . where—?" said Hildreth in a shocked voice.

Conlon waved a hand at the dimming landscape. "There's almost as much water as there is land around here," he said. "Lake, marshes, even quicksand. She had such a horror of things eaten up in the water, remember?"

"Stop!" said Hildreth with genuine violence. "You mustn't talk about her as though—Besides, Marian was happy, she would never have—"

"Committed suicide, or disappeared on purpose?" said Conlon when it was apparent that Hildreth was not going to finish. "Oh, I never thought she had. As you say, I knew Marian . . . here we are."

The car had descended a gentle twisting curve. At the bottom, opposite a stand of birches and set perhaps a hundred feet in from the road, was the pond, as round and clear as a wondering eye, lashed by willows that looked lamplit in the approaching dusk.

On the far side of it, on a slight rise, stood the creamy new structure, the remodeled barn, which six months ago had been weather-beaten planks and a wobbly brown-painted door. There was no breath of wind; the house and reflection met themselves in a mirror stillness.

Howard Hildreth gazed, and his heart raced with such horror that he wondered if he was about to have a stroke. He wrenched at his horn-rimmed glasses with a trembling hand, and heard Conlon say curiously, "Are you all right, Howard?"

"Yes. These damned glasses—the doctor warned me that I needed new ones." Even the effort of speaking calmly seemed to put a nut-cracker pressure on his heart. "You've done a beautiful job of remodeling the barn, Bill. The photographs you sent didn't do it justice. Shall we go on in?"

The drive up to the house itself was screened by willows. By the time Conlon had helped him inside with his bags, Hildreth was able to say almost normally, "Well, here we are. You'll have a drink, won't you?"

Conlon shook his head. He said with a hand on the doorknob, "Sarah—Sarah Wilde, you know—ordered a few essentials for the kitchen, so you ought to get through the night without starving. Well—"

Hildreth did not press him to stay. He said, standing in the open doorway, "These friends of yours that I had to disappoint—do I know them? What's their name?"

"Pocock," said Conlon promptly, and it was so unlikely a name that Hildreth had to believe him. Or was it meant to be a shortened version of poppycock?

He did not even look around at the long studio that took up most of the lower front of the house. He waited tensely for the final retreat of Conlon's motor, and when even the echoes were gone he opened the door and walked the length of the driveway in the lonely frog-sounding dusk.

And there was light enough—just enough—to show him the same sickening apparition. On the far side of the pond stood the new barn, radiantly pale, bearing no resemblance to its former weather-beaten brown. But at his feet, glassily etched on the surface of the water, lay the old barn, with its knotholes and weather stains and the wide brown-painted door.

Hildreth drew a long uneven breath. There was no one to see him step squashily to the reed-grown edge of the pond and dip a hand in the icy water. The old barn quaked under the willows, and shook and was presently still again—but it was still the old barn. . . .

★   ★   ★

He did not drink—Marian had—but he took a tranquilizer and headed for his reviews like a child to its mother's skirts. The *Times, Tribune, Daily News,* the out-of-town papers. "Last night at the Odeon Theatre this critic was refreshingly jolted. . . ."

"*The Far Cry* is just that in a season so far noted for its weary offerings. . . ." "Let us hope we do not have to wait another eight years for the next Hildreth play. . . ."

And presently he knew what had happened to him out there at the pond's edge. Autosuggestion, hallucination—at any rate, there was an accepted term for it; if beauty lay in the beholder's eye, so did other things. He knew what was under that pleasant and pastoral surface, and at the subconscious tension of his mind, because Conlon had been with him, his retina had produced the appropriate setting.

But not for Conlon, with all his suspicions—and in retrospect, the man had exuded suspicion. Conlon had looked at the pond and seen nothing amiss; for him, the still water had reflected only his personal creation of shored-up beams and plaster and creamy paint and whatever else went into his remodeling of an old structure. The thought gave Hildreth a satisfaction that, keyed up as he was, bordered on triumph.

What a joke on them all, he mused as he broiled the steak Sarah Wilde had left in the refrigerator, if only he, Hildreth, could see this watery witness, gaze at it in their presence, say casually, "Lovely day, isn't it?"—and stand there calmly and casually in the midst of their blindness.

Not that the reflection would be on the pond in the morning. Tonight it had simply been a product of nerves and fatigue, and a good night's sleep would erase it. Still, he was shaken, and he prudently avoided his after-dinner coffee. He darkened the downstairs, flipped on the staircase switch, and went up to his bedroom.

And came face to face with a portrait of Marian which he never knew had been taken.

As the blood came and went from his heart more slowly, he realized that the matted and mounted photograph on the bureau was not a portrait but an enlarged snapshot; on closer inspection it bore a telltale grain and blurriness. It was in color and it showed Marian laughing. There was a halo of sunlight on the close curls that scrambled over her beautifully shaped head, and the same light picked out the comma of mirth beside her mouth although her short, soft, full white throat was in shadow.

Marian laughing . . .

. . . laughing at his play, which she was not supposed to have seen at all until he had written the final word—*Curtain.* Managing to say through the laughter, "My dear playwright, you don't mean to say you've been muddling around with this thing for eight years and missed the whole *point?* It ought to be satire at the end, don't you see, and you fox the audience in the third act instead of this heavy Russian gloom going on and on? It would have such a wonderful, final crack-the-whip effect, and you could get rid of Anna coming in and saying"—she draggled at her hair, which was much too short and curly for draggling—"whatever that long lugubrious speech is."

Her face was brilliant with excited laughter. "Oh, *wait* till I tell Bill and Sarah we've found a way to finish the Odyssey at last! They'll be so—Howard, for heaven's sake, I'm only—*Howar*—"

For such a full throat, it was as soft and weak as a child's. . . .

In the morning Hildreth looked at the pond, and the old weather-beaten barn was still there, shaken and distorted under a gently falling rain. Disturbingly, he was not terrified or shocked or even very surprised; it was as though, at some point during his sleep, his brain had accepted this phenomenon as readily as the pond had accepted Marian.

After breakfast he made arrangements for renting a car, and then he called Sarah Wilde.

It was through Sarah, who also had an apartment in the building on East Tenth Street, that he had met Marian Guest. Sarah and Marian were copywriters in the same advertising agency, and although Hildreth had a sober loathing of advertising copy and all the people who wrote it—there was a flippancy about them that appalled him—Sarah was well connected. An aunt of hers was a best-selling novelist, and it had never harmed any hopeful playwright to have even a hearsay acquaintance with a publisher. He had cultivated Sarah in the elevator, lent her an umbrella one day, and ultimately wound up at a party in her apartment.

And there was Marian, sitting on the floor although there were chairs available. She wore black slacks and an expensive-looking white silk shirt with a safety pin where a button should have been, and, profile tilted in the lamplight, she was explaining with zest how she had come by her black eye and scraped cheekbone. She had been walking her dog George and had fallen over a sheep on a leash. "The man said it was a Bedlington but he was obviously trying to cover up his own confusion. Poor George bit him, not the man, and I think he's got a hair ball."

Although there were two or three other girls present, all with a just-unboxed Madison Avenue attractivess, the attention seemed to cluster about Marian. She said presently to Howard Hildreth in her boyish and uninhibited voice, "You look terribly broody. What are you hatching?"

"A play," he told her distantly, and it might have been the very distance that attracted her, as it was the attention focused on her that attracted him. At any rate, he ended up taking her home to her apartment on Barrow Street, drinking innumerable cups of black coffee, and telling her about his play. He began challengingly, prepared for amusement when she learned that he had already been working on it for three years; but she listened, her light clear eyes as wide and sober as a child's.

She said, "What do you do—for an income, I mean?"

When he said flatly, "I'm a shoe clerk," she stared past him with a kind of wondering sadness.

"How marvelous," she had said, "to give that much of a damn about anything."

There was Marian, summed up in a single sentence; even after they were married she never told him anything as self-revelatory as that. And under the influence of her respect for his dedication, his work, which had always been his Work to him, was able to come out in the open with its capital letter. Until she had defected—

But Hildreth had learned to discipline his mind, and he did it now.

He said into the telephone, "Sarah? I'm an ingrate for not calling you last night to tell you how much I like the way you've done the place—as well as providing my dinner—but. . . ."

Sarah Wilde cut him off easily. "Do you like it? I'm glad. It's rather a lot of lavender, but you did specify—"

"Yes," Hildreth gazed, secretly entertained, at the lavender draperies, the lavender cushions, round and square and triangular, piled on the black tweed couch. Lavender—Marian's favorite color. Any doubters close to Marian could not help saying to themselves, "Well, if he can live with that. . . ."

"It's very soothing," he said to Sarah with the defensive air of a husband standing up for his wife's vagaries. "Very restful. I like the picture on my bureau, by the way."

It was as though the telephone cord had been pulled taut between them. "It is a good one, isn't it? I took it—oh, some time last summer, I think, and I'd forgotten all about it until Bill Conlon happened to see it and thought you'd like an enlargement."

"It was very thoughtful of you both," said Hildreth with perfect evenness. "That's the way I think of her, you know. Laughing. I suppose Bill's told you that I haven't given up hope."

"Of course you haven't," said Sarah, bright and artificial.

Between them, in the small silence that followed, lay the many trips that he and Conlon had taken to view unidentified female bodies which corresponded even roughly with Marian's age and height. It was grim work, which helped; he was always a thoroughly pale and shaken man. And with each fruitless trip, because of the very nature of such an errand, the official belief that Marian Hildreth was dead had grown. Hildreth could tell that Sarah believed it too—in which, of course, she was quite right.

She was veering quickly away from the subject now, saying something about dinner this week. Hildreth accepted for Thursday evening, adding with a deprecating little laugh that he trusted it wouldn't be an Occasion; he'd come up here to get started on his new play.

"No, just two or three people," Sarah assured him. "I did tell you, didn't I, how much I liked *The Far Cry?* I thought I knew what was coming in the third act, but it was one time I loved being made a fool of."

Hildreth thanked her, a trifle aloofly, and there was not the smallest alarm along his nerves. He suspected that Sarah and Conlon, mere acquaintances six months ago, would be married before the year was out, but the fact that they had undoubtedly seen the play together didn't matter. They could not say, "That last act sounds like Marian," because as far as they knew Marian had never laid eyes on the script—she had said wryly, in fact, two or three days before that last night, "Howard thinks I'll mark his baby, like a gypsy. . . ."

(What a very tellable joke it would have been, what an irresistible nugget for gossip columns, because Marian's was not a secret-keeping nature: that Howard Hildreth had toiled unremittingly over his play for eight years, and in the space of a single hour his wife, who had never written anything but tongue-in-cheek praise of vinyl tile and slide fasteners, had offhandedly supplied the satirical twist that made it a success.)

Even at the thought Hildreth felt a qualm of nausea. Although his portable typewriter stood ready on the desk at the far end of the studio, with a fresh ream of yellow paper beside it, he let himself out the front door into the falling rain and walked to the pond's edge. There was the old barn, shaking dimly under the falling drops, and he knew that in some terrible way he was drawing strength from this private vision, locked under the willows for his eyes, and apparently for his alone. . . .

A notion of incipient madness slid across his mind, but he looked quickly about him and everything else was sane and clear. If Marian thought to retaliate after death. . . .

He drew himself up sharply.

In the afternoon he was gracious to the editor of the local newspaper, with the result that his favorite publicity picture appeared in the next morning's issue. He was holding his horn-rimmed glasses with one earpiece casually collapsed, and the three-quarter turn of his head almost concealed the double chin developed since those lean days.

" . . . seeking inspiration for his new play," said the account below, proudly, and, "Residents will recall the still-unresolved disappearance of Mrs. Marian Hildreth six months ago. Mrs. Hildreth, 38, told her husband late on the evening of October 4, 1963, that she was going out for a walk. She did not return, and no trace of her has since been found. Mr. Hildreth maintains his staunch belief that his wife is still alive, possibly suffering from a loss of memory. . . ."

Hildreth read with calm pleasure the rest of the telling—how the pond on the property land had been dragged without result. The police had indeed dragged it over his demurs—"Oh, come now, she wouldn't fall into a pond she's lived beside for five years"—and then came the heavily tactful, "Mr. Hildreth, your wife wasn't—er . . . ?"

Because Marian's more madcap exploits were not unknown to the local police. They viewed her with a tolerant and even an indulgent eye—that was the effect she had on people; but under the circumstances they could not rule out a tragic and alcoholic whim.

"No," Hildreth had said with transparent stoutness. "Oh, she may have had a highball or two after dinner. . . ."

He knew, he had known at the moment of her death, that the marital partner was usually Suspect Number One. But that had not actually held true in little Ixton, Connecticut. If there had been any whisper of discord, any suggestion of dalliance by either party, any prospect of inheriting money—or even if Marian's life had been insured—the police might have looked deeper than they did. As it was, they walked past the burlaped yew, the burlaped roses, Marian's burlaped body, and then announced that they would drag the pond.

This procedure netted them two ancient inner tubes, a rotted and hinged object which had once been the hood of a convertible, and a rust-fretted oil drum which seemed to have spawned a great many beer cans. If the police had returned at just after dark, when one particular piece of burlap among the yews had been lifted free of its stiffened secret, and the secret transferred to the now officially blameless water . . . but, predictably, they had not.

They could have no further reason for dragging the pond now—indeed, thought Hildreth, they would need a warrant. And for a warrant they would need evidence.

That was the safety element in a spur-of-the-moment murder. The cleverest planners—Hildreth rejected the word *killers*—had come to grief over elaborate timetables, unsuspected correspondence, a hint of fear dropped somewhere. There could be none of that in this case. Neither he nor Marian had known what was coming until that moment of her crowing laughter, that intolerable tearing-down of the secrecy and seriousness of his Work.

It was not so much that Marian had burst the bonds of curiosity and somehow contrived to unlock the desk drawer which housed his script, nor even that she had slipped at least temporarily into the ranks of the people who found him clownishly amusing. It was that she was right. Like someone engaged on a painstaking tapestry, he had been following stitch after stitch and lost sight of the pattern, which had leaped at once to Marian's unbothered and mischievous eye.

It was as if . . . he could not say at the time, because his logic had smoked away like cellophane in a flame. Later, more calmly, he could compare himself to a woman who, after a long and difficult labor, watches the doctor merrily bearing the infant off to his own home.

But there was no evidence, and he would not be tricked or trapped. His visit here—the first since the five weeks or so after he had reported Marian missing—would proclaim his innocence. Not to the police—he wasn't worried about them—but to Bill Conlon and Sarah Wilde, the only people who, close to Marian, might just possibly. . . .

Hildreth arranged yellow paper beside his uncovered typewriter in the white-walled lavender-and-black studio, but he did not, that morning or the next or the one after that, commence even the roughest work on a new play.

He told himself defensively that he had spent several months under considerable strain; a man didn't bounce back from that right away. And critical success was paralyzing in itself: there was the inevitable restudying of the first work in search of the magic ingredient, and the equally inevitable fear of comparison with a second.

At no time did he allow it to cross his mind that there were one-play playwrights as there were one-book novelists, and that his one play would still be in various stages of rewriting except for Marian's unruly wit. But there was a moment when, seated blankly at the typewriter, he thought, *Do I look like the pond?* and got up and crossed the room to examine himself in a mirror.

But no; he hadn't changed at all in spite of his damp little tremor of fright. And if he could see the truth on the pond's surface, surely he could see it on his own? There was the gained weight, granted, but his dark eyes gave back their old serious look, his eyebrows were forbiddingly level, a lock of hair—now pampered by his New York barber— still hung with dedication.

But when he stared long enough and hard enough, moving his face to within an inch or two of the mirror, tiny little Howard Hildreths peeked out of the pupils, and behind them—

Ah, behind *them*. . . .

He developed a kind of triumphant passion for the pond. He watched it ballooned with clouds, or covered with nervous little wrinkles under a sudden wind. He saw the weather-beaten planks and the brown door warp and fly to pieces under the miniature tidal waves caused by water bugs or perhaps frogs. Pretending to enjoy a cigarette in the course of a stroll, he took note of the passing cars that slowed for an admiring view of the clean creamy little house behind the willowed pond, and no car jerked to a shocked halt, no one screamed.

Hildreth had a Polaroid camera, and one afternoon, in a fascinated test, he took a picture of the pond. Conlon's photographs had shown no abnormality, but this time it was he who was pressing the shutter. The day warranted color film—the willows dripped and candled about the round eye of water, enameled so perfectly that it might have been a brooch.

Wouldn't it be odd, thought Hildreth, counting excitedly to sixty, if only the camera and I—?

He was peeling the paper shield away when Sarah Wilde's voice said at his shoulder, "Oh, may I see?"

The print and its fluttering attachment dropped to the ground.

Hildreth got only a swinging glimpse of Sarah's slanted white cheek, caught only the beginning of the rueful, "I'm sorry, I didn't mean—" before he bent, barely circumventing her; if necessary he would have put his shoe on the print.

As it was, he snatched it up and turned away, manufacturing a cough, while he finished stripping the shield. He said a second later, turning back, "Not bad, is it?" and handed the innocent color print to Sarah. No, not the camera and himself—only himself.

Sarah, he thought watchfully, was a remarkably beautiful young woman. Her dropped lashes were a thick unretouched silver-brown, her polished hair a slightly deeper brown; her gaze, when she lifted it, would be gray. With the suave red lipstick to counterpoint the water-color effect, she was quietly startling in any gathering.

"Very good indeed," she said, handing the print back by its edges. "The pond's so pretty, isn't it? Especially now."

She glanced at the circle of water and then back at Hildreth, who following her gaze had still seen the placidly mirrored old barn. A tremble of nerves ran along his throat. To control a wild impulse toward laughter he said in a considering, landownerish way, "It seems quite full, but you've had heavy rains this month, haven't you?" and he slid the print casually into his coat pocket.

"Yes, it is full," said Sarah in his own considering tone, and there was no doubt about it; the eyes that moved from the pond to his face held some kind of—doubt? Challenge? Hildreth said coolly, "Well, if you'll excuse me, it's back to the typewriter," and he took a step away.

"Wait, I almost forgot what I came for," Sarah was dripping into her calf handbag. "Here—the mailman put this in my box instead of yours. Wonderful to get fan mail. Don't forget about dinner tonight—cocktails at six thirty."

It wasn't fan mail which Hildreth opened when the red Volkswagen had disappeared over the hill, but one of the many letters which, the police had told him, always arrived in the wake of a disappearance. This one was from "Someone Who Can Help," and in exchange for two hundred dollars mailed to an enclosed box number in Vermont the writer would put him in touch with his missing wife.

The maddening part of these communications was that they could not be ignored—at least, not by a man in whom hope supposedly sprang eternal. Hildreth, sitting down to write the form reply that thanked the writer and said he was turning the letter over to the officers in charge of the investigation, thought angrily that there ought to be a law.

The afternoon passed slowly. Conlon telephoned to say that there would be a plumber coming over to do something to the downstairs bath, and Hildreth said pettishly, "Really, Bill, forgive me, but I thought all that had been taken care of. One doesn't greet plumbers in the middle of Scene One, you know."

He was mollified a little later by a delegation from the local high-school magazine, asking humbly for a "Best Wishes from Howard Hildreth" to be photostated for the graduation issue. One of the shiny-haired, wide-eyed girls ventured close to his typewriter, in which Hildreth foresightedly kept a typed yellow sheet—the opening scene of *The Far Cry*—and he said at once, austerely, "Please don't—I have a 'thing' about work in progress."

It only added to their awe. But he had had it, thought Hildreth, presently seeing them to the door, he had had all the local adulation he wanted. Imperiously buying delicacies at the only market that carried them, he had seen the fawning face of the manager who only a year ago had told him that if his bill wasn't settled promptly he would find himself in the small-claims court.

He had been pointed out respectfully on the main street, and had declined invitations from the town's reigning hostess. More importantly, he had been accepted everywhere without a trace of suspicion; if there was any sentiment in the air, it was one of embarrassed pity for a man who so courageously continued to hope.

In a day or two he could go back to New York, having established to Bill Conlon and Sarah Wilde and everybody else that there was no question of his selling or even renting the property with its pretty, deadly pond.

He was all the more shocked, in the midst of these comfortable reflections, when at a little after three he had a call from a Sergeant Fisk at the police station. Some little girls looking for pussy willows in a field on the outskirts of the town had discovered a woman's leather handbag and part of a dress with some suggestive stains; would Hildreth please come down and see if he could identify them?

"Certainly," said Hildreth, staring angrily out the window. "Of course, being out in the weather, I imagine they're pretty well—?"

"No, sir, they were stuffed in the remains of an old stone wall and they're still in fair condition. Recognizable, anyway."

"I'll leave right away," said Hildreth, tempering his eagerness with the right amount of dread.

At the police station he was asked to wait—Sergeant Fisk would be right with him.

By four o'clock Sergeant Fisk still was not with him; at four thirty, fuming, Hildreth walked up to the uniformed man at the switchboard and said sharply, "I came here at the request of Sergeant Fisk to look at some objects for identification, and I cannot wait any longer. Please leave a message—"

"Just a minute, sir," said the policeman unruffledly, and slipped a plug into its socket and inquired for Sergeant Fisk. "There's a Mr. Hildreth here, been waiting since—okay, I'll tell him to go right in."

But the handbag and dress fragment, when Hildreth reached Sergeant Fisk's office, had been transferred to Lieutenant Martin's office, where there was some question as to their possible connection with the vanishing of a Colorado couple making a cross-country tour four months ago. Hildreth contained his temper as he went with the sergeant to Martin's office; he was, he remembered, a man who would do anything to find a clue to his wife's fate.

He was badly tempted when, at after five o'clock, he surveyed a rotted and mildewed navy calf handbag, empty, and the sleeve and half the bodice of what had once been a yellow wool dress. Why not say, "Yes, they're my wife's," and bury his face in his hands and be done with it?

Because, he thought with a feeling of having stepped back from the edge of a cliff, Marian had never worn yellow—she said it made her look like a two-legged hangover; and there was a suggestion of something on the leather lining of the bag that could easily be a nearly obliterated name or monogram. Hildreth had read what modern police laboratories could do with things like that. So he shook his head and said, "They're not my wife's," and with a shudder at the stains on the rotting yellow wool, "Thank God."

Three hours, he thought as he drove home seething in the rainy dusk; three hours on a fool's errand which he could not have risked refusing. Just barely time to dress for dinner at Sarah Wilde's—and then get out of here, tomorrow.

He was restored at the thought, and at the glimpse of the old barn quivering on the pond in the last of the light as he drove to Sarah's. His temper was further improved by Sarah's big, casually gay living room—two rooms thrown together in a very old saltbox—and the contrast between an open fire and a cold rattling rain on the windows.

The other guests were already established with drinks—Conlon, a Mr. and Mrs. Slater, and Mrs. Slater's decorative visiting sister.

Hildreth thawed, physically and temperamentally. He felt a slight jar of recognition when he was introduced to the Slaters, but he had undoubtedly encountered them on a station platform at some forgotten time, or in a local store. He noted with approval that Sarah had obviously got someone in for the evening, because there were sounds of kitchen activity while Sarah sat on the couch, in black and pearls, beside Conlon.

On the rare occasions when he and Marian had entertained, Marian had charged in and out like a demented puppy, crying, "My God, who's been watching the beans? Nobody!" Or, abashedly, "We all like nutmeg instead of pepper in our mashed potatoes, don't we?"

Sarah had turned her head and was gazing at him; somebody had clearly asked a question. Hildreth used a handkerchief on his suddenly damp forehead and temples and said, "I got wetter than I thought— that's really quite a downpour," and he got up to stand by the fire.

And the bad moment was gone, further wiped out by Sarah's "You said you mightn't be here long on this visit, Howard, so we're having your favorite dinner—you know, what you won't eat in restaurants."

"Don't tell me . . . ?" said Hildreth, delighted, but it was: trout, a crisp deep-gold outside, succulent white within, delicately enhanced by herbs that only hinted at themselves. He ate with deliberate pleasure, not succumbing until close to the end of dinner to his habit of providing backgrounds for people.

The extraordinarily good-looking sister from New Haven—her name was Vivian Hughes—seemed the kind of young woman who, convinced in her teens that she could have any man she wanted, had ended up with none; there was a kind of forced grace to the frequent turn of her head, and lines of discontent around her really striking green eyes.

Mrs. Slater wasn't a fair test, because she had ticketed herself earlier by a reference to the young twins they had left with a baby-sitter, and by her very casualness she had given herself away. She was the new and on the whole the best breed of mother, thought Hildreth approvingly; slender, amiable, intelligent, she kept her maternal dotings strictly for hearth and home.

Slater? Hildreth gazed obliquely through candlelight at the other man, perhaps a year or two younger than his own forty. The lean, polished, ruddy face suggested an outdoorsman, but everything else pointed to an executive. He went on gazing, and like an exposed print washed gently back and forth in developer, outlines began to emerge.

A desk, not executive grain, but scarred oak. Two telephones on it. A uniformed man in a far doorway saying, "Yes, sir, right away," then disappearing down one of a warren of corridors.

Yes, Slater was a police officer of some sort, or a detective, glimpsed or perhaps even talked to in the first stages of the investigation six months ago. And Sarah and Conlon hoped that he would be terrified by this recognition, and go to pieces. That was the whole point of this friendly little gathering.

How very disappointed they must be. Hildreth stirred his coffee tranquilly, because no motive for murder had existed until sixty seconds before Marian died, and there wasn't a single clue. In an enjoyment of the attention he now knew to be trained on him he said in a well-fed voice, "Marvelous dinner, Sarah. I don't know when I've had trout like that," and Sarah said, "As a matter of fact, you never have."

She was leaning forward a little in the candlelight, her gaze cool and removed. "The trout were from your pond, Howard, and they were caught this afternoon while you were down at the police station. You didn't know that Marian had had the pond stocked for you, as a birth-day present, just before she—disappeared, because you love trout but never trust it in restaurants. We didn't know about it either until the friend who did it for her stopped by to see Bill a couple of weeks ago."

Hildreth's neck felt caught in one of those high white collars you saw on injured people; he could not turn it even when he heard Conlon's, "Nice fat trout, I thought, but lazy. They bite at anything."

. . . while he had sat in the police station, decoyed there by a tele-phone call.

"You all ate it," said Hildreth triumphantly, in a candlelight that had begun to tremble and dampen his face. "You all—"

"No. Ours was perch from the Old Town Fish Market," said Sarah, and although she continued to hold his gaze, her forehead had a cold glimmer and her mouth seemed clenched against a scream.

Hildreth lost them all then. He dropped his eyes, but instead of his dessert cup he saw his dinner plate, with the neat spiny bones from which all the succulent white flesh had been forked away. Marian's soft white throat, and the busy, inquisitive, nibbling mouths at the bottom of the pond, and the plump things placed on his plate—

He heard his chair go crashing back, and the gagging cry of horror that issued from his own throat as he plunged blindly for some-where to be sick; and, from a mist, Slater's voice saying, " . . . looks like it. Very definitely. We'll get at it first thing in the morning. . . ."

Margaret Maron is the multiple Agatha and Anthony Award–winning author of the Deborah Knott series, about a district judge in North Carolina. Before that, she wrote about Sigrid Harald, a New York City police lieutenant. A past president of Sisters in Crime, she is also active in the Mystery Writers of America and the Carolina Crime Writers Association. Recent novels include Killer Market and Shoveling Smoke. In the following story, Lieutenant Harald goes on a modern-day treasure hunt and uncovers a most unusual prize.

Lieutenant Harald and the *Treasure Island* Treasure

Margaret Maron

I thought you liked puzzles," argued Oscar Nauman's disembodied voice.

"I do," Lieutenant Sigrid Harald answered, balancing the telephone receiver on her shoulder as she struggled with a balky can opener. "That's one of the reasons I joined the NYPD. I get paid for it, Nauman. I don't have to waste a free weekend."

"But this is a real buried treasure. One of my former students is going to lose her inheritance if it isn't found soon, and I told her we'd help."

As one of America's leading abstract artists, Oscar Nauman could have sold one or two paintings a year and lived in comfortable retirement on some Mediterranean island. Instead, he continued to chair the art department at Vanderlyn College over on the East River where Sigrid first met him during a homicide investigation. The end of the case hadn't been the end of their acquaintance, though. He kept walking in and out of her life as if he had a right there, lecturing, bullying, and keeping her off balance. Her prickly nature seemed to amuse him, and Sigrid had quit trying to analyze why he persisted.

Or why she allowed it.

"We can drive up tonight," said Nauman. "Unless," he added craftily, knowing her aversion to sunrises, "you'd rather leave around six tomorrow morning?"

"Now listen, Nauman, I don't—" The can opener slipped. "Oh, damn! I just dumped soup all over the blasted stove."

"Throw it out. I'll pick you up in thirty minutes and we'll have dinner on the way."

"I am *not* going to Connecticut," she said firmly, but he had already hung up.

Fourteen hours later, she sat on the terrace of Nauman's Connecticut house and placidly bit into a second Danish. A good night's sleep had removed most of her annoyance at being dragged from the city and hurtled through the night at Nauman's usual speed-of-light driving. The sun was shining, the air was warm, and she had found an unworked double-crostic in an elderly issue of the New York *Times*.

She looked contented as a cat, thought Nauman. Her long dark hair was pinned at the nape more loosely than usual, and her faded jeans and cream-colored knit shirt were more becoming than those shapeless pantsuits she wore in town. Thin to the point of skinniness, with a mouth too wide for conventional beauty and a neck too long, her cool grey eyes were her best feature, but these were presently engrossed in her paper.

He'd been up for hours and was so impatient to be off that he swept cups, carafe, and the remaining sweet rolls back onto the large brass tray and carted it all away without asking Sigrid if she'd finished.

"I thought your friend wasn't expecting us before ten," she said, following Nauman to the kitchen where she retrieved her cup and refilled it while he loaded the dishwasher.

"It'll take us about that long to walk over." He took her cup and poured it in the sink.

"Walk?" Sigrid was appalled.

"Less than a mile as the crow flies. You walk more than that every day."

"But that's on concrete," she protested. "In the city. You're talking about trees and snakes and briars, aren't you?"

"It used to be an Indian trading path," Nauman coaxed, leading her out through the terrace gate. "It'll be like a walk through Central Park."

"I hate walking in Central Park," Sigrid muttered, but she followed him across a narrow meadow to a scrub forest. As Nauman disappeared behind a curtain of wild grapevines, she hesitated a moment, then took a deep breath and plunged in after him.

Ten minutes later, sweaty, her ankles whipped by thorns, a stinging scratch on her arm, she was ready for mutiny. "No Indians ever walked through this jungle."

"Not this part. We're taking a shortcut. The path is just past those tall oaks."

"If it isn't, I'm going back."

But it was; and once they were on it, the walk became more pleasant. Sigrid was used to covering twenty-five or thirty city blocks at a stretch, but she was deeply suspicious of nature in the raw. Still, it was cooler under the massive trees in this part of the forest. The path angled downward and was so broad that no branches caught at her clothing. She began to relax. They crossed a small stream on stepping stones and the path rose gently again.

As Nauman paused to re-tie his sneaker, a large black bird lazily flapped along overhead in their general direction.

"That crow of navigational fame, no doubt," said Sigrid.

Her smiles were so rare, thought Oscar, that one forgot they transformed her face. She was more than twenty-five years younger than he and nearly as tall and she photographed badly, but perhaps a painting? He hadn't attempted a portrait since his student days.

"Hi, Oscar!" came a lilting voice from the top of the path. "Welcome to Treasure Island."

To Sigrid, Jemima Bullock looked like a thoroughly nice child as she ran down to meet them in cut-off jeans. She was sturdily built, athletic rather than buxom, with short reddish-blonde hair, an abundance of freckles on every inch of visible skin, and an infectious grin as Nauman effected introductions.

"Jemima's the art world's contribution to oceanography."

"What Oscar means is that he's eternally grateful I didn't stay an art major at Vanderlyn," Jemima explained cheerfully. "My technical drawing was good, but I bombed in creativity."

"At least you had the native wit to admit it," Nauman said.

At the top of the path, they rounded a hummock of wisteria and honeysuckle vines to find an old cottage of undressed logs. A wide porch ran its length and gave good views of rolling woodlands and of Jemima's battered VW van, which was parked on the drive beneath an enormous oak.

"My uncle was caretaker for the Rawlings estate," said Jemima, leading them up on the porch and pulling wicker chairs around a bamboo table. "The main house is farther down the drive, but no one's lived there for years. Uncle Jim mostly had the place to himself."

What looked like a small telescope on a tripod stood at the far end of the porch. "He called this Spyglass Hill, but that's really a surveyor's transit."

"Nauman said his hobby was Robert Louis Stevenson," said Sigrid. "Is that why you welcomed us to Treasure Island?"

"Partly, but Uncle Jim was nutty about only one of Stevenson's books: TREASURE ISLAND. He was my mother's favorite uncle, see, and their name was Hawkins; so when he was a kid, he used to pretend he was the Jim Hawkins in the book. Mom named me Jemima Hawkins Bullock after him, and since he never married, we were pretty close. I used to spend a month up here every summer when I was growing up. He's the one who got me interested in oceanography, though it started off with treasure maps. Every summer he'd have a new one waiting for me."

She darted into the house and reappeared a moment later with a book and a large leather-bound portfolio of charts which she spread out on the porch table.

"This is a survey map of the area," she said. Her finger stabbed a small black square. "Here's this cottage." She traced a short route. "Here's Oscar's house and the path and stream you crossed. See the way the stream comes up and intersects the creek here? And then the creek runs back down and around where a second stream branches off and merges again with the first stream."

"So, technically, we really are on an island," said Sigrid, obscurely pleased with that idea.

"A body of land surrounded by water," Nauman agreed. He pulled out his pipe and worked at getting it lit.

"The freaky thing is that it's actually shaped like the original Treasure Island," said Jemima. She flipped the book open to an illustration. To Sigrid's eyes the two were only roughly similar, but she supposed that wishful thinking could rationalize the differences.

"Uncle Jim made all these treasure maps for me. So many paces to a certain tree while I was small; later he taught me to use a sextant and I'd have to shoot the stars to get the proper bearing. He didn't make it easy, either. It usually took two or three days and several false starts to find the right place to dig. It was worth it, though."

Sigrid leafed through the sheaf of hand-drawn charts. Although identical in their outlines, each was exquisitely embellished with different colored inks: tiny sailing ships, mermaids, and dolphins sported in blue waters around elaborate multipointed compasses. Latitude and longitude lines had been carefully lettered in India ink, along with minute numbers and directions. Sigrid peered closely and read, "Bulk of treasure here."

"He never made much money as a caretaker," said Jemima, "but the treasures he used to hide! Chocolates wrapped in gold and purple foil, a pair of binoculars I still use, maps and drawing pads and compasses so I could draw my own." There was a wistful note in her voice as of a child describing never-to-come-again Christmas mornings.

"Tell her about the real treasure," Nauman prompted, bored with the preliminaries.

"I'm coming to it, Oscar. Be patient. She has to understand how Uncle Jim's mind worked first—the way he liked making a mystery out of things. It wasn't only his maps," she told Sigrid. "He never talked freely about his life, either. He'd trained as a surveyor but seldom held a steady job till after his leg was hurt—just bummed around the world till he was past thirty. I guess he might've seen or done some things he didn't want to tell a kid; but when he was feeling loose, he'd talk about a treasure he brought home from England during World War II. Nothing direct, just a brief mention. If you asked too many questions, he'd cut you off. I used to think it might be gold, then again it'd sound like jewels. Whatever it was, he got it in London. He was on leave there and the building he was in was hit by a buzz bomb. Crushed his left leg.

"That London hospital was where he really got into the TREASURE ISLAND thing. The nurses kept bringing him different editions of the book. Because of his name, you see. He'd always had a flair for precision drawing—from the surveying—and when he started mapping the wards on scrap paper, they brought him sketch pads and pens and he was off to the races. I think they made a pet out of him because they knew his leg would never heal properly. Anyhow, he let it slip once that if the nurses hadn't liked him, he never would have recognized the treasure when it appeared."

She looked at Sigrid doubtfully through stubby sandy lashes. "That doesn't sound much like gold or diamonds, does it?"

"He never revealed its nature?"

"Nope. Anyhow, Uncle Jim knew it takes an M.S. to get anywhere in oceanography. That means an expensive year or two at some school like Duke, and I just don't have the money. In fact, I haven't been able to get up here much these last four years because I've had to work summers and part time just to stay at Vanderlyn. Uncle Jim said not to worry, that he was going to give me the treasure for graduation so I could sell it for enough to finance my post-graduate work.

"When he called three weeks ago to make sure I was coming, he said he was drawing up a new map. The heart attack must have hit him within the hour. I drove up the next morning and found him slumped over the table inside. He'd just finished sketching in the outline. It was going to be our best treasure hunt."

An unembarrassed tear slipped down her freckled cheek, and she brushed it away with the back of her hand.

"The trustees for the Rawlings estate have been very understanding, but they do need the cottage for the new caretaker. Uncle Jim left everything to me, so they've asked if I can clear out his things by the end of the month. You're my last hope, Lieutenant Harald. Oscar said you're good at solving puzzles. I hope you can figure out this one 'cause nobody else can."

Sigrid looked at Nauman. "But I don't know a thing about sextants or surveyor's transits, and anyhow, if he died before he finished the map—"

"Nobody's asking you to go tramping through hill and dale with a pickax," Nauman said, correctly interpreting her horrified expression. "Jemima doesn't think he'd buried it yet."

"Come inside and I'll show you," said the girl.

In essence the cottage was one big room, with kitchen equipment at one end and two small sleeping alcoves at the other end separated by a tiny bath. A shabby couch and several comfortable looking armchairs circled an enormous stone fireplace centered on the long rear wall. A bank of windows overlooked the porch and underneath were shelves crammed with books of all shapes and sizes. Most were various editions of—"What else?" said Jemima—TREASURE ISLAND. In the middle of the room was a round wooden table flanked by six ladderback chairs, one of which was draped in an old and worn woollen pea jacket with heavy brass buttons. A rusty metal picnic cooler sat beside one chair with its lid ajar to reveal a porcelain interior.

"Things are pretty much as Uncle Jim left them. That cooler is our treasure chest because it was watertight. As you can see, there was nothing in it."

Sigrid circled the table, carefully cataloguing its contents: an uncapped bottle of India Ink, a fine-nibbed drawing pen, a compass, a ruler, four brushes, a twelve by eighteen inch block of watercolor paper with the top half of the island sketched in, a set of neatly arranged watercolors and a clean tray for mixing them. Across from these, a book was opened to a reproduction of the map Robert Louis Stevenson had drawn so many years ago, and several more books formed a prop for two framed charts. Sigrid scanned the cottage and found the light oblongs on the whitewashed walls where a chart had hung on either side of the stone chimney.

"Uncle Jim often used them as references when he was drawing a new map," explained Jemima. "The right one's a copy of the survey map. It's the first one he drew after he took the job here and realized that the streams and creek made this place an island almost like the real Treasure Island. The other one's the first copy he made when he was in the hospital. I guess he kept it for sentimental reasons even though the proportions aren't quite right."

Sigrid peered through the glass at the sheet of yellowed watercolor paper, which was frayed around the edges and showed deep crease lines where it had once been folded into quarters. It, too, was minutely detailed with hillocks, trees, sailing ships, and sounding depths although, as Jemima had noted, it wasn't an accurate copy.

She turned both frames over and saw that the paper tape that sealed the backings to the frames had been torn.

"We took them apart," Jemima acknowledged. "A friend of mine came over from the rare book library at Yale to help appraise the books, and he thought maybe the treasure was an autographed letter from Stevenson or something like that which Uncle Jim might've hidden inside the matting."

"None of the books are rare?" asked Sigrid. That had seemed the most likely possibility.

"He thought they might bring a few hundred dollars if I sold them as a collection," said the girl, "but individually, nothing's worth over forty dollars at the most. And we thumbed through every one of them in case there really was a letter or something. No luck."

Sigrid's slate gray eyes swept through the large, shabby room. Something jarred, but she couldn't quite put her finger on the source.

"Not as simple as a double-crostic, is it?" Nauman said.

Sigrid shrugged, unnettled by his light gibe. "If a treasure's here, logic will uncover it."

"But we've *been* logical!" Jemima said despairingly. "Last week my mom and I and two cousins went over every square inch of this place. We looked behind knotholes, jiggled every stone in the fireplace, checked for loose floorboards, and examined mattress seams and cushion covers. Nothing, and my cousins are home ec majors," she added to buttress her statement.

"Mom even separated out all the things Uncle Jim might have brought from England." She gestured to a small heap of books stacked atop the window case. "Luckily he dated all his books. My Yale friend says none of those is worth more than a few dollars."

Sigrid lifted one. The blue cloth binding was familiar, and when she read the publication date—1932—she realized it was the same edition of TREASURE ISLAND as the one her father had owned as a boy and which she had read as a child herself. Memories of lying on her stomach on a window ledge, munching toasted cheese sandwiches while she read, came back to Sigrid as she paused over a well-remembered illustration of Jim Hawkins shooting Israel Hands. Inscribed on the flyleaf was *A very happy Christmas to our own Jim Hawkins from Nurse Fromyn and staff.* Underneath, a masculine hand had added 12/5/1944.

The other four books in the heap carried dates which spanned the early months of 1945. "Mom said he was brought home in the summer of '45," said Jemima, peering around Sigrid's shoulder.

"What else did he bring?"

"That first map he drew," she answered promptly, "a shaving kit, that jacket on the chair, and Mom thinks that leather portfolio, too." She fetched it in from the porch and carefully removed the charts it held before handing it over. It measured about eighteen by twenty inches.

The leather was worn by forty years of handling, but when Nauman turned it over, they could still read the tooled letters at the edge of the case. "Bartlelow's," he said. "They're still the best leather goods shop in London. And the most expensive."

Sigrid found a worn spot in the heavy taffeta lining. Carefully, she slipped her thin fingers inside and worked the fabric away from the leather. Had any slip of paper been concealed there, her search should have found it. Nothing.

The shaving kit and threadbare pea jacket were equally barren of anything remotely resembling treasure. "My cousins thought those heavy brass buttons might be worth five dollars apiece," Jemima said ruefully. She looked around the big shabby room and sighed. "If only Uncle Jim hadn't loved secrets so much."

"If he hadn't, your childhood would have been much duller," Oscar reminded her sensibly. He knocked his pipe out on the hearth. "You promised us lunch, and I for one am ready for it. Food first, ratiocination afterwards. Lead us to your galley, Jemima Hawkins, and if it's water biscuits and whale blubber, you'll walk the plank."

"It's cold chicken and fresh salad," Jemima giggled, "but we'll have to pick the greens ourselves. Uncle Jim's garden is just down the drive."

Sigrid looked dubious and Oscar grinned. "Don't worry. I know you can't distinguish lettuce and basil from poison oak and thistles. You stay and detect; we'll pick the salad."

Left alone, Sigrid circled the room again. Although spartan in its furnishings, the area itself was so large that another thorough search was impractical. One would have to trust the home ec cousins' expertise. As a homicide detective with her own expertise, she had told Nauman that logic would uncover a treasure if it were there to be found, but perhaps she'd spoken too soon.

If there were a treasure. . . .

She stared again at the forlorn table where Jemima's uncle had died so peacefully. At the drawing paraphernalia and the uncompleted map. At the empty chest on the floor, its lid ajar to receive a treasure as soon as old Jim Hawkins had mapped its burial site. She lingered over the two framed charts and a sudden thought made her measure the older one against the leather portfolio.

Jemima said this had been the very first TREASURE ISLAND map her uncle had attempted and that he'd kept it for sentimental reasons. But what if this were the map Robert Louis Stevenson had drawn himself? Wouldn't that be a real treasure? And what better place to hide it than in plain sight, passed off as Hawkins' own work?

She strode across the rough-planked floor and pulled two likely books from the shelves beneath the windows. One was a fairly recent biography of Stevenson, the other a facsimile copy of the first edition of TREASURE ISLAND. Both contained identical reproductions of the author's map, and the biography's version was labeled *Frontispiece of the first edition as drawn by RLS in his father's office in Edinburgh.*

She carried the books over to the table, but there was no denying the evidence of her eyes: the embellishments were different and the map Hawkins had brought home from London was misproportioned. The uncle's island had been drawn slightly longer and not quite as wide as Stevenson's original version.

Disappointed, Sigrid returned the books to their former slots and continued circling the room. Surely that expensive portfolio had something to do with the treasure. Or was it only a bon voyage gift from the nurses when Hawkins was shipped home?

She paused in the door of the tiny bath and inspected the battered shaving kit again. Had such a homely everyday pouch once held diamonds or gold?

Nothing about the cottage indicated a taste for luxury. Devising modest treasures and drawing exquisitely precise maps for his young namesake seemed to have been the caretaker's only extravagance. Otherwise, he lived almost as a hermit, spare and ascetic, still making do with an ancient pea jacket whose eight brass buttons were probably worth more than everything else in his wardrobe.

She paused by the chair which held the jacket and again tried to make herself take each item on the table top separately and significantly.

And then she saw it.

When Jemima and Oscar reentered the cottage, hilarious with the outrageous combination of herbs and salad greens they had picked, they found Sigrid standing by the window with her finger marking a place in the blue clothbound book she'd read as a child. Jemima started to regale her with their collection, but Oscar took one look at Sigrid's thin face and said, "You found it."

Her wide gray eyes met his and a smile almost brushed her lips. "Can you phone your expert at Yale?" she asked Jemima.

"Sure, but he checked all the books before. Or did you find a hidden one?"

Sigrid shook her head. "Not a book. The map." She pointed to the older of the framed charts.

"What's special about Uncle Jim's map? It's not the original, if that's what you're thinking. Charlie told me that one was auctioned off in the forties and he's pretty sure the same person still owns it."

Nauman had found a reproduction of the original and silently compared it to the faded chart on the table. "Look, Siga, the proportions are wrong."

"I know," she said, and there was definite mischief in her eyes now. "That's precisely why you should call him, Jemima."

"You mean the books are all wrong?" asked the girl.

Sigrid opened the blue book to the forward. "Listen," she said. With one hand hooked into the pocket of her jeans, she leaned against the stone chimney and read in a cool clear voice Stevenson's own version of how he came to write TREASURE ISLAND; of how, in that rainy August of 1881, he and his stepson "with the aid of pen and ink and shilling box of water colours," had passed their afternoon drawing.

On one of these occasions, I made a map of an island . . . the shape of it took my fancy beyond expression . . . and I ticketed it "Treasure Island" . . . the next thing I knew, I had some papers before me and was writing out a list of characters.

Sigrid turned the pages. "The next is familiar territory. The story was written, serialized in a magazine and then was to be published in book form." She read again,

I sent in my manuscript, and the map along with it . . . the proofs came, they were corrected, but I heard nothing of the map. I wrote and asked; was told it had never been received, and sat aghast. It is one thing to draw a map at random, set a scale in one corner of it . . . and write up a story to the measurements. It is quite another to have to examine a whole book, make an inventory of it, and, with a pair of compasses, painfully design a map to suit the data. I did it; and the map was drawn in my father's office . . . but somehow it was never Treasure Island to me.

Sigrid closed the book. "If you'll look closely, Jemima, you'll see the handwriting on that map's a lot closer to Stevenson's than to your uncle's."

Oscar compared the maps with an artist's eye, then lifted the phone and wryly handed it to Jemima. "Call your friend."

It took several calls around New Haven and surrounding summer cottages to chase Jemima's expert to earth. While they waited, Oscar created an elaborate dressing for their salad and sliced the cold chicken. Lunch was spread on the porch and Sigrid was trying to decide if she really approved mixing basil and parsley together when Jemima danced through the open doorway.

"He's going to call Sotheby's in New York!" she caroled. "And he's coming out himself just to make sure; but if it's genuine, he says it'll pay for at least two years in any M.S. program in the United States!"

Oscar removed an overlooked harlequin beetle from the salad bowl and filled Jemima's plate. "Admit it, though," he said to Sigrid. "It was the coincidence of remembering that passage from your childhood book that made you suspect the map, not logic."

"It was logic," she said firmly, forking through the salad carefully in case more beetles had been overlooked. She was not opposed to food foraged in a garden instead of in a grocery, but Nauman was entirely too casual about the wildlife.

"Show me the logic," Oscar challenged, and Jemima looked at her expectantly, too.

"All right," said Sigrid. "Why would your uncle acquire an expensive portfolio if not to bring home something special?"

"It didn't have to be that map."

"No? What else was the right size?"

"Even so," objected Oscar, "why not assume he was taking pains with it because it was the first copy he'd drawn himself?"

"Because it's been folded. You can still see the crease lines. If he'd ever folded it up himself, why buy a leather case to carry it flat? We'll probably never know exactly how the map disappeared in the 1880s and reappeared during the Blitz, but I'd guess one of the publisher's clerks misfiled it or maybe an office boy lifted it and then was afraid to own up."

"So that it rattled around in someone's junk room until it caught a nurse or corpsman's eye and they thought it would cheer up their Yank patient? Maybe," Oscar conceded. He cocked a skeptical eye at Sigrid. "So, on the basis of some old crease marks, you instantly deduced this was the original Stevenson-drawn TREASURE ISLAND map?"

"They helped. Made it seem as if that paper hadn't been carefully handled from the beginning." She peered at a suspicious dark fleck beneath a leaf of spinach. "Too, he'd told Jemima that if it hadn't been for the nurses, he wouldn't have recognized the treasure when it appeared. Lying there in bed, he would have read the book they'd given him from cover to cover wouldn't he? Including the foreword about the missing map? I'm sure it would have interested him because of his own mapping skills. That's really what made me look twice: the map was all wrong.

"Jemima's uncle was far too skilled to have miscopied a map with the book right there in front of him. I don't care how sentimental he might later have been over a first attempt, I couldn't see him framing and hanging a misdrawn, ill-proportioned copy.

"And *that*," she concluded triumphantly as she presented Oscar with a potato beetle done in by his dressing, "is logic."

Edward D. Hoch is another Edgar Award–winning author who has quietly produced some of the finest crime fiction around. A master of the short story, he has published his work in every issue of Ellery Queen's Mystery Magazine *since 1973. When he's not writing, he edits anthologies and has put together twenty volumes of* The Year's Best Mystery and Suspense Stories. *Luckily he doesn't edit all the time; if he did, he wouldn't have time to turn out perfect little stories like "The Problem of the Snowbound Cabin."*

The Problem of the Snowbound Cabin

Edward D. Hoch

D r. Sam Hawthorne settled down in this favorite chair, took a sip of brandy, and said, "I wanted to tell you about my vacation in Maine back in January of 'thirty-five and I suppose you wonder why any sane person would drive up to Maine in the middle of winter, especially in the days before turnpikes and expressways. Well, I suppose it was because of the car . . ."

My major weakness (Dr. Sam continued) has always been sports-cars. When I completed my internship, my father and mother presented me with a yellow 1921 Pierce-Arrow Runabout and it was the pride of my life until it was destroyed in an explosion. The cars I owned after that, in the early 1930s, were unsatisfactory shadows of that great vehicle. Then, in early '35, I finally found the car of my dreams—a Mercedes-Benz 500K Special Roadster in glorious red. It was expensive, of course, but by that time I'd been a practicing physician for over twelve years and in my single state I'd managed to save a fair amount of money from my country practice.

I purchased the car in Boston, and when I drove up to the office wing at Pilgrim Memorial Hospital with it, my nurse, April, couldn't believe her eyes.

"You *bought* it, Sam? It's *yours?*"

"That's right. Hawthorne's folly."

She ran her hands over the red lacquer, admiring the long sleek lines of the engine housing. We tried out the rumble seat together and examined the twin spare tires mounted behind it. Then I let her take the car for a drive around the hospital parking lot. "It's a dream, Sam!" she said. "I never saw anything like it!"

April had been with me since I came to Northmont, and a decade earlier we'd had a brief vacation on Cape Cod together, but our relationship had remained platonic. I liked April as a friend and found her perfect as a nurse, but no spark of romance had ever developed between us. She was a few years older than I, in her late thirties, but still an attractive woman for the right man. Though we never discussed her private life, I had the feeling the right man hadn't yet appeared within the confines of Northmont.

It was against this background that I impulsively said, as she climbed out of the Mercedes, "Let's drive it up to Maine."

"Maine? In January?"

"Why not? It's been a fairly open winter and the roads are clear. We might even try some skiing."

"No, thanks, I don't want a leg in a cast." But I could see the idea of a vacation intrigued her. "What would we do about your patients?"

"Doc Handleman's offered to take care of them if I want to get away for a week. I'm filling in for him in March when he goes to Florida."

"Let's do it," April decided with an impish grin. "But remember, no skiing . . . !"

We set off at the beginning of the following week, driving north through Massachusetts and into New Hampshire. The car handled like a dream, and though it was far too cold to drive with the convertible top down, the right-hand steering wheel and the long hood gave the feeling of driving something foreign and fast. I'd telephoned ahead and made reservations at a vacation lodge north of Bangor, so even after we crossed the state line into Maine we had a long drive ahead of us.

"It's starting to snow," April pointed out as the first fine flakes hit the windshield.

"I guess we were lucky to get this far without it."

The snow was light but steady for the remainder of our journey, and when we reached the Greenbush Inn a few inches had accumulated on the road. I parked in the shelter of a large pine tree and took our bags out of the rumble seat where they'd been stored. The lodge was a large structure built entirely of logs, reminding me of the number one resource of the Maine woods. Inside a cheery lobby with the fireside atmosphere of a cozy living room, we were greeted by a tall dark man in his forties whose speech held just a hint of an accent.

"Good afternoon and welcome to Greenbush. I am your host, Andre Mulhone."

"Dr. Sam Hawthorne," I said, extending my hand. "And this is—"

"Ah, Mrs. Hawthorne!"

"No—", I continued my introduction, "—I've booked separate rooms."

Andre Mulhone smiled. "Separate but connecting. If you'll sign the register, I'll show them to you."

"We'll be here for six nights."

"Very good."

Our rooms were pleasant and when we went down for dinner an hour later, Mulhone motioned us to join him at his table. "I despise dining alone," he said. "Please dine with me."

It was an enjoyable meal, and I could see April warming to Andre. He told us about his French–Irish background and about his wife who had been killed the previous winter when her car skidded off the road. "What was her name?" April asked sympathetically.

"Lois. I have a picture of her in my wallet. When she went out of my life, I had very little to keep me going. We had no children and the inn was all I had to occupy myself."

He showed us a snapshot of a pleasant-looking woman about his age. "What a nice smile," April commented.

Mulhone's conversation at dinner reflected cosmopolitan interests I found surprising in the Maine Woods. At one moment he'd be speaking of Thoreau's visit there a century earlier and the next he was discussing Adolf Hitler, who was threatening all of Europe. It wasn't the sort of discussion I ever had back in Northmont.

"What's there to do around here?" I asked, adding, "Neither of us ski."

Andre Mulhone shrugged. "Skiing is an Alpine sport. I often wonder if it will be as popular in America as it is in Switzerland and Norway. I understand, though, that it is gaining popularity in Minnesota among the Scandinavians. And who knows? There is a new invention called the ski lift, which could revolutionize the pastime. One can ski downhill and ride back up."

"But you have no skiing at Greenbush?" April asked.

"No. But we have snowshoeing and hiking. Let me fit you both out with some snowshoes in the morning and I'll show you a bit of the countryside."

I was sure Mulhone's special interest in us had more to do with April than with me, but I had no cause for complaint. He was a charming man and an excellent conversationalist. I went to bed looking forward to the morning.

It was bright and brisk, with a north wind that made us turn up our collars as we waited for Andre to join us in front of the lodge. April had her eyes on the door and I let mine wander to the pine tree where I'd parked my Mercedes. I was startled to see a young man in a plaid jacket hovering by it. In one hand he carried a shotgun.

I strolled over. "Admiring the car?" I said.

"It's a beauty. Is it yours?"

"That's right."

"You staying at the lodge?"

I nodded. "My name is Sam Hawthorne."

"I'm Gus Laxault. I do some odd jobs around here."

"With a shotgun?"

"Been out shootin' varmints. When there's a snow cover and they can't get food easily, they come in to our rubbish dump. Got me a bobcat this morning."

"I didn't realize we were that close to nature."

Laxault was more interested in the Mercedes. "First one of these I've seen," he said, running his hand over the fender. "I'll bet it set you back a good piece of money."

"It wasn't cheap." I didn't want to pursue the conversation any longer. When I moved away from the car, I was relieved that he followed along.

Mulhone had arrived by this time, carrying three pairs of snowshoes. He frowned at Laxault and seemed about to say something, then to think better of it. The varmint-hunter veered off and disappeared around the back of the lodge.

"Oh, it's a perfect morning!" April was radiant.

"We had snow last night back in the hills," Andre said. "You'll find it quite deep in spots." He knelt to fit April's snowshoes while I struggled with the pair he gave me.

"How many people do you employ here?" I asked.

"It depends on how busy we are. If we have many reservations for a particular weekend, I call on some temporary help from town."

"Is Laxault one of your temporaries?"

"He does odd jobs, but he's a bit unreliable."

"He told me he shot a bobcat this morning."

"He probably did. During the winter they come looking for food."

We started out, heading north across a frozen lake and up the side of a gentle hill. April and I were unaccustomed to snowshoes and walking with them wasn't as easy as it looked. My leg muscles were aching before we'd covered the first mile.

"We can rest at Ted Shorter's cabin on the other side of this hill," Mulhone suggested. "It's hard walking in this cold wind if you're not used to it."

"Who's Ted Shorter?"

"A retired stockbroker who moved up here a few years ago. He lives by himself, but he's friendly enough if you come to visit."

Once we reached the crest of the hill, the cabin came into view. A Ford sedan was parked nearby, but the road was completely buried by the snow that had drifted across the cabin's front door. There was smoke coming from the chimney.

"He must be home," Mulhone observed. "The fireplace is going and there are no tracks out of the house."

Following his lead, we made our way down the hill. April pointed off to the left. "Are those bobcat tracks?"

Mulhone went closer to them and said, "I think so. They're about nine inches apart. It might be the one Gus Laxault shot." The tracks wandered toward the corner of the cabin and then went off in the other direction. The drifted snow grew deeper near the cabin and I doubted we could have made it without snowshoes. When we reached the door, Mulhone pounded on it with a gloved fist.

When no one came, he tried the knob. "It's unlocked," he said and carefully pushed it open, letting the drifted snow fall in on the floor. He turned a switch and a single overhead light came on. Over his shoulder, I saw a pleasant room with a large easy chair drawn up to the fire. Sunshine from a skylight in the roof flooded in the room. I could make out a sleeping loft with an unmade bed and some dirty breakfast dishes on a dining table.

We could see the top of someone's head in the easy chair and Mulhone hurried forward while April and I waited in the doorway. "Ted, it's Andre. I was out snowshoeing and stopped to—" He bent over the chair, shaking the man slightly. Then I saw his face change.

"What is it?" I asked, starting forward.

"My God—he's been stabbed."

I took one look and saw it was true. And that the man in the chair was dead.

Mulhone used the crank phone on the wall to call the authorities.

When he arrived a half hour later, Sheriff Petty proved to be quite different from Sheriff Lens, my best friend back home in Northmont. He seemed out of place in the backwoods—a tall, slim, frowning man who wore an expensive leather coat over his tailored uniform. He wanted to know what had brought us to the cabin that morning. Though he'd ignored me during the initial questioning, he perked up when he learned I was a doctor.

"We don't have a full-time coroner right now," he said. "Is there any chance you could estimate the time of death for us, Dr. Hawthorne?"

"I could try," I told him, "but the body was so close to the fireplace it's hard to be accurate. There's no sign of rigor mortis. He could have been dead anywhere from a few minutes to a few hours. Certainly no longer than a few hours. The fact that the fire was still burning when we entered the cabin tells us something. It would have burned itself out over a longer period."

"Then he was killed after sunrise."

"I'd say so, yes. It was around ten o'clock when we found him. There were unwashed breakfast dishes and the lights were out."

"The snow stopped before the sun was up," Sheriff Petty turned to Mulhone. "There was no one else here when you entered the cabin?"

"Only poor Shorter."

"And no tracks leading in or out?"

Andre shook his head.

"No tracks," I confirmed. "We searched the cabin and looked out in all directions. This is the only door and the snow was drifted against it when we arrived. The windows were all closed and latched against the cold. Nothing came near the place except for a bobcat."

"The killer must have been here all night," the sheriff decided. "But then how did he get away without leaving tracks?"

"Suicide," Mulhone said. "It's the only answer."

Sheriff Petty's frown deepened. "If it's suicide, what happened to the weapon?"

It was a fair enough question, and for the moment we had no answer.

They took the body away, pulling it on a sled up the snow-covered hill, then down the other side till they reached the road that was clear. We headed back to the lodge.

"Tell me about Shorter," I said to Andre. "Who do you think would want to kill him?"

The innkeeper shrugged. "Someone from his past, I suppose. I doubt if he saw enough people around here to make enemies. As I said before, he was friendly enough but he kept to himself."

"Did he ever come over to the lodge?"

"Hardly at all." Then he snapped his fingers at a sudden thought. "But he did show up just a few days ago. He came to visit a woman who's staying here. I remember being surprised to see him, but then I thought no more about it."

"Is she still here?"

"Mrs. Deveroux—yes, I believe she is."

I left April enjoying Andre's company and sought out the number of Mrs. Deveroux's room. The desk clerk pointed across the lobby at a slim woman in her thirties who was glancing through a fashion magazine. I thanked him and walked over to her. "Pardon me. Mrs. Deveroux?"

She turned and smiled. "Yes. Do I know you?"

"I haven't had the pleasure. My name is Sam Hawthorne."

"And I'm Faith Deveroux, as you seem to know. What can I do for you?" She put down the magazine.

"It's about Ted Shorter. I understand you knew him."

"Knew?"

"I'm sorry. I thought you'd heard by now. Mr. Shorter was found dead in his cabin this morning."

She swayed and started to fall out of her chair. I caught her just in time.

When she'd regained her composure, Faith Deveroux took a sip of the brandy I'd ordered and said, "You'll have to excuse me. I haven't fainted in years."

"I'm sorry my news was such a shock."

She leaned back against the sofa in the lobby. There had been no fuss—only the desk clerk had seen her fall and I had quickly revived her. "It shouldn't have been, really. He was someone I knew a long time ago. What was it—a heart attack?"

"He was stabbed in the chest."

"You mean someone *killed* him?" Her pallid face might have grown a shade paler.

"It might have been suicide, but that's doubtful. Could you tell me something about him, about why he chose to live here away from everyone?"

"That's simple enough. Ted was a stockbroker. He was wiped out in the crash and never recovered from it. He not only lost his own money but that of hundreds of small investors as well. Some of them blamed him for their losses. He finally reached the point where he couldn't face it any more. He moved up here from Boston about three years ago and he's been alone ever since."

"Were you one of his investors?" I asked.

She gave me a sad smile. "No. I was his wife."

It was my turn to be shocked. "You were divorced?"

Faith Deveroux nodded. "It had nothing to do with the crash. I met Glen Deveroux early in 1929 and we fell in love. I told Ted I wanted a divorce a few months later. I was sorry when I heard what happened to him, but it had no connection with me."

"You're up here now without your husband?"

"Yes. He's a construction engineer working on the new Golden Gate Bridge in San Francisco. Sometimes he's out there for months at a time. I got lonesome, so I came up here for a week."

"Did you know your former husband was living here?"

"I knew he was in the general area."

"Did you phone him when you arrived?"

By this time her patience had worn thin. "What are you, Mr. Hawthorne, some sort of detective? What's the meaning of all these questions?"

"I'm a doctor. I've had some experience with crimes of this type and I thought I might help the local police."

"What do you mean, crimes of this type?"

"The circumstances seem somewhat bizarre, even impossible. Mr. Shorter was stabbed while he was alone in a cabin surrounded by unmarked snow. The killer couldn't have entered or left once the snow stopped before dawn. Yet there is no weapon pointing to suicide."

"Do the police suspect *me* of killing him?" she asked.

"I don't think at this point they're even aware of your existence."

"I'd appreciate it if that continued to be the case, Dr. Hawthorne. I assure you I know nothing of my ex-husband's death. We dined together the other night and that was all."

There was nothing more to be learned just then. I thanked her for her time and went to my room, where I sat by the window and tried to recall the details of the dead man's cabin. It was one large room with a sleeping loft and a small kitchen area. An outhouse was located at the rear. There had been some books, mainly about business and the stock market, and the remains of breakfast, confirming that Shorter had probably died after dawn. I wondered if a man would make breakfast if he intended to kill himself—and decided that stranger things had happened.

★   ★   ★

I didn't see April until after dinner. Then she seemed happier than I'd ever seen her.

"Have you been with Andre all day?" I asked, thinking I was making a joke.

To my surprise, she nodded. "I really like him, Sam. We had dinner in his office, just the two of us."

"This is getting serious," I said.

She changed the subject. "Do you have any leads on the killing?"

"Nothing much. I met a woman here at the lodge who turns out to be Shorter's former wife. It's interesting that she should be on the scene at the time he died, but she swears she knows nothing about it."

"Why would anyone kill a man who lived by himself in the woods?"

"I don't know. He lost a great deal of money in the crash and so did a number of people whose investments he handled. Perhaps one of them followed him up here for revenge."

"After more than five years?"

"It's happened before. Sometimes the anger at a supposed wrong will build in a person's mind until it blossoms into a homicidal rage. Shorter may have been here in hiding from just such a person."

We strolled out around the lodge, and the conversation shifted to Northmont and the people there. April spoke of it with something like nostalgia, as if remembering the home she'd left long ago. The conversation bothered me, and later in my room I sat for a long time at the window, staring out at the snow and the few lights that reflected off it.

Once I saw a figure moving, passing beneath one of the lights. It was Gus Laxault, carrying his shotgun, perhaps on the trail of another bobcat.

In the morning, April was gone from her room when I knocked at the door. I went down to breakfast and avoided joining Faith Deveroux, who was seated alone on the other side of the room.

April appeared as I was finishing my coffee. "I'm sorry I'm late," she said a bit sheepishly.

"That's all right. We're both on our own up here. Have you had breakfast?"

"Yes."

"How about a walk, then?"

"Sounds good. Where to?"

"I was thinking of taking another look at Shorter's cabin."

"Won't we need snowshoes?"

"I imagine Sheriff Petty's people have worn a path to the door by now. Let's find out."

We followed our route of the previous day, encountering deep snow at only one point. April sank in up to her waist and I had to pull her out. We were still laughing when we finally reached the top of the hill overlooking Shorter's cabin.

"I think someone's in there," I said. "The door's standing open."

It proved to be a bearded man in a fur parka, sent by the telephone company to remove the phone from the wall. "Guess he won't have any more need for this," he told us. "We don't like to leave our equipment around in an empty house."

"Did you know Ted Shorter?" I asked him.

"Not really." He kept working as he talked. "Met him once when I came out here to string some new line."

"Was he alone?"

"No—one of the fellas from the lodge was here with him."

"Andre Mulhone?"

"No, a handyman who works there. Laxault, I think his name is."

"Gus Laxault." I thought about that. "Ever see any bobcats around here?"

"Sure, once in a while. Mostly they mind their own business."

After he'd gone, April and I examined the cabin. It was much as I remembered it from the previous day, except that now there was no warming heat from the fireplace. I stood by the chair in which Shorter had been found dead, looking in every direction for some clue I might have missed. "Any ideas?" I asked April.

She giggled, this lighthearted new April I'd never seen before. "You sound like Sherlock Holmes. All right, how's this? He stabs himself with a knife tied to a piece of rubber cut from an inner tube or something. When he lets go of the knife, it's yanked away out of sight by this long rubber band."

"Where out of sight?"

April looked up and pointed. "Through that skylight to the roof."

It was just crazy enough to have happened. I moved a sturdy table over, placed a chair on top of it, and was able to reach the skylight. It opened easily, but the snow on the roof appeared unmarked. I felt around the edge of the window but there was no hidden knife.

I climbed back down to the floor. "Nothing up there," I said.

After replacing the furniture, I looked up the chimney, remembering a story I'd read about a weapon pulled up a chimney after a suicide, but there, too, I found nothing. I tried to reconstruct the events of the previous morning, talking as much to myself as to April. "He got up, probably shortly after dawn, and fixed breakfast. He started a fire, either before or after breakfast."

"Maybe the killer started the fire," April suggested, "to keep the body warm and confuse the time of death."

That was a possibility I'd overlooked. "But that still doesn't tell us how the killer got in and out," I said.

"During the night, before the snow stopped."

I shook my head. "You're forgetting breakfast."

"The killer could have faked that."

"But there's still the fire. It would have died down if it was unattended for that long."

"I suppose you're right," she admitted. Then her eyes fastened on something on the floor near the door, almost hidden by a scatter rug. "What's that?"

It was a slim gold lead-pencil with the initials *G.D.* engraved on its side. "Maybe it's a clue," I said, though I doubted it. Sheriff Petty's people wouldn't be likely to miss it. Perhaps one of the investigators had used it to draw a map of the cabin and dropped it. I put it in my pocket and looked around the room. "I guess we've done all the looking that makes sense, April," I said.

As we walked back to the lodge, April became serious. "Sam, what would you do if I left you someday to take another job?"

"Probably close up my practice and become a monk."

"No, seriously."

"You've been with me thirteen years, April. As long as I've had my practice. Aren't you happy? Do you want more money?"

"It has nothing to do with money."

"I thought you were happy. You've certainly been happy the last couple of days."

"Yes."

"Then, what—"

"Andre's asked me to stay up here."

I was dumbfounded. "He offered you a job?"

"He wants to marry me."

"April! You'd marry a man you met only two days ago?"

"No."

I sighed with relief. "That's something, anyway."

"But maybe I'd like to say here a while longer, to get to know him better."

"His wife was killed in an auto accident last year. He's just lonesome."

"So am I."

"What?"

"I'm thirty-nine years old, Sam."

"I never thought of you as wanting—"

"I know you didn't." There was a new note of sharpness in her voice. "Sometimes, I've wondered if you thought of me as a woman at all."

I didn't want to talk about it any more. "We've got a few more days here," I said. "Let's just see what happens."

That night after dinner, I joined Faith Deveroux at her table for a little sherry. "I'll be leaving tomorrow," she confided, "going back to Boston."

"You're not staying for Shorter's funeral?"

She shook her head. "He hasn't meant anything to me in years. I was foolish to come up here at all."

I saw April standing in the doorway, looking around the room. When she saw me, she waved and headed for the table. "What is it?" I asked, standing up to greet her.

"Can you come with me? Andre thinks he's solved the mystery. I want you to hear it."

"I'd be happy to."

Faith Deveroux was on her feet, too. "May I come?"

I introduced her to April and we both followed along to Andre's office. He was seated behind his desk and seemed surprised to see Mrs. Deveroux, but he quickly offered her a chair. "You must excuse me, Mrs. Deveroux. I wasn't aware Ted's former wife was a guest here. I have a theory about his death which seems to fit the facts, and April thought Dr. Hawthorne should hear it."

"Go right ahead," she said.

"If you can explain how he was killed in that cabin with no tracks nearby except those of a wandering bobcat," I told him, "I'll certainly be interested in hearing it."

Andre nodded. "It's so simple I can tell you in one sentence. Ted Shorter stabbed himself with a dagger of ice, which promptly melted in the heat from the fireplace."

Faith Deveroux and I were silent, but April was quick to praise the theory. "That's the sort of thing you'd come up with, Sam! I just know it has to be right."

"April—" I started to say, and then directed my remarks directly to Mulhone. "Have you ever tried cutting the skin with a sharp piece of ice? It's not as easy as it sounds, even outdoors. Indoors, next to that fire, it would be impossible. What happens is that the edge of the ice, no matter how sharp it is, immediately begins to melt and grow dull." I turned to Faith. "Would your ex-husband have gained anything by concealing the fact of his suicide?"

She shook her head. "Nothing. After the divorce, he turned in his insurance policy for its cash value. He told me after he moved up here that there was no one who needed his insurance money."

"I still think your theory is possible, Andre," April insisted.

"No, Dr. Hawthorne is right," Mulhone said graciously. "I hadn't thought it through. I suppose I was trying to dispel the notion of a killer at large in the area."

Later, as I relaxed over a billiard table in the lodge's game room, April sought me out. "Sam, I want to talk."

"All right. In the bar?"

"I'd rather go upstairs."

I took her to my room and relaxed in a chair while she sat stiffly on the bed. "Now tell me what's troubling you," I said, dreading what might be coming.

"You hate Andre, don't you? Ever since I told you about us."

"You're wrong, April."

"What is it, then?"

I felt drained of energy. What I was about to say was the most difficult thing I'd ever done. "We have to face facts. Shorter's death wasn't a suicide, and certainly that wandering bobcat didn't kill him. No one entered that cabin between the time the snow stopped and we entered to find him. No one could have. The windows were latched and the snow at the door and on the roof was undisturbed."

"But—"

"Ted Shorter was alive when we entered, perhaps dozing by the fire. Andre, the first one to reach his chair, stabbed him when he bent over to shake him. That's the only way it could have been. I'm sorry, April.—Perhaps he lost money with Shorter's firm some years ago."

"*No!*" She threw herself down on the bed and sobbed, beating at the spread with her fists. There was nothing I could say or do. I'd said too much already.

I slept badly that night, but I finally dozed off near dawn and awakened with a clear head. My brain seemed to have been working even while I slept, and I had a fresh grasp of the situation that hadn't been obvious before. I lay in bed for a time, staring at the ceiling, then finally got up and telephoned Sheriff Petty. I told him what I wanted to do, without explaining why.

"It may be too late, Sheriff, but I'd like you to go with me to Shorter's cabin. This morning."

"What for?"

"I'd rather not say until I'm more certain."

"Don't tell me you believe that old chestnut about the murderer returning to the scene of the crime."

"Something like that," I admitted.

I met him there shortly after eight o'clock, having suggested he leave his car out of sight on the main road. There had been no further snow, so we were able to enter the cabin along the well trodden path without leaving new prints. Once inside, I suggested we take cover in the sleeping loft.

"Who are you expecting to come?" Petty wanted to know.

"I'd like to wait to see if I'm right. There'll be plenty of time for explanations later."

But as the hours dragged on, I could see the sheriff's patience wearing him. "It's after ten o'clock, Dr. Hawthorne. I have other duties, you know."

"Give me one more hour. If nothing happens by eleven, we'll call it—"

Below us, the cabin door started to open. I touched Petty's arm, warning him to silence. A man I'd never seen before entered and began looking around the floor. "Who—?" Sheriff Petty started to whisper, but I squeezed his arm, tensing myself to leap out of the sleeping loft.

I landed not six feet from the searching man, bringing him up straight with a look of surprise on his face. "Is this what you're looking for?" I asked, holding out the pencil April and I had found the previous day.

He looked at me oddly, then reached out his hand. "Yes, it is."

"Sheriff," I called out, "you'd better join us!"

An expression of panic crossed the man's face and I thought he might try to flee, but he stood his ground. "What's going on here, anyway?"

With Petty at my side, I felt a surge of confidence. "You dropped your pen yesterday morning when you were wearing your false beard and posing as the telephone man. You had to remove the phone wires before we figured out how you got into this cabin without leaving tracks. Sheriff, I want you to arrest this man for murder. He's the husband of Shorter's ex-wife. His name is Glen Deveroux."

I had to explain it all to the sheriff before he took Deveroux away, and then later, back at the Greenbush Inn, I told April and Andre about it. Faith Deveroux, shocked by her husband's arrest, had gone to the county jail to be with him.

"I'm sorry about last night," I told April at the beginning. "My mind wasn't functioning right."

"We understand," Andre said. Obviously he'd heard the details from April.

"Glen Deveroux is a construction engineer, supposedly working for long periods on the Golden Gate Bridge in San Francisco. Apparently he mistrusted his wife and would sneak back to Boston to check up on her. This time he followed her up here, wearing a beard for disguise, and found her having dinner with her ex-husband. Maybe they did more than have dinner. Posing as a telephone lineman, Deveroux went to Shorter's cabin and strung a couple of thin steel cables—the sort he uses in bridge construction. From a distance they looked just like ordinary telephone or electric wires. They were so much part of the scenery that we never noticed them as we approached the cabin, but they had to be there. The cabin had electric lights and a crank telephone. I suppose our attention was diverted by the bobcat tracks."

"You mean," Andre asked, "that this man walked across to the cabin on the telephone wire?"

"On a steel cable," I corrected, "with another steel cable to hang on to. Not a difficult task for a bridge builder. Once he reached the roof, he lifted the skylight and entered that way, lowering himself with another length of cable. When Shorter encountered him at work, he wasn't alarmed because Deveroux had visited him before in his guise of a telephone lineman. Deveroux stabbed Shorter and left the way he came. Any tracks he might have left on the roof would be easily smoothed over and the wind would finish the job of obliterating them."

April had a question. "If Deveroux met Shorter on a previous visit to the cabin, why didn't he simply kill the man then? Why go to all this trouble?"

"Because Shorter wasn't alone the first time. Gus Laxault was with him. Deveroux used this method in the hope the death would be taken for suicide. But he was so anxious to get out of there, he forgot to leave the weapon."

"How do you know this, Sam?" April asked. "Last night you thought Andre was guilty."

"I remembered the sunshine coming through the skylight when we entered the cabin to find the body. There wasn't time for all the snow to have melted from that glass, even with the heat from the cabin. Remember it was a cold morning. There was no snow on the skylight because it slid off when the skylight was opened. It wasn't latched like the windows. In fact, it opened quite easily. I asked myself, If the killer came through the skylight, how did he reach the roof?

"The wires, those unseen but necessary wires, were the answer. But could telephone and electric wires support the weight of a man across that distance? Not unless they were special wires, especially anchored on either end. When the lineman was there, removing the phone not twenty-four hours after the murder, I had to suspect him.

"Then there was the matter of the pencil. It had the initials G.D. on it, which could have stood for Glen Deveroux. It hadn't been dropped at the time of the murder or the police would have found it. If it didn't belong to Sheriff Petty or his people, it must have been dropped by that telephone man. If the phone man was Glen Deveroux in disguise, everything fell into place, including the motive. This morning I took a chance he'd come back to the cabin, looking for his pencil."

Andre stood up when I'd finished and shook my hand. "We owe you our thanks, April and I."

She kissed me on the cheek. "Can you ever forgive me for the way I behaved last night?"

"If you can forgive me," I looked at my watch. "I think I'll be starting back today. What are your plans?"

"I'll stay for the rest of the week, Sam. Then I'll come back to help train my replacement. You deserve a month's notice after all these years."

"April and Andre were married in the spring (Dr. Sam Hawthorne concluded). Of course, I hated to see April go, but they were happy together and had a fine marriage. I was the godfather for their child. Things didn't go as smoothly with April's replacement, though, as I'll tell you next time."

Janwillem van de Wetering brings the sights and sounds of the desolate Maine coastline home for his readers, having lived there for over twenty years. Whether exploring the New England landscape or solving crime in the city of Amsterdam, his characters attempt to come to grips with themselves almost as much as they try to solve whatever case they're on. It's an intriguing mixture of Zen philosophy and clever mystery wrapped up in a series of books.

A Great Sight

Janwillem van de Wetering

No, it wasn't easy. It took a great deal of effortful dreaming to get where I am now. Where I am is Moose Bay, on the Maine coast, which is on the east of the United States of America, in case you haven't been looking at maps lately. Moose Bay is long and narrow, bordered by two peninsulas and holding some twenty square miles of water. I've lived on the south shore for almost thirty years now, always alone—if you don't count a couple of old cats—and badly crippled. Lost the use of my legs thirty years ago, and that was my release and my ticket to Moose Bay. I've often wondered whether the mishap was really an accident. Sure enough, the fall was due to faulty equipment (a new strap that broke) and quite beyond my will. The telephone company that employed me acknowledged their responsibility easily enough, paying me handsomely so that I could be comfortably out of work for the rest of my life. But didn't I, perhaps, dream myself into that fall? You see, I wasn't exactly happy being a telephone repairman. Up one post and down another, climbing or slithering up and down forever, day after day, and not in the best of climates. For years I did that and there was no way I could see in which the ordeal would ever end. So I began to dream of a way out, and of where I would go. To be able to dream is a gift. My father didn't have the talent. No imagination the old man had. In Holland, where he lived and I was born, he had a similar job to what I would have later. He was a window-cleaner and I guess he could only visualize death, for when *he* fell it was the last thing he ever did. I survived, with mashed legs. I never dreamed of death, I dreamed of the great sights I would still see, whisking myself to a life on a rocky coast, where I would be alone, maybe with a few old cats, in a cedar log cabin with a view of the water, the sky, and a line of trees on the other shore. I would see, I dreamed, rippling waves or the mirror-like surface of a great expanse of liquid beauty on a windless day. I never gave that up, the possibility of seeing great sights, and I dreamed myself up here, where everything is as I thought it might be, only better.

Now don't get me wrong, I'm not your dreamy type. No long hair and beads for me, no debts unpaid or useless things just lying about in the house. Everything is spic-and-span with me; the kitchen works, there's an ample supply of staples, each in their own jar, I have good vegetables from the garden, an occasional bird I get with the shotgun, and fish caught off my dock. I can't walk so well, but I get about on my crutches and the pickup has been changed so that I can drive it with my hands. No fleas on the cats, either, and no smell from the outhouse. I have all I need and all within easy reach. There must be richer people in the world (don't I see them sometimes, sailing along in their hundred-foot skyscrapers?), but I don't have to envy them. May they live happily for as long as it takes; I'll just sit here and watch the sights from my porch.

Or I watch them from the water. I have an eight-foot dory and it rows quite well in the bay if the waves aren't too high, for it *will* ship water when the weather gets rough. There's much to see when I go rowing. A herd of harbor seals lives just out of my cove and they know me well, coming to play around my boat as soon as I sing out to them. I bring them a rubber ball that they push about for a bit, and throw even, until they want to go about their own business again and bring it back. I've named them all and can identify the individuals when they frolic in the spring, or raise their tails and heads, lolling in the summer sun.

I go out most good days, for I've taken it upon myself to keep this coast clean. Garbage drifts in, thrown in by the careless, off ships I suppose, and by the city people, the unfortunates who never look at the sights. I get beer cans to pick up in my net, and every variety of plastic container, boards with rusty nails in them and occasionally a complete vessel, made out of crumbly foam. I drag it all to the same spot and burn the rubbish. Rodney, the fellow I share Moose Bay with—he lives a mile down from me in a tar-papered shack—makes fun of me when I perform my duty. He'll come by in his smart powerboat, flat on the water and sharply pointed, with a loud engine pushing it that looks like three regular outboards stacked on top of each other. Rodney can really zip about in that thing. He's a thin, ugly fellow with a scraggly black beard and big slanted eyes above his crooked nose. He's from here, of course, and he won't let me forget his lawful nativity. Much higher up the scale than me, he claims, for what am I but some itinerant, an alien washed up from nowhere, tolerated by the locals? If I didn't happen to be an old codger, and lame, Rodney says, he would drown me like he does his kittens. Hop into the sack, weighted down with a good boulder, and away with the mess. But being what I am, sort of human in a way, he puts up with my presence for a while provided I don't trespass on his bit of the shore, crossing the high-tide line, for then he'll have to shoot me with the deer rifle he now uses for poaching. Rodney has a vegetable patch garden, too, even though he doesn't care for greens. The garden is a trap for deer so that he can shoot them from his shack, preferably at night, after he has frozen them with a flashlight.

There are reasons for me not to like Rodney too much. He shot my friend, the killer whale that used to come here some summers ago. Killer whales are a rare sight on this coast, but they do pop up from time to time. They're supposed to be wicked animals, that will push your boat over and gobble you up when you're thrashing about, weighed down by your boots and your oilskins. Maybe they do that, but my friend didn't do it to me. He used to float alongside my dory, which he could have tipped with a single flap of his great triangular tail. He would roll over on his side, all thirty feet of him, and grin lazily from the corner of his huge curved mouth. I could see his big gleaming teeth and mirror my face in his calm, humorous eye, and I would sing to him. I haven't got a good loud voice, but I would hum away, making up a few words here and there, and he'd lift a flipper in appreciation and snort if my song wasn't long enough for his liking. Every day that killer whale came to me; I swear he was waiting for me out in the bay, for as soon as I'd splash my oars I'd see his six-foot fin cut through the waves, and a moment later his black-and-white head, always with that welcoming grin.

Now we don't have any electricity down here, and kerosene isn't as cheap as it used to be, so maybe Rodney was right when he said that he shot the whale because he needed the blubber. Blubber makes good fuel, Rodney says. Me, I think he was wrong, for he never got the blubber anyway. When he shot the whale while zipping past it in the powerboat, he got the animal between the eyes with his deer rifle and it just sank. I never saw its vast body wash up. Perhaps it didn't die straight-away and could make it to the depth of the ocean, to die there in peace.

He's a thief, too, Rodney is. He'll steal anything he can get his hands on, to begin with his welfare. There's nothing wrong with Rodney's back but he's stuffed a lot of complaints into it, enough so that the doctors pay attention. He collects his check and his food stamps, and he gets his supplies for free. There's a town, some fifty miles further along, and they employ special people there to give money to the poor, and counselors to listen to pathetic homemade tales, and there's a soci-ety that distributes gifts on holiday. Rodney even gets his firewood every year, brought by young religious men on a truck; they stack it right where Rodney points—no fee.

"Me against the world," Rodney says, "for the world owes me a living. I never asked to be born but here I am, and my hands are out." He'll be drinking when he talks like that, guzzling my Sunday bourbon on my porch, and he'll point his long finger at me. "You some sort of Kraut?"

I say I'm Dutch. The Dutch fought the Krauts during the war; I fought a bit myself until they caught me and put me in a camp. They were going to kill me, but then the Americans came. "Saved you, did we?" Rodney will say, and fill up his glass again. "So you owe us now, right? So how come you're living off the fat of this land, you with the crummy legs?" He'll raise his glass and I'll raise mine.

Rodney lost his wife. He still had her when I settled in my cabin, I got to talk to her at times and liked her fine. She would talk to Rodney, about his ways, and he would leer at her, and he was still leer-ing when she was found at the bottom of the cliff. "Never watched where she was going," Rodney said to the sheriff, who took the corpse away. The couple had a dog, who was fond of Rodney's wife and unhappy when she was gone. The dog would howl at night and keep Rodney awake, but the dog happened to fall off the cliff too. Same cliff. Maybe I should have reported the coincidence to the authorities, but it wasn't much more than a coincidence and, as Rodney says, accidents will happen. Look at me, I fell down a telephone post, nobody pushed *me,* right? It was a brand-new strap that snapped when it shouldn't have; a small event, quite beyond my control.

No, I never went to the sheriff and I've never stood up to Rodney. There's just the two of us on Moose Bay. He's the bad guy who'll tip his garbage into the bay and I'm the in-between guy who's silly enough to pick it up. We also have a good guy, who lives at the end of the north peninsula, at the tip, facing the ocean. Michael his name is, Michael the lobsterman. A giant of a man, Michael is, with a golden beard and flashing teeth. I can see his smile when his lobster boat enters the bay. The boat is one of these old-fashioned jobs, sturdy and white and square, puttering along at a steady ten knots in every sort of weather. Michael's got a big winch on it, for hauling up the heavy traps, and I can see him taking the lobsters out and putting the bait in and throwing them back. Michael has some thousand traps, all along the coast, but his best fishing is here in Moose Bay. Over the years we've got to know each other and I sometimes go out with him, much further than the dory can take me. Then we see the old squaws flock in, the diver ducks that look as if they've flown in from a Chinese painting with their thin curved tail-feathers and delicately-drawn wings and necks. Or we watch the big whales, snorting and spouting, and the haze on the horizon where the sun dips causing indefinably soft colors, or we just smell the clear air coming to cool the forests in summer. Michael knows Rodney, too, but he isn't the gossipy kind. He'll frown when he sees the powerboat lurking in Moose Bay and gnaw his pipe before he turns away. When Michael doesn't stop at my dock he'll wave and make some gesture in lieu of conversation—maybe he'll hold his hands close together to show me how far he could see when he cut through the fog, or he'll point at a bird flying over us, a heron in slow flight, or a jay, hurrying from shore to shore, gawking and screeching, and I'll know what he means.

This Michael is a good guy, I knew it the first time I saw his silhouette on the lobster boat, and I've heard good stories about him too. A knight in shining armor who has saved people about to drown in storms or marooned and sick on the islands. A giant and a genius, for he's built his own boat and his gear—even his house, a big sprawling structure made out of driftwood on pegged beams. And he'll fight when he has to, for it isn't always cozy here. He'll be out in six-foot waves, and I've seen him when the bay is frozen up, excepting the channel where the current rages, with icicles on his beard and snow driving against his bow—but he'll still haul up his traps.

I heard he was out in the last war, too, flying an airplane low above the jungle, and he still flies now, on Sundays, for the National Guard.

Rodney got worse. I don't know what devil lives in that man but the fiend must have been thrown out of the lowest hells. Rodney likes new games and he thought it would be fun to chase me a bit. My dory sits pretty low in the water, but there are enough good days here and I can get out quite a bit. When I do Rodney will wait for me, hidden behind the big rocks east of my cove, and he'll suddenly appear, revving his engine, trailing a high wake. When his curly waves hit me I have to bail for my life, and as soon as I'm done the fear will be back, for he'll be after me again.

I didn't quite know what to do then. Get a bigger boat? But then he would think of something else. There are enough games he can play. He knows my fondness for the seals, he could get them one by one, as target practice. There's my vegetable garden too, close to the track; he could back his truck into it and get my cats as an afterthought, flattening them into the gravel, for they're slow these days, careless with old age. The fear grabbed me by the throat at night as I watched my ceiling remembering his dislike of my cabin and thinking how easily it would burn, being made of old cedar with a roof of shingles. I knew it was him who took the battery out of my truck, making me hitchhike to town for a new one. He was also sucking my gas, but I keep a drum of energy near the house. Oh, I'm vulnerable here all right with the sheriff coming down only once a year. Suppose I talk to the law, suppose the law talks to Rodney, suppose *I* fall down that cliff too?

I began to dream again like I had done before when I was still climbing the telephone posts like a demented monkey. I was bored then, hopelessly bored, and now I was hopelessly afraid. Hadn't I dreamed my way out once before? Tricks can be repeated.

My dream gained strength; it had to for Rodney was getting rougher. His powerboat kept less distance and went faster. I couldn't see myself sticking to the land. I need to get out on the bay, to listen to the waves lapping the rocks, to hear the seals blow when they clear their nostrils, to hear the kingfishers and the squirrels whirr in the trees on shore, and to spot the little ring-necked ducks busily investigating the shallows peering eagerly out of their tufted heads. There are the quiet herons stalking the mudflats and the ospreys whirling slowly; there are even eagles diving and splashing when the alewives run from the brooks. Would I have to potter about in the vegetable patch all the time, leaning on a crutch while pushing a hoe with my free hand?

I dreamed up a bay free of Rodney. There was a strange edge to the dream; some kind of quality there that I couldn't quite see, but it was splendid, a great sight and part of my imagination although I couldn't quite make it out.

One day, fishing off my dock, I saw Michael's lobster boat nosing into the cove. I waved and smiled and he waved back, but he didn't smile.

He moored the boat and jumped onto the jetty, light as a great cat, touching my arm. We walked up to my porch and I made some strong coffee.

"There's a thief," Michael said, "stealing my lobsters. He used to take a few, few enough to ignore maybe, but now he's taking too many."

"Oho," I said, holding my mug. Michael wouldn't be referring to me. Me? Steal lobsters? how could I ever haul up a trap? The channel is deep in the bay. A hundred feet of cable and a heavy trap at the end of it, never. I would need a winch, like Rodney has on his powerboat.

Besides, doesn't Michael leave me a lobster every now and then? Lying on my dock in the morning, its claws neatly tied with a bit of yellow string?

"Any idea?" he asked.

"Same as yours," I said, "but he's hard to catch. The powerboat is fast. He nips out of the bay before he does his work, to make sure you aren't around."

"Might get the warden," Michael said, "and then he might go to jail and come out again and do something bad."

I agreed. "Hard to prove, it would be," I said. "A house burns down, yours or mine. An accident maybe."

Michael left. I stayed on the porch, dreaming away, expending some power. A little power goes a long way in a dream.

It happened the next day, a Sunday it was. I was walking to the shore for it was low tide and I wanted to see the seals on their rocks. It came about early, just after sunrise. I heard an airplane. A lot of airplanes come by here. There's the regular commuter plane from the town to the big city, and the little ones the tourists fly in summer, and the flying club. There are also big planes dirtying up the sky, high up, some of them are Russians they say; the National Guard has to be about to push them back. The big planes rumble, but this sound was different, light but deadly, far away still. I couldn't see the plane, but when I did it was coming silently, ahead of its own sound, it was that fast. Then it slowed down, surveying the bay.

I've seen fighter planes during World War II, Germans and Englishmen flew them, propeller jobs that would spin around each other above the small Dutch lakes, until one of the planes came down trailing smoke. Jet planes I only saw later, here in America. They looked dangerous enough, even while they gambolled about, and I felt happy watching them for I was in the States and they were protecting me from the bad guys lurking in the east.

This airplane was a much-advanced version of what I had seen in the late '40s. Much longer it was and sleek and quiet as it lost height, aiming for the channel. A baby-blue killer with twin rudders sticking up elegantly far behind the large gleaming canopy up front reflecting the low sunlight. I guessed her to be seventy feet long, easily the size of the splendid yachts of the rich summer people, but there was no pleasure in her; she was all functional, programmed for swift pursuit and destruction only. I grinned when I saw her American stars set in circles with a striped bar sticking out at each side. When she was closer I thought I could see the pilot all wrapped up in his tight suit and helmet, the living brain controlling this deadly superfast vessel of the sky.

I saw that the plane was armed, with white missiles attached to its slender streamlined belly. I had read about those missiles. Costly little mothers they are. Too costly to fire at Rodney's boat, busily stealing away right in front of my cove. Wouldn't the pilot have to explain the loss of one of his slick rockets? He'd surely be in terrible trouble if he returned to base incomplete.

Rodney was thinking the same way for he was jumping up and down in his powerboat grinning and sticking two fingers at the airplane hovering above the bay.

Then the plane roared and shot away, picking up speed at an incredible rate. I was mightily impressed and grateful, visualizing the enemy confronted with such force, banking, diving, rising again at speeds much faster than sound.

The plane had gone and I·was alone again, with Rodney misbehaving in the bay, taking the lobsters out as fast as he could—one trap shooting up after another, yanked up by his nastily whining little winch.

The plane came back, silently, with the roar of its twin engines well behind it. It came in low, twenty-five feet above the short choppy waves. Rodney, unaware, busy, didn't even glance over his shoulder. I was leaning on the railing of my porch, gaping stupidly. Was the good guy going to ram the bad guy? Would they go down together? This had to be the great sight I had been dreaming up. Perhaps I should have felt guilty.

Seconds it took, maybe less than one second. Is there still time at five thousand miles an hour?

Then there was the flame, just after the plane passed the powerboat. A tremendous cloud of fire, billowing, deep orange with fiery red tongues, blotting out the other shore, frayed with black smoke at the edges. The flame shot out of the rear of the plane and hung sizzling around Rodney's boat. The boat must have dissolved instantly, for I never found any debris. Fried to a cinder. Did Rodney's body whizz away inside that hellish fire? It must have, bones, teeth and all.

I didn't see where the plane went. There are low hills at the end of the bay, so it must have zoomed up immediately once the afterburners spat out the huge flame.

Michael smiled sadly when he visited me a few days later and we were having coffee on my porch again.

"You saw it happen?"

"Oh yes," I said. "A great sight indeed."

"Did he leave any animals that need taking care of?"

"Just a cat," I said. The cat was on my porch, a big marmalade tom that had settled in already.

Time has passed again since then. The bay is quiet now. We're having a crisp autumn and I'm enjoying the cool days rowing about on the bay, watching the geese gather, honking majestically as they get ready to go south.

Linda Barnes makes her home city of Boston come alive in the novels featuring Carlotta Carlyle, an ex-cop/taxi driver turned private detective. The first Carlyle novel, A Trouble of Fools, was nominated for the Edgar Award. Carlyle's first appearance, however, in the following story, did win her creator the Edgar for best short fiction. Without further ado, here it is.

Lucky Penny

Linda Barnes

Lieutenant Mooney made me dish it all out for the record. He's a good cop, if such an animal exists. We used to work the same shift before I decided—wrongly—that there was room for a lady PI in this town. Who knows? With this case under my belt, maybe business'll take a 180-degree spin, and I can quit driving a hack.

See, I've already written the official report for Mooney and the cops, but the kind of stuff they wanted: date, place, and time, cold as ice and submitted in triplicate, doesn't even start to tell the tale. So I'm doing it over again, my way.

Don't worry, Mooney. I'm not gonna file this one.

The Thayler case was still splattered across the front page of the *Boston Globe*. I'd soaked it up with my midnight coffee and was puzzling it out—my cab on automatic pilot, my mind on crime—when the mad tea party began.

"Take your next right, sister. Then pull over, and douse the lights. Quick!"

I heard the bastard all right, but it must have taken me thirty seconds or so to react. Something hard rapped on the cab's dividing shield. I didn't bother turning around. I hate staring down gun barrels.

I said, "Jimmy Cagney, right? No, your voice is too high. Let me guess, don't tell me—"

"Shut up!"

"*Kill* the lights, *turn off* the lights, okay. But *douse* the lights? You've been tuning in too many old gangster flicks."

"I hate a mouthy broad," the guy snarled. I kid you not.

"*Broad*," I said. "Christ! *Broad*? You trying to grow hair on your balls?"

"Look, I mean it, lady!"

"*Lady's* better. Now you wanna vacate my cab and go rob a phone booth?" My heart was beating like a tin drum, but I didn't let my voice shake, and all the time I was gabbing at him, I kept trying to catch his face in the mirror. He must have been crouching way back on the passenger side. I couldn't see a damn thing.

"I want all your dough," he said.

Who can you trust? This guy was a spiffy dresser: charcoal-gray three-piece suit and rep tie, no less. And picked up in front of the swank Copley Plaza. I looked like I needed the bucks more than he did, and I'm no charity case. A woman can make good tips driving a hack in Boston. Oh, she's gotta take precautions, all right. When you can't smell a disaster fare from thirty feet, it's time to quit. I pride myself on my judgment. I'm careful. I always know where the police checkpoints are, so I can roll my cab past and flash the old lights if a guy starts acting up. This dude fooled me cold.

I was ripped. Not only had I been conned, I had a considerable wad to give away. It was near the end of my shift, and like I said, I do all right. I've got a lot of regulars. Once you see me, you don't forget me— or my cab.

It's gorgeous. Part of my inheritance. A '59 Chevy, shiny as new, kept on blocks in a heated garage by the proverbial dotty old lady. It's the pits of the design world. Glossy blue with those giant chromium fins. Restrained decor: just the phone number and a few gilt curlicues on the door. I was afraid all my old pals at the police department would pull me over for minor traffic violations if I went whole hog and painted "Carlotta's Cab" in ornate script on the hood. Some do it anyway.

So where the hell were all the cops now? Where are they when you need 'em?

He told me to shove the cash through that little hole they leave for the passenger to pass the fare forward. I told him he had it backwards. He didn't laugh. I shoved bills.

"Now the change," the guy said. Can you imagine the nerve?

I must have cast my eyes up to heaven. I do that a lot these days.

"I mean it." He rapped the plastic shield with the shiny barrel of his gun. I checked it out this time. Funny how big a little .22 looks when it's pointed just right.

I fished in my pockets for change, emptied them.

"Is that all?"

"You want the gold cap on my left front molar?" I said.

"Turn around," the guy barked. "Keep both hands on the steering wheel. High."

I heard jingling, then a quick intake of breath.

"Okay," the crook said, sounding happy as a clam, "I'm gonna take my leave—"

"Good. Don't call this cab again."

"Listen!" The gun tapped. "You cool it here for ten minutes. And I mean frozen. Don't twitch. Don't blow your nose. Then take off."

"Gee, thanks."

"Thank *you*," he said politely. The door slammed.

At times like that, you just feel ridiculous. You *know* the guy isn't going to hang around, waiting to see whether you're big on insubordination. *But*, he might. And who wants to tangle with a .22 slug? I rate pretty high on insubordination. That's why I messed up as a cop. I figured I'd give him two minutes to get lost. Meantime I listened.

Not much traffic goes by those little streets on Beacon Hill at one o'clock on a Wednesday morn. Too residential. So I could hear the guy's footsteps tap along the pavement. About ten steps back, he stopped. Was he the one in a million who'd wait to see if I turned around? I heard a funny kind of *whooshing* noise. Not loud enough to make me jump, and anything much louder than the ticking of my watch would have put me through the roof. Then the footsteps patted on, straight back and out of hearing.

One minute more. The only saving grace of the situation was the location: District One. That's Mooney's district. Nice guy to talk to.

I took a deep breath, hoping it would have an encore, and pivoted quickly, keeping my head low. Makes you feel stupid when you do that and there's no one around.

I got out and strolled to the corner, stuck my head around a building kind of cautiously. Nothing, of course.

I backtracked. Ten steps, then *whoosh*. Along the sidewalk stood one of those new "Keep Beacon Hill Beautiful" trash cans, the kind with the swinging lid. I gave it a shove as I passed. I could just as easily have kicked it; I was in that kind of funk.

Whoosh, it said, just as pretty as could be.

Breaking into one of those trash cans is probably tougher than busting into your local bank vault. Since I didn't even have a dime left to fiddle the screws on the lid, I was forced to deface city property. I got the damn thing open and dumped the contents on somebody's front lawn, smack in the middle of a circle of light from one of those snooty Beacon Hill gas street lamps.

Halfway through the whisky bottles, wadded napkins, and beer cans, I made my discovery. I was doing a thorough search. If you're going to stink like garbage anyway, why leave anything untouched, right? So I was opening all the brown bags—you know, the good old brown lunch-and-bottle bags—looking for a clue. My most valuable find so far had been the moldy rind of a bologna sandwich. Then I hit it big: one neatly creased bag stuffed full of cash.

To say I was stunned is to entirely underestimate how I felt as I crouched there, knee-deep in garbage, my jaw hanging wide. I don't know what I'd expected to find. Maybe the guy's gloves. Or his hat, if he'd wanted to get rid of it fast in order to melt back into anonymity. I pawed through the rest of the debris. My change was gone.

I was so befuddled I left the trash right on the front lawn. There's probably still a warrant out for my arrest.

District One headquarters is off the beaten path, over on New Sudbury Street. I would have called first, if I'd had a dime.

One of the few things I'd enjoyed about being a cop was gabbing with Mooney. I like driving a cab better, but, face it, most of my fares aren't scintillating conversationalists. The Red Sox and the weather usually covers it. Talking to Mooney was so much fun, I wouldn't even consider dating him. Lots of guys are good at sex, but conversation—now there's an art form.

Mooney, all six-feet-four, 240 linebacker pounds of him, gave me the glad eye when I waltzed in. He hasn't given up trying. Keeps telling me he talks even better in bed.

"Nice hat," was all he said, his big fingers pecking at the typewriter keys.

I took it off and shook out my hair. I wear an old slouch cap when I drive to keep people from saying the inevitable. One jerk even misquoted Yeats at me: "Only God, my dear, could love you for yourself alone and not your long red hair." Since I'm seated when I drive, he missed the chance to ask me how the weather is up here. I'm six-one in my stocking feet and skinny enough to make every inch count twice. I've got a wide forehead, green eyes, and a pointy chin. If you want to be nice about my nose, you say it's got character.

Thirty's still hovering in my future. It's part of Mooney's past.

I told him I had a robbery to report and his dark eyes steered me to a chair. He leaned back and took a puff of one of his low-tar cigarettes. He can't quite give 'em up, but he feels guilty as hell about 'em.

When I got to the part about the bag in the trash, Mooney lost his sense of humor. He crushed a half-smoked butt in a crowded ashtray.

"Know why you never made it as a cop?" he said.

"Didn't brown-nose enough."

"You got no sense of proportion! Always going after crackpot stuff!"

"Christ, Mooney, aren't you interested? Some guy heists a cab, at gunpoint, then tosses the money. Aren't you the least bit *intrigued*?"

"I'm a cop, Ms. Carlyle. I've got to be more than intrigued. I've got murders, bank robberies, assaults—"

"Well, excuse me. I'm just a poor citizen reporting a crime. Trying to help—"

"Want to help, Carlotta? Go away." He stared at the sheet of paper in the typewriter and lit another cigarette. "Or dig me up something on the Thayler case."

"You working that sucker?"

"Wish to hell I wasn't."

I could see his point. It's tough enough trying to solve any murder, but when your victim is *the* Jennifer (Mrs. Justin) Thayler, wife of the famed Harvard Law prof, and the society reporters are breathing down your neck along with the usual crime-beat scribblers, you got a special kind of problem.

"So who did it?" I asked.

Mooney put his size twelves up on his desk. "Colonel Mustard in the library with the candlestick! How the hell do I know? Some scumbag housebreaker. The lady of the house interrupted his haul. Probably didn't mean to hit her that hard. He must have freaked when he saw all the blood, 'cause he left some of the ritziest stereo equipment this side of heaven, plus enough silverware to blind your average hophead. He snatched most of old man Thayler's goddamn idiot artworks, collections, collectibles—whatever the hell you call 'em—which ought to set him up for the next few hundred years, if he's smart enough to get rid of them."

"Alarm system?"

"Yeah, they had one. Looks like Mrs. Thayler forgot to turn it on. According to the maid, she had a habit of forgetting just about anything after a martini or three."

"Think the maid's in on it?"

"Christ, Carlotta. There you go again. No witnesses. No finger-prints. Servants asleep. Husband asleep. We've got word out to all the fences here and in New York that we want this guy. The pawnbrokers know the stuff's hot. We're checking out known art thieves and shady museums—"

"Well, don't let me keep you from your serious business," I said, getting up to go. "I'll give you the collar when I find out who robbed my cab."

"Sure," he said. His fingers started playing with the typewriter again.

"Wanna bet on it?" Betting's an old custom with Mooney and me.

"I'm not gonna take the few piddling bucks you earn with that ridiculous car."

"Right you are, boy. I'm gonna take the money the city pays you to be unimaginative! Fifty bucks I nail him within the week."

Mooney hates to be called "boy." He hates to be called "unimagi-native." I hate to hear my car called "ridiculous." We shook hands on the deal. Hard.

Chinatown's about the only chunk of Boston that's alive after mid-night. I headed over to Yee Hong's for a bowl of wonton soup.

The service was the usual low-key, slow-motion routine. I used a newspaper as a shield; if you're really involved in the *Wall Street Journal*, the casual male may think twice before deciding he's the answer to your prayers. But I didn't read a single stock quote. I tugged at strands of my hair, a bad habit of mine. Why would somebody rob me and then toss the money away?

Solution Number One: He didn't. The trash bin was some mob drop, and the money I'd found in the trash had absolutely nothing to do with the money filched from my cab. Except that it was the same amount—and that was too big a coincidence for me to swallow.

Two: The cash I'd found was counterfeit and this was a clever way of getting it into circulation. Nah. Too baroque entirely. How the hell would the guy know I was the pawing-through-the trash type?

Three: It was a training session. Some fool had used me to perfect his robbery technique. Couldn't he learn from TV like the rest of the crooks?

Four: It was a frat hazing. Robbing a hack at gunpoint isn't exactly in the same league as swallowing goldfish.

I closed my eyes.

My face came to a fortunate halt about an inch above a bowl of steaming broth. That's when I decided to pack it in and head for home. Wonton soup is lousy for the complexion.

I checked out the log I keep in the Chevy, totaled my fares: $4.82 missing, all in change. A very reasonable robbery.

By the time I got home, the sleepiness had passed. You know how it is: one moment you're yawning, the next your eyes won't close. Usually happens when my head hits the pillow; this time I didn't even make it that far. What woke me up was the idea that my robber hadn't meant to steal a thing. Maybe he'd left me something instead. You know, something hot, cleverly concealed. Something he could pick up in a few weeks, after things cooled off.

I went over that backseat with a vengeance, but I didn't find anything besides old Kleenex and bent paperclips. My brainstorm wasn't too clever after all. I mean, if the guy wanted to use my cab as a hiding place, why advertise by pulling a five-and-dime robbery?

I sat in the driver's seat, tugged my hair, and stewed. What did I have to go on? The memory of a nervous thief who talked like a B movie and stole only change. Maybe a mad toll-booth collector.

I live in a Cambridge dump. In any other city, I couldn't sell the damned thing if I wanted to. Here, I turn real estate agents away daily. The key to my home's value is the fact that I can hoof it to Harvard Square in five minutes. It's a seller's market for tar-paper shacks within walking distance of the Square. Under a hundred thou only if the plumbing's outside.

It took me a while to get in the door. I've got about five locks on it. Neighborhood's popular with thieves as well as gentry. I'm neither. I inherited the house from my weird Aunt Bea, all paid for. I consider the property taxes my rent, and the rent's getting steeper all the time.

I slammed my log down on the dining room table. I've got rooms galore in that old house, rent a couple of them to Harvard students. I've got my own office on the second floor, but I do most of my work at the dining room table. I like the view of the refrigerator.

I started over from square one. I called Gloria. She's the late-night dispatcher for the Independent Taxi Owners Association. I've never seen her, but her voice is as smooth as mink oil and I'll bet we get a lot of calls from guys who just want to hear her say she'll pick 'em up in five minutes.

"Gloria, it's Carlotta."

"Hi, babe. You been pretty popular today."

"Was I popular at one-thirty-five this morning?"

"Huh?"

"I picked up a fare in front of the Copley Plaza at one-thirty-five. Did you hand that one out to all comers or did you give it to me solo?"

"Just a sec." I could hear her charming the pants off some caller in the background. Then she got back to me.

"I just gave him to you, babe. He asked for the lady in the '59 Chevy. Not a lot of those on the road."

"Thanks, Gloria."

"Trouble?" she asked.

"Is mah middle name," I twanged. We both laughed and I hung up before she got a chance to cross-examine me.

So. The robber wanted my cab. I wished I'd concentrated on his face instead of his snazzy clothes. Maybe it was somebody I knew, some jokester in mid-prank. I killed that idea; I don't know anybody who'd pull a stunt like that, at gunpoint and all. I don't want to know anybody like that.

Why rob my cab, then toss the dough?

I pondered sudden religious conversion. Discarded it. Maybe some robber was some perpetual screwup who'd ditched the cash by mistake.

Or . . . Maybe he got exactly what he wanted. Maybe he desperately desired my change.

Why?

Because my change was special, valuable beyond its $4.82 replacement cost.

So how would somebody know my change was valuable?

Because he'd given it to me himself, earlier in the day.

"Not bad," I said out loud. "Not bad." It was the kind of reasoning they'd bounced me off the police force for, what my so-called superiors termed the "fevered product of an overimaginative mind." I leapt at it because it was the only explanation I could think of. I do like life to make some sort of sense.

I pored over my log. I keep pretty good notes: where I pick up a fare, where I drop him, whether he's a hailer or a radio call.

First, I ruled out all the women. That made the task slightly less impossible: sixteen suspects down from thirty-five. Then I yanked my hair and stared at the blank white porcelain of the refrigerator door. Got up and made myself a sandwich: ham, Swiss cheese, salami, lettuce and tomato, on rye. Ate it. Stared at the porcelain some more until the suspects started coming into focus.

Five of the guys were just plain fat and one was decidedly on the hefty side; I'd felt like telling them all to walk. Might do them some good, might bring on a heart attack. I crossed them all out. Making a thin person look plump is hard enough; it's damn near impossible to make a fatty look thin.

Then I considered my regulars: Jonah Ashley, a tiny blond southern gent; muscle-bound "just-call-me-Harold" at Longfellow Place; Dr. Homewood getting his daily ferry from Beth Israel to MGH; Marvin of the gay bars; and Professor Dickerman, Harvard's answer to Berkeley's sixties radicals.

I crossed them all off. I could see Dickerman holding up the First Filthy Capitalist Bank, or disobeying civilly at Seabrook, even blowing up an oil company or two. But my mind boggled at the thought of the great liberal Dickerman robbing some poor cabbie. It would be like Robin Hood joining the sheriff of Nottingham on some particularly rotten peasant swindle. Then they'd both rape Maid Marian and go off pals together.

Dickerman *was* a lousy tipper. That ought to be a crime.

So what did I leave? Eleven out of sixteen guys cleared without leaving my chair. Me and Sherlock Holmes, the famous armchair detectives.

I'm stubborn; that was one of my good cop traits. I stared at that log till my eyes bugged out. I remembered two of the five pretty easily; they were handsome and I'm far from blind. The first had one of those elegant bony faces and far-apart eyes. He was taller than my bandit. I'd ceased eyeballing him when I noticed the ring on his left hand; I never fuss with the married kind. The other one was built, a weight lifter. Not an Arnold Schwarzenegger extremist, but built. I think I'd have noticed that bod on my bandit. Like I said, I'm not blind.

That left three.

Okay. I closed my eyes. Who had I picked up at the Hyatt on Memorial Drive? Yeah, that was the salesman guy, the one who looked so uncomfortable that I'd figured he'd been hoping to ask his cabbie for a few pointers concerning the best skirt-chasing areas in our fair city. Too low a voice. Too broad in the beam.

The log said I'd picked up a hailer at Kenmore Square when I'd let out the salesman. Ah, yes, a talker. The weather, mostly. Don't you think it's dangerous for you to be driving a cab? Yeah, I remembered him, all right: a fatherly type, clasping a briefcase, heading to the financial district. Too old.

Down to one. I was exhausted but not the least bit sleepy. All I had to do was remember who I'd picked up on Beacon near Charles. A hailer. Before five o'clock, which was fine by me because I wanted to be long gone before rush hour gridlocked the city. I'd gotten onto Storrow and taken him along the river into Newton Center. Dropped him off at the Bay Bank Middlesex, right before closing time. It was coming back. Little nervous guy. Pegged him as an accountant when I'd let him out at the bank. Measly, undernourished soul. Skinny as a rail, stooped, with pits left from teenage acne.

Shit. I let my head sink down onto the dining room table when I realized what I'd done. I'd ruled them all out, every one. So much for my brilliant deductive powers.

I retired to my bedroom, disgusted. Not only had I lost $4.82 in assorted alloy metals, I was going to lose fifty dollars to Mooney. I stared at myself in the mirror, but what I was really seeing was the round hole at the end of a .22, held in a neat, gloved hand.

Somehow, the gloves made me feel better. I'd remembered another detail about my piggy-bank robber. I consulted the mirror and kept the recall going. A hat. The guy wore a hat. Not like my cap, but like a hat out of a forties gangster flick. I had one of those: I'm a sucker for hats. I plunked it on my head, jamming my hair up underneath—and I drew in my breath sharply.

A shoulder-padded jacket, a slim build, a low slouched hat. Gloves. Boots with enough heel to click as he walked away. Voice? High. Breathy, almost whispered. Not unpleasant. Accentless. No Boston *r*.

I had a man's jacket and a couple of ties in my closet. Don't ask. They may have dated from as far back as my ex-husband, but not necessarily so. I slipped into the jacket, knotted the tie, tilted the hat down over one eye.

I'd have trouble pulling it off. I'm skinny, but my build is decidedly female. Still, I wondered—enough to traipse back downstairs, pull a chicken leg out of the fridge, go back to the log, and review the feminine possibilities. Good thing I did.

Everything clicked. One lady fit the bill exactly: mannish walk and clothes, tall for a woman. And I was in luck. While I'd picked her up in Harvard Square, I'd dropped her at a real address, a house in Brookline: 782 Mason Terrace, at the top of Corey Hill.

JoJo's garage opens at seven. That gave me a big two hours to sleep.

I took my beloved car in for some repair work it really didn't need yet and sweet-talked JoJo into giving me a loaner. I needed a hack, but not mine. Only trouble with that Chevy is it's too damn conspicuous.

I figured I'd lose way more than fifty bucks staking out Mason Terrace. I also figured it would be worth it to see old Mooney's face.

She was regular as clockwork, a dream to tail. Eight-thirty-seven every morning, she got a ride to the Square with a next-door neighbor. Took a cab home at five-fifteen. A working woman. Well, she couldn't make much of a living from robbing hacks and dumping the loot in the garbage.

I was damn curious by now. I knew as soon as I looked her over that she was the one, but she seemed so blah, so *normal*. She must have been five-seven or -eight, but the way she stooped, she didn't look tall. Her hair was long and brown with a lot of blond in it, the kind of hair that would have been terrific loose and wild, like a horse's mane. She tied it back with a scarf. A brown scarf. She wore suits. Brown suits. She had a tiny nose, brown eyes under pale eyebrows, a sharp chin. I never saw her smile. Maybe what she needed was a shrink, not a session with Mooney. Maybe she'd done it for the excitement. God knows, if I had her routine, her job, I'd probably be dressing up like King Kong and assaulting skyscrapers.

See, I followed her to work. It wasn't even tricky. She trudged the same path, went in the same entrance to Harvard Yard, probably walked the same number of steps every morning. Her name was Marcia Heidegger and she was a secretary in the admissions office of the college of fine arts.

I got friendly with one of her coworkers.

There was this guy typing away like mad at a desk in her office. I could just see him from the side window. He had grad student written all over his face. Longish wispy hair. Gold-rimmed glasses. Serious. Given to deep sighs and bright velour V necks. Probably writing his thesis on "Courtly Love and the Theories of Chrétien de Troyes."

I latched onto him at Bailey's the day after I'd tracked Lady Heidegger to her Harvard lair.

Too bad Roger was so short. Most short guys find it hard to believe that I'm really trying to pick them up. They look for ulterior motives. Not the Napoleon type of short guy; he assumes I've been waiting years for a chance to dance with a guy who doesn't have to bend to stare down my cleavage. But Roger was no Napoleon. So I had to engineer things a little.

I got into line ahead of him and ordered, after long deliberation, a BLT on toast. While the guy made it up and shoved it on a plate with three measly potato chips and a sliver of pickle you could barely see, I searched through my wallet, opened my change purse, counted out silver, got to $1.60 on the last five pennies. The counterman sang out, "That'll be a buck, eighty-five." I pawed through my pockets, found a nickel, two pennies. The line was growing restive. I concentrated on looking like a damsel in need of a knight, a tough task for a woman over six feet.

Roger (I didn't know he was Roger then) smiled ruefully and passed over a quarter. I was effusive in my thanks. I sat at a table for two, and when he'd gotten his tray (ham-and-cheese and a strawberry ice cream soda), I motioned him into my extra chair.

He was a sweetie. Sitting down, he forgot the difference in our height, and decided I might be someone he could talk to. I encouraged him. I hung shamelessly on his every word. A Harvard man, imagine that. We got around slowly, ever so slowly, to his work at the admissions office. He wanted to duck it and talk about more important issues, but I persisted. I'd been thinking about getting a job at Harvard, possibly in admissions. What kind of people did he work with? Were they congenial? What was the atmosphere like? Was it a big office? How many people? Men? Women? Any soulmates? Readers? Or just, you know, office people?

According to him, every soul he worked with was brain dead. I interrupted a stream of complaint with "Gee, I know somebody who works for Harvard. I wonder if you know her."

"It's a big place," he said, hoping to avoid the whole endless business.

"I met her at a party. Always meant to look her up." I searched through my bag, found a scrap of paper and pretended to read Marcia Heidegger's name off it.

"Marcia? Geez, I work with Marcia. Same office."

"Do you think she likes her work? I mean I got some strange vibes from her," I said. I actually said "strange vibes" and he didn't laugh his head off. People in the Square say things like that and other people take them seriously.

His face got conspiratorial, of all things, and he leaned closer to me.

"You want it, I bet you could get Marcia's job."

"You mean it?" What a compliment—a place for me among the brain dead.

"She's gonna get fired if she doesn't snap out of it."

"Snap out of what?"

"It was bad enough working with her when she first came over. She's one of those crazy neat people, can't stand to see papers lying on a desktop, you know? She almost threw out the first chapter of my thesis!"

I made a suitably horrified noise and he went on.

"Well, you know, about Marcia, it's kind of tragic. She doesn't talk about it."

But he was dying to.

"Yes?" I said, as if he needed egging on.

He lowered his voice. "She used to work for Justin Thayler over at the law school, that guy in the news, whose wife got killed. You know, her work hasn't been worth shit since it happened. She's always on the phone, talking real soft, hanging up if anybody comes in the room. I mean, you'd think she was in love with the guy or something, the way she . . ."

I don't remember what I said. For all I know, I may have volunteered to type his thesis. But I got rid of him somehow and then I scooted around the corner of Church Street and found a pay phone and dialed Mooney.

"Don't tell me," he said. "Somebody mugged you, but they only took your trading stamps."

"I have just one question for you, Moon."

"I accept. A June wedding, but I'll have to break it to Mother gently."

"Tell me what kind of junk Justin Thayler collected."

I could hear him breathing into the phone.

"Just tell me," I said, "for curiosity's sake."

"You onto something, Carlotta?"

"I'm curious, Mooney. And you're not the only source of information in the world."

"Thayler collected Roman stuff. Antiques. And I mean old. Artifacts, statues—"

"Coins?"

"Whole mess of them."

"Thanks."

"Carlotta—"

I never did find out what he was about to say because I hung up. Rude, I know. But I had things to do. And it was better Mooney shouldn't know what they were, because they came under the heading of illegal activities.

When I knocked at the front door of the Mason Terrace house at 10:00 A.M. the next day, I was dressed in dark slacks, a white blouse, and my old police department hat. I looked very much like the guy who reads your gas meter. I've never heard of anyone being arrested for impersonating the gasman. I've never heard of anyone really giving the gasman a second look. He fades into the background and that's exactly what I wanted to do.

I knew Marcia Heidegger wouldn't be home for hours. Old reliable had left for the Square at her usual time, precise to the minute. But I wasn't 100 percent sure Marcia lived alone. Hence the gasman. I could knock on the door and check it out.

Those Brookline neighborhoods kill me. Act sneaky and the neighbors call the cops in twenty seconds, but walk right up to the front door, knock, talk to yourself while you're sticking a shim in the crack of the door, let yourself in, and nobody does a thing. Boldness is all.

The place wasn't bad. Three rooms, kitchen and bath, light and airy. Marcia was incredibly organized, obsessively neat, which meant I had to keep track of where everything was and put it back just so. There was no clutter in the woman's life. The smell of coffee and toast lingered, but if she'd eaten breakfast, she'd already washed, dried, and put away the dishes. The morning paper had been read and tossed in the trash. The mail was sorted in one of those plastic accordion files. I mean, she folded her underwear like origami.

Now coins are hard to look for. They're small; you can hide 'em anywhere. So this search took me one hell of a long time. Nine out of ten women hide things that are dear to them in the bedroom. They keep their finest jewelry closest to the bed, sometimes in the nightstand, sometimes right under the mattress. That's where I started.

Marcia had a jewelry box on top of her dresser. I felt like hiding it for her. She had some nice stuff and a burglar could have made quite a haul with no effort.

The next favorite place for women to stash valuables is the kitchen. I sifted through her flour. I removed every Kellogg's Rice Krispy from the giant economy-sized box—and returned it. I went through her place like no burglar ever will. When I say thorough, I mean thorough.

I found four odd things. A neatly squared pile of clippings from the *Globe* and the *Herald*, all the articles about the Thayler killing. A manila envelope containing five different safe-deposit-box keys. A Tupperware container full of superstitious junk, good luck charms mostly, the kind of stuff I'd never have associated with a straight-arrow like Marcia: rabbits' feet galore, a little leather bag on a string that looked like some kind of voodoo charm, a pendant in the shape of a cross surmounted by a hook, and, I swear to God, a pack of worn tarot cards. Oh, yes, and a .22 automatic, looking a lot less threatening stuck in an ice cube tray. I took the bullets; the loaded gun threatened a defenseless box of Breyers' mint chocolate-chip ice cream.

I left everything else just the way I'd found it and went home. And tugged my hair. And stewed. And brooded. And ate half the stuff in the refrigerator. I kid you not.

At about one in the morning, it all made blinding, crystal-clear sense.

The next afternoon, at five-fifteen, I made sure I was the cabbie who picked up Marcia Heidegger in Harvard Square. Now cabstands have the most rigid protocol since Queen Victoria; you do not grab a fare out of turn or your fellow cabbies are definitely not amused. There was nothing for it but bribing the ranks. This bet with Mooney was costing me plenty.

I got her. She swung open the door and gave the Mason Terrace number. I grunted, kept my face turned front, and took off.

Some people really watch where you're going in a cab, scared to death you'll take them a block out of their way and squeeze them for an extra nickel. Others just lean back and dream. She was a dreamer, thank God. I was almost at District One headquarters before she woke up.

"Excuse me," she said, polite as ever, "that's Mason Terrace in *Brookline*."

"Take the next right, pull over, and douse your lights," I said in a low Bogart voice. My imitation was not that good, but it got the point across. Her eyes widened and she made an instinctive grab for the door handle.

"Don't try it, lady," I Bogied on. "You think I'm dumb enough to take you in alone? There's a cop car behind us, just waiting for you to make a move."

Her hand froze. She was a sap for movie dialogue.

"Where's the cop?" was all she said on the way up to Mooney's office.

"What cop?"

"The one following us."

"You have touching faith in our law-enforcement system," I said.

She tried to bolt, I kid you not. I've had experience with runners a lot trickier than Marcia. I grabbed her in approved cop hold number three and marched her into Mooney's office.

He actually stopped typing and raised an eyebrow, an expression of great shock for Mooney.

"Citizen's arrest," I said.

"Charges?"

"Petty theft. Commission of a felony using a firearm." I rattled off a few more charges, using the numbers I remembered from cop school.

"This woman is crazy," Marcia Heidegger said with all the dignity she could muster.

"Search her," I said. "Get a matron in here. I want my four dollars and eighty-two cents back."

Mooney looked like he agreed with Marcia's opinion of my mental state. He said, "Wait up, Carlotta. You'd have to be able to identify that four dollars and eighty-two cents as yours. Can you do that? Quarters are quarters. Dimes are dimes."

"One of the coins she took was quite unusual," I said. "I'm sure I'd be able to identify it."

"Do you have any objection to displaying the change in your purse?" Mooney said to Marcia. He got me mad the way he said it, like he was humoring an idiot.

"Of course not," old Marcia said, cool as a frozen daiquiri.

"That's because she's stashed it somewhere else, Mooney," I said patiently. "She used to keep it in her purse, see. But then she goofed. She handed it over to a cabbie in her change. She should have just let it go, but she panicked because it was worth a pile and she was just babysitting it for someone else. So when she got it back, she hid it somewhere. Like in her shoe. Didn't you ever carry your lucky penny in your shoe?"

"No," Mooney said. "Now, Miss—"

"Heidegger," I said clearly. "Marcia Heidegger. She used to work at Harvard Law School." I wanted to see if Mooney picked up on it, but he didn't. He went on: "This can be taken care of with a minimum of fuss. If you'll agree to be searched by—"

"I want to see my lawyer," she said.

"For four dollars and eighty-two cents?" he said. "It'll cost you more than that to get your lawyers up here."

"Do I get my phone call or not?"

Mooney shrugged wearily and wrote up the charge sheet. Called a cop to take her to the phone.

He got JoAnn, which was good. Under cover of our old-friend-long-time-no-see greetings, I whispered in her ear.

"You'll find it fifty well spent," I said to Mooney when we were alone.

JoAnn came back, shoving Marcia slightly ahead of her. She plunked her prisoner down in one of Mooney's hard wooden chairs and turned to me, grinning from ear to ear.

"Got it?" I said. "Good for you."

"What's going on?" Mooney said.

"She got real clumsy on the way to the pay phone," JoAnn said. "Practically fell on the floor. Got up with her right hand clenched tight. When we got to the phone, I offered to drop her dime for her. She wanted to do it herself. I insisted and she got clumsy again. Somehow this coin got kicked clear across the floor."

She held it up. The coin could have been a dime, except the color was off: warm, rosy gold instead of dead silver. How I missed it the first time around I'll never know.

"What the hell is that?" Mooney said.

"What kind of coins were in Justin Thayler's collection?" I asked. "Roman?"

Marcia jumped out of the chair, snapped her bag open, and drew out her little .22. I kid you not. She was closest to Mooney and she just stepped up to him and rested it above his left ear. He swallowed, didn't say a word. I never realized how prominent his Adam's apple was. JoAnn froze, hand on her holster.

Good old reliable, methodical Marcia. Why, I said to myself, *why* pick today of all days to trot your gun out of the freezer? Did you read bad luck in your tarot cards? Then I had a truly rotten thought. What if she had two guns? What if the disarmed .22 was still staring down the mint chocolate-chip ice cream?

"Give it back," Marcia said. She held out one hand, made an impatient waving motion.

"Hey, you don't need it, Marcia," I said. "You've got plenty more. In all those safe deposit boxes."

"I'm going to count to five—" she began.

"Were you in on the murder from day one? You know, from the planning stages?" I asked. I kept my voice low, but it echoed off the walls of Mooney's tiny office. The hum of everyday activity kept going in the main room. Nobody noticed the little gun in the well-dressed lady's hand. "Or did you just do your beau a favor and hide the loot after he iced his wife? In order to back up his burglary tale? I mean, if Justin Thayler really wanted to marry you, there is such a thing as divorce. Or was old Jennifer the one with the bucks?"

"I want that coin," she said softly. "Then I want the two of you"— she motioned to JoAnn and me—"to sit down facing that wall. If you yell, or do anything before I'm out of the building, I'll shoot this gentleman. He's coming with me."

"Come on, Marcia," I said, "put it down. I mean, look at you. A week ago you just wanted Thayler's coin back. You didn't want to rob my cab, right? You just didn't know how else to get your good luck charm back with no questions asked. You didn't do it for the money, right? You did it for love. You were so straight you threw away the cash. Now here you are with a gun pointed at a cop—"

"Shut up!"

I took a deep breath and said, "You haven't got the style, Marcia. Your gun's not even loaded."

Mooney didn't relax a hair. Sometimes I think the guy hasn't ever believed a word I've said to him. But Marcia got shook. She pulled the barrel away from Mooney's skull and peered at it with a puzzled frown. JoAnn and I both tackled her before she got a chance to pull the trigger. I twisted the gun out of her hand. I was almost afraid to look inside. Mooney stared at me and I felt my mouth go dry and a trickle of sweat worm its way down my back.

I looked.

No bullets. My heart stopped fibrillating, and Mooney actually cracked a smile in my direction.

So that's all. I sure hope Mooney will spread the word around that I helped him nail Thayler. And I think he will; he's a fair kind of guy. Maybe it'll get me a case or two. Driving a cab is hard on the backside, you know?

Donald E. Westlake's series characters couldn't be more different than oil and water. Parker is a hard-boiled professional thief who makes a well-deserved return after almost twenty years in the novel Comeback. *Dortmunder is a bumbling burglar whose capers inevitably fall apart, the only question being how spectacularly it happens. The short story "Too Many Crooks" garnered Dortmunder's creator an Edgar Award, proving that it's not always the hard-boiled or serious mystery stories that deserve recognition. In the following story, the protagonist finds that you can find more than you bargained for when you look back at family history.*

Never Shake a Family Tree

Donald E. Westlake

Actually, I have never been so shocked in all my born days, and I am seventy-three my last birthday and eleven times a grandmother and twice a great-grandmother. But never in all my born days did I see the like, and that's the truth.

Actually, it all began with my interest in genealogy, which I got from Mrs. Ernestine Simpson, a lady I met at Bay Arbor, in Florida, when I went there three summers ago. I certainly didn't like Florida— far too expensive, if you ask me, and far too bright, and with just too many mosquitoes and other insects to be believed—but I wouldn't say the trip was a total loss, since it did interest me in genealogical research, which is certainly a wonderful hobby, as well as being very valuable, what with one thing and another.

Actually, my genealogical researches had been valuable in more ways than one, since they have also been instrumental in my meeting some very pleasant ladies and gentlemen, although some of them only by postal, and of course it was through this hobby that I met Mr. Gerald Fowlkes in the first place.

But I'm getting far ahead of my story, and ought to begin at the beginning, except that I'm blessed if I know where the beginning actually is. In one way of looking at things, the beginning is my introduction to genealogy through Mrs. Ernestine Simpson, who has since passed on, but in another way the beginning is really almost two hundred years ago, and in still another way the story doesn't really begin until the first time I came across the name of Euphemia Barber.

Well. Actually, I suppose, I really ought to begin by explaining just what genealogical research is. It is the study of one's family tree. One checks marriage and birth and death records, searches old family Bibles and talks to various members of one's family, and one gradually builds up a family tree, showing who fathered whom and what year, and when so-and-so died, and so on. It's really a fascinating work, and there are any number of amateur genealogical societies throughout the country, and when one has one's family tree built up for as far as one wants— seven generations, or nine generations, or however long one wants— then it is possible to write this all up in a folder and bequeath it to the local library, and then there is a *record* of one's family for all time to come, and I for one think that's important and valuable to have even if my youngest boy Tom does laugh at it and say it's just a silly hobby. Well, it *isn't* a silly hobby. After all, I found evidence of murder that way, didn't I?

So, actually, I suppose the whole thing really begins when I first came across the name of Euphemia Barber. Euphemia Barber was John Anderson's second wife. John Anderson was born in Goochland County, Virginia, in 1754. He married Ethel Rita Mary Rayborn in 1777, just around the time of the Revolution, and they had seven chil- dren, which wasn't at all strange for that time, though large families have, I notice, gone out of style today, and I for one think it's a shame.

At any rate, it was John and Ethel Anderson's third child, a girl named Prudence, who is in my direct line on my mother's father's side, so of course I had them in my family tree. But then, in going through Appomattox County records—Goochland County being now a part of Appomattox, and no longer a separate county of its own—I came across the name of Euphemia Barber. It seems that Ethel Anderson died in 1793, in giving birth to her eighth child—who also died—and three years later, 1796, John Anderson remarried, this time marrying a widow named Euphemia Barber. At that time, he was forty-two years of age, and her age was given as thirty-nine.

Of course, Euphemia Barber was not at all in my direct line, being John Anderson's second wife, but I was interested to some extent in her pedigree as well, wanting to add her parents' names and her place of birth to my family chart, and also because there were some Barbers fairly distantly related on my father's mother's side, and I was wondering if this Euphemia might be kin to them. But the records were very incomplete, and all I could learn was that Euphemia Barber was not a native of Virginia, and had apparently only been in the area for a year or two when she had married John Anderson. Shortly after John's death in 1798, two years after their marriage, she had sold the Anderson farm, which was apparently a somewhat prosperous location, and had moved away again. So that I had neither birth nor death records on her, nor any record of her first husband, whose last name had apparently been Barber, but only the one lone record of her marriage to my great-great-great-great-great-grandfather on my mother's father's side.

Actually, there was no reason for me to pursue the question further, since Euphemia Barber wasn't in my direct line anyway, but I had worked diligently and, I think, well, on my family tree, and had it almost complete back nine generations, and there was really very little left to do with it, so I was glad to do some tracking down.

Which is why I included Euphemia Barber in my next entry in the Genealogical Exchange. Now, I suppose I ought to explain what the Genealogical Exchange is. There are any number of people throughout the country who are amateur genealogists, concerned primarily with their own family trees, but of course family trees do interlock, and any one of these people is liable to know about just the one record which has been eluding some other searcher for months. And so there are magazines devoted to the exchanging of some information, for nominal fees. In the last few years, I had picked up all sorts of valuable leads in this way. And so my entry in the summer issue of the Genealogical Exchange read:

BUCKLEY, Mrs. Henrietta Rhodes, 119A Newbury St., Boston, Mass. Xch data on *Rhodes, Anderson, Richards, Pryor, Marshall, Lord.* Want any info Euphemia *Barber,* m. John Anderson, Va. 1796.

Well. The Genealogical Exchange had been helpful to me in the past, but I never received anywhere near the response caused by Euphemia Barber. And the first response of all came from Mr. Gerald Fowlkes.

It was a scant two days after I received my own copy of the summer issue of the Exchange. I was still poring over it myself, looking for people who might be linked to various branches of my family tree, when the telephone rang. Actually, I suppose I was somewhat irked at being taken from my studies, and perhaps I sounded a bit impatient when I answered.

If so, the gentleman at the other end gave no sign of it. His voice was most pleasant, quite deep and masculine, and he said, "May I speak, please, with Mrs. Henrietta Buckley?"

"This is Mrs. Buckley," I told him.

"Ah," he said. "Forgive my telephoning, please, Mrs. Buckley. We have never met. But I noticed your entry in the current issue of the Genealogical Exchange—"

"Oh?"

I was immediately excited, all thought of impatience gone. This was surely the fastest reply I'd ever had to date!

"Yes," he said. "I noticed the reference to Euphemia Barber. I do believe that may be the Euphemia Stover who married Jason Barber in Savannah, Georgia, in 1791. Jason Barber is in my direct line, on my mother's side. Jason and Euphemia had only the one child, Abner, and I am descended from him."

"Well," I said. "You certainly do seem to have complete information."

"Oh, yes," he said. "My own family chart is almost complete. For twelve generations, that is. I'm not sure whether I'll try to go back farther than that or not. The English records before 1600 are so incomplete, you know."

"Yes, of course," I said. I was, I admit, taken aback. Twelve generations! Surely that was the most ambitious family tree I had ever heard of, though I had read sometimes of people who had carried particular branches back as many as fifteen generations. But to actually be speaking to a person who had traced his entire family back twelve generations!

"Perhaps," he said, "it would be possible for us to meet, and I could give you the information I have on Euphemia Barber. There are also some Marshalls in one branch of my family; perhaps I can be of help to you there, as well." He laughed, a deep and pleasant sound, which reminded me of my late husband, Edward, when he was most particularly pleased. "And, of course," he said, "there is always the chance that you may have some information on the Marshalls which can help me."

"I think that would be very nice," I said, and so I invited him to come to the apartment the very next afternoon.

At one point the next day, perhaps half an hour before Gerald Fowlkes was to arrive, I stopped my fluttering around to take stock of myself and to realize that if ever there were an indication of second childhood taking over, my thoughts and actions preparatory to Mr. Fowlkes' arrival were certainly it. I had been rushing hither and thither, dusting, rearranging, polishing, pausing incessantly to look in the mirror and touch my hair with fluttering fingers, all as though I were a flighty teenager before her very first date. "Henrietta," I told myself sharply, "you are seventy-three years old, and all that nonsense is well behind you now. Eleven times a grandmother, and just look at how you carry on!"

But poor Edward had been dead and gone these past nine years, my brothers and sisters were all in their graves, and as for my children, all but Tom, the youngest, were thousands of miles away, living their own lives—as of course they should—and only occasionally remembering to write a duty letter to Mother. And I am much too aware of the dangers of the clinging mother to force my presence too often upon Tom and his family. So I am very much alone, except of course for my friends in the various church activities and for those I have met, albeit only by postal, through my genealogical research.

So it *was* pleasant to be visited by a charming gentleman caller, and particularly so when that gentleman shared my own particular interests.

And Mr. Gerald Fowlkes, on his arrival, was surely no disappointment. He looked to be no more than fifty-five years of age, though he swore to sixty-two, and had a fine shock of gray hair above a strong and kindly face. He dressed very well, with that combination of expense and breeding so little found these days, when the well-bred seem invariably to be poor and the well-to-do seem invariably to be horribly plebeian. His manner was refined and gentlemanly, what we used to call courtly, and he had some very nice things to say about the appearance of my living room.

Actually, I make no unusual claims as a housekeeper. Living alone, and with quite a comfortable income having been left me by Edward, it is no problem at all to choose tasteful furnishings and keep them neat. (Besides, I had scrubbed the apartment from top to bottom in preparation for Mr. Fowlkes' visit.)

He had brought his pedigree along, and what a really beautiful job he had done. Pedigree charts, photostats of all sorts of records, a running history typed very neatly on bond paper and inserted in a looseleaf notebook—all in all, the kind of careful, planned, well-thought-out perfection so unsuccessfully striven for by all amateur genealogists.

From Mr. Fowlkes, I got the missing information on Euphemia Barber. She was born in 1765, in Salem, Massachusetts, the fourth child of seven born to John and Alicia Stover. She married Jason Barber in Savannah in 1791. Jason, a well-to-do merchant, passed on in 1794, shortly after the birth of their first child, Abner. Abner was brought up by his paternal grandparents, and Euphemia moved away from Savannah. As I already knew, she had then gone to Virginia, where she had married John Anderson. After that, Mr. Fowlkes had no record of her, until her death in Cincinnati, Ohio, in 1852. She was buried as Euphemia Stover Barber, apparently not having used the Anderson name after John Anderson's death.

This done, we went on to compare family histories and discover an Alan Marshall of Liverpool, England, around 1680, common to both trees. I was able to give Mr. Fowlkes Alan Marshall's birth date. And then the specific purpose of our meeting was finished. I offered tea and cakes, it then being four-thirty in the afternoon, and Mr. Fowlkes graciously accepted my offering.

And so began the strangest three months of my entire life. Before leaving, Mr. Fowlkes asked me to accompany him to a concert on Friday evening, and I very readily agreed. Then, and afterward, he was a perfect gentleman.

It didn't take me long to realize that I was being courted. Actually, I couldn't believe it at first. After all, at *my* age! But I myself did know some very nice couples who had married late in life—a widow and a widower, both lonely, sharing interests, and deciding to lighten their remaining years together—and looked at in that light it wasn't at all as ridiculous as it might appear at first.

Actually, I had expected my son Tom to laugh at the idea, and to dislike Mr. Fowlkes instantly upon meeting him. I suppose various fictional works that I have read had given me this expectation. So I was most pleasantly surprised when Tom and Mr. Fowlkes got along famously together from their very first meeting, and even more surprised when Tom came to me and told me Mr. Fowlkes had asked him if he would have any objection to his, Mr. Fowlkes', asking for my hand in matrimony. Tom said he had no objection at all, but actually thought it a wonderful idea, for he knew that both Mr. Fowlkes and myself were rather lonely, with nothing but our genealogical hobbies to occupy our minds.

As to Mr. Fowlkes' background, he very early gave me his entire history. He came from a fairly well-to-do family in upstate New York, and was himself now retired from his business, which had been a stock brokerage in Albany. He was a widower these last six years, and his first marriage had not been blessed with any children, so that he was completely alone in the world.

The next three months were certainly active ones. Mr. Fowlkes—Gerald—squired me everywhere, to concerts and to museums and even, after we had come to know one another well enough, to the theater. He was at all times most polite and thoughtful, and there was scarcely a day went by but what we were together.

During this entire time, of course, my own genealogical researches came to an absolute standstill. I was much too busy, and my mind was much too full of Gerald, for me to concern myself with family members who were long since gone to their rewards. Promising leads from the Genealogical Exchange were not followed up, for I didn't write a single letter. And though I did receive many in the Exchange, they all went unopened into a cubbyhole in my desk. And so the matter stayed, while the courtship progressed.

After three months, Gerald at last proposed. "I am not a young man, Henrietta," he said. "Nor a particularly handsome man"—though he most certainly was very handsome, indeed—"nor even a very rich man, although I do have sufficient for my declining years. And I have little to offer you, Henrietta, save my own self, whatever poor companionship I can give you, and the assurance that I will be ever at your side."

What a beautiful proposal! After being nine years a widow, and never expecting even in fanciful daydreams to be once more a wife, what a beautiful proposal and from what a charming gentleman!

I agreed at once, of course, and telephoned Tom the good news that very minute. Tom and his wife, Estelle, had a dinner party for us, and then we made our plans. We would be married three weeks hence. A short time? Yes, of course, it was, but there was really no reason to wait. And we would honeymoon in Washington, D.C., where my oldest boy, Roger, has quite a responsible position with the State Department. After which, we would return to Boston and take up our residence in a lovely old home on Beacon Hill, which was then for sale and which we would jointly purchase.

Ah, the plans! The preparations! How newly filled were my so-recently empty days!

I spent most of the last week closing my apartment on Newbury Street. The furnishings would be moved to our new home by Tom, while Gerald and I were in Washington. But, of course, there was ever so much packing to be done, and I got at it with a will.

And so at last I came to my desk, and my genealogical researches lying as I had left them. I sat down at the desk, somewhat weary, for it was late afternoon and I had been hard at work since sunup, and I decided to spend a short while getting my papers into order before packing them away. And so I opened the mail which had accumulated over the last three months.

There were twenty-three letters. Twelve asked for information on various family names mentioned in my entry in the Exchange, five offered to give me information, and six concerned Euphemia Barber. It was, after all, Euphemia Barber who had brought Gerald and me together in the first place, and so I took time out to read these letters.

And so came the shock. I read the six letters, and then I simply sat limp at the desk, staring into space, and watched the monstrous pattern as it grew in my mind. For there was no question of the truth, no question at all.

Consider: Before starting the letters, this is what I knew of Euphemia Barber: She had been born Euphemia Stover in Salem, Massachusetts, in 1765. In 1791, she married Jason Barber, a widower of Savannah, Georgia. Jason died two years later, in 1793, of a stomach upset. Three years later, Euphemia appeared in Virginia and married John Anderson, also a widower. John died two years thereafter, in 1798, of stomach upset. In both cases, Euphemia sold her late husband's property and moved on.

And here is what the letters added to that, in chronological order:

From Mrs. Winnie Mae Cuthbert, Dallas, Texas: Euphemia Barber, in 1800, two years after John Anderson's death, appeared in Harrisburg, Pennsylvania, and married one Andrew Cuthbert, a widower and a prosperous feed merchant. Andrew died in 1801, of a stomach upset. The widow sold his store, and moved on.

From Miss Ethel Sutton, Louisville, Kentucky: Euphemia Barber, in 1804, married Samuel Nicholson of Louisville, a widower and a well-to-do tobacco farmer. Samuel Nicholson passed on in 1807, of a stomach upset. The widow sold his farm, and moved on.

From Mrs. Isabelle Padgett, Concord, California: in 1808, Euphemia Barber married Thomas Norton, then Mayor of Dover, New Jersey, and a widower. In 1809, Thomas Norton died of a stomach upset.

From Mrs. Luella Miller, Bicknell, Utah: Euphemia Barber married Jonas Miller, a wealthy shipowner of Portsmouth, New Hampshire, a widower, in 1811. The same year, Jonas Miller died of a stomach upset. The widow sold his property and moved on.

From Mrs. Lola Hopkins, Vancouver, Washington: In 1813, in southern Indiana, Euphemia Barber married Edward Hopkins, a widower and a farmer. Edward Hopkins died in 1816, of a stomach upset. The widow sold the farm, and moved on.

From Mr. Roy Cumbie, Kansas City, Missouri: In 1819, Euphemia Barber married Stanley Thatcher of Kansas City, Missouri, a river barge owner and a widower. Stanley Thatcher died, of a stomach upset, in 1821. The widow sold his property, and moved on.

The evidence was clear, and complete. The intervals of time without dates could mean that there had been other widowers who had succumbed to Euphemia Barber's fatal charms, and whose descendants did not number among themselves an amateur genealogist. Who could tell just how many husbands Euphemia had murdered? For murder it quite clearly was, brutal murder, for profit. I had evidence of eight murders, and who knew but what there were eight more, or eighteen more? Who could tell, at this late date, just how many times Euphemia Barber had murdered for profit, and had never been caught?

Such a woman is inconceivable. Her husbands were always widowers, sure to be lonely, sure to be susceptible to a wily woman. She preyed on widowers, and left them all a widow.

Gerald.

The thought came to me, and I pushed it firmly away. It couldn't possibly be true; it couldn't possibly have a single grain of truth.

But what did I know of Gerald Fowlkes, other than what he had told me? And wasn't I a widow, lonely and susceptible? And wasn't I financially well off?

Like father, like son, they say. Could it be also, like great-great-great-great-great-grandmother, like great-great-great-great-great-grandson?

What a thought! It came to me that there must be any number of widows in the country, like myself, who were interested in tracing their family trees. Women who had a bit of money and leisure, whose children were grown and gone out into the world to live their own lives, and who filled some of the empty hours with the hobby of genealogy. An unscrupulous man, preying on well-to-do widows, could find no better introduction than a common interest in genealogy.

What a terrible thought to have about Gerald! And yet, I couldn't push it from my mind, and at last I decided that the only thing I could possibly do was try to substantiate the autobiography he had given me, for if he had told the truth about himself, then he could surely not be a beast of the type I was imagining.

A stockbroker, he had claimed to have been, in Albany, New York. I at once telephoned an old friend of my first husband's, who was himself a Boston stockbroker, and asked him if it would be possible for him to find out if there had been, at any time in the last fifteen or twenty years, an Albany stockbroker named Gerald Fowlkes. He said he could do so with ease, using some sort of directory he had, and would call me back. He did so, with the shattering news that no such individual was listed!

Still I refused to believe. Donning my coat and hat, I left the apartment at once and went directly to the telephone company, where, after an incredible number of white lies concerning genealogical research, I at last persuaded someone to search for an old Albany, New York, telephone book. I knew that the main office of the company kept books for other major cities, as a convenience for the public, but I wasn't sure they would have any from past years. Nor was the clerk I talked to, but at last she did go and search, and came back finally with the 1946 telephone book from Albany, dusty and somewhat ripped, but still intact, with both the normal listings and the yellow pages.

No Gerald Fowlkes was listed in the white pages, or in the yellow pages under Stocks & Bonds.

So. It was true. And I could see exactly what Gerald's method was. Whenever he was ready to find another victim, he searched one or another of the genealogical magazines until he found someone who shared one of his own past relations. He then proceeded to effect a meeting with that person, found out quickly enough whether or not the intended victim was a widow, of the peoper age range, and with the properly large bank account, and then the courtship began.

I imagined that this was the first time he had made the mistake of using Euphemia Barber as the go-between. And I doubted that he even realized he was following in Euphemia's footsteps. Certainly, none of the six people who had written to me about Euphemia could possibly guess, knowing only of one marriage and death, what Euphemia's role in life had actually been.

And what was I to do now? In the taxi, on the way back to my apartment, I sat huddled in a corner, and tried to think.

For this *was* a severe shock, and a terrible disappointment. And could I face Tom, or my other children, or any one of my friends, to whom I had already written the glad news of my impending marriage? And how could I return to the drabness of my days before Gerald had come to bring gaiety and companionshiip and courtly grace to my days?

Could I even call the police? I was sufficiently convinced myself, but could I possibly convince anyone else?

All at once, I made my decision. And, having made it, I immediately felt ten years younger, ten pounds lighter, and quite a bit less foolish. For, I might as well admit, in addition to everything else, this had been a terrible blow to my pride.

But the decision was made, and I returned to my apartment cheerful and happy.

And so we were married.

Married? Of course. Why not?

Becuase he will try to murder me? Well, of course he *will* try to murder me. As a matter of fact, he has already tried, half a dozen times.

But Gerald is working at a terrible disadvantage. For he cannot murder me in any way that looks like murder. It must appear to be a natural death, or, at the very worst, an accident. Which means that he must be devious, and he must plot and plan, and never come at me openly to do me in.

And there is the source of his disadvantage. For I am forewarned, and forewarned is forearmed.

But what, really, do I have to lose? At seventy-three, how many days on this earth do I have left? And how *rich* life is these days! How rich compared to my life before Gerald came into it! Spiced with the thrill of danger, the excitement of cat and mouse, the intricate moves and countermoves of the most fascinating game of all.

And, of course, a pleasant and charming husband. Gerald *has* to be pleasant and charming. He can never disagree with me, at least not very forcefully, for he can't afford the danger of my leaving him. Nor can he afford to believe that I suspect him. I have never spoken of the matter to him, and so far as he is concerned I know nothing. We go to concerts and museums and the theater together. Gerald is attentive and gentlemanly, quite the best sort of companion at all times.

Of course, I can't allow him to feed me breakfast in bed, as he would so love to do. No, I told him I was an old-fashioned woman, and believed that cooking was a woman's job, and so I won't let him near the kitchen. Poor Gerald!

And we don't take trips, no matter how much he suggests them.

And we've closed off the second story of our home, since I pointed out that the first floor was certainly spacious enough for just the two of us, and I felt I was getting a little old for climbing stairs. He could do nothing, of course, but agree.

And, in the meantime, I have found another hobby, though of course Gerald knows nothing of it. Through discreet inquiries, and careful perusal of past issues of the various genealogical magazines, the use of the family names in Gerald's family tree, I am gradually compiling another sort of tree. Not a family tree, no. One might facetiously call it a hanging tree. It is a list of Gerald's wives. It is in with my genealogical files, which I have willed to the Boston library. Should Gerald manage to catch me after all, what a surprise is in store for the librarian who sorts out those files of mine! Not as big a surprise as the one in store for Gerald, of course.

Ah, here comes Gerald now, in the automobile he bought last week. He's going to ask me again to go for a ride with him.

But I shan't go.

Brendan Du Bois's home turf is the New England countryside, and few writers know the ins and outs of their chosen backdrop so well. From the taciturn inhabitants to the magnificent landscape, he makes both the beauty and the hardness of the region spring to life. "The Dark Snow," nominated for the Edgar Award, is a prime example of his work.

The Dark Snow

Brendan Du Bois

When I get to the steps of my lakeside home, the door is open. I slowly walk in, my hand reaching for the phantom weapon at my side, everything about me extended and tingling as I enter the strange place that used to be mine. I step through the small kitchen, my boots crunching the broken glassware and dishes on the tile floor. Inside the living room with its cathedral ceiling the furniture has been upended, as if an earthquake had struck.

I pause for a second, looking out the large windows and past the enclosed porch, down to the frozen waters of Lake Marie. Off in the distance are the snow-covered peaks of the White Mountains. I wait, trembling, my hand still curving for that elusive weapon. They are gone, but their handiwork remains. The living room is a jumble of furniture, torn books and magazines, shattered pictures and frames. On one clear white plaster wall, next to the fireplace, two words have been written in what looks to be ketchup: GO HOME.

This is my home. I turn over a chair and drag it to the windows. I sit and look out at the crisp winter landscape, my legs stretched out, holding both hands still in my lap, which is quite a feat.

For my hands at that moment want to be wrapped around someone's throat.

After a long time wandering, I came to Nansen, New Hampshire, in the late summer and purchased a house along the shoreline of Lake Marie. I didn't waste much time, and I didn't bargain. I made an offer that was about a thousand dollars below the asking price, and in less than a month it belonged to me.

At first I didn't know what to do with it. I had never had a residence that was actually mine. Everything before this had been apartments, hotel rooms or temporary officer's quarters. The first few nights I couldn't sleep inside. I would go outside to the long dock that extends into the deep blue waters of the lake, bundle myself up in a sleeping bag over a thin foam mattress and stare up at the stars, listening to the loons getting ready for their long winter trip. The loons don't necessarily fly south; the ones here go out to the cold Atlantic and float with the waves and currents, not once touching land the entire winter.

As I snuggled in my bag I thought it was a good analogy for what I'd been doing. I had drifted too long. It was time to come back to dry land.

After getting the power and other utilities up and running and moving in the few boxes of stuff that belonged to me, I checked the bulky folder that had accompanied my retirement and pulled out an envelope with a doctor's name on it. Inside were official papers that directed me to talk to him, and I shrugged and decided it was better than sitting in an empty house getting drunk. I phoned and got an appointment for the next day.

His name was Ron Longley and he worked in Manchester, the state's largest city and about an hour's drive south of Lake Marie. His office was in a refurbished brick building along the banks of the Merrimack River. I imagined I could still smell the sweat and toil of the French Canadians who had worked here for so many years in the shoe, textile and leather mills until their distant cousins in Georgia and Alabama took their jobs away.

I wasn't too sure what to make of Ron during our first session. He showed me some documents that made him a Department of Defense contractor and gave his current classification level, and then, after signing the usual insurance nonsense, we got down to it. He was about ten years younger than I, with a mustache and not much hair on top. He wore jeans, a light blue shirt and a tie that looked as if about six tubes of paint had been squirted onto it, and he said, "Well, here we are."

"That we are," I said. "And would you believe I've already forgotten if you're a psychologist or a psychiatrist?"

That made for a good laugh. With a casual wave of his hand, he said, "Makes no difference. What would you like to talk about?"

"What should I talk about?"

A shrug, one of many I would eventually see. "Whatever's on your mind."

"Really?" I said, not bothering to hide the challenge in my voice. "Try this one on then, doc. I'm wondering what I'm doing here. And another thing I'm wondering about is paperwork. Are you going to be making a report down south on how I do? You working under some deadline, some pressure?"

His hands were on his belly and he smiled. "Nope."

"Not at all?"

"Not at all," he said. "If you want to come in here and talk baseball for 50 minutes, that's fine with me."

I looked at him and those eyes. Maybe it's my change of view since retirement, but there was something trustworthy about him. I said, "You know what's really on my mind?"

"No, but I'd like to know."

"My new house," I said. "It's great. It's on a big lake and there aren't any close neighbors, and I can sit on the dock at night and see stars I haven't seen in a long time. But I've been having problems sleeping."

"Why's that?" he asked, and I was glad he wasn't one of those stereotypical head docs, the ones who take a lot of notes.

"Weapons."

"Weapons?"

I nodded. "Yeah, I miss my weapons." A deep breath. "Look, you've seen my files, you know the places Uncle Sam has sent me and the jobs I've done. All those years, I had pistols or rifles or heavy weapons, always at my side, under my bed or in a closet. But when I moved into that house, well, I don't have them anymore."

"How does that make you feel?" Even though the question was friendly, I knew it was a real doc question and not a from-the-next-barstool type of question.

I rubbed my hands. "I really feel like I'm changing my ways. But damn it . . ."

"Yes?"

I smiled. "I sure could use a good night's sleep."

As I drove back home, I thought, Hell, it's only a little white lie. The fact is, I did have my weapons.

They were locked up in the basement, in strongboxes with heavy combination locks. I couldn't get to them quickly, but I certainly hadn't tossed them away.

I hadn't been lying when I told Ron I couldn't sleep. That part was entirely true.

I thought, as I drove up the dirt road to my house, scaring a possum that scuttled along the side of the gravel, that the real problem with living in my new home was so slight that I was embarrassed to bring it up to Ron.

It was the noise.

I was living in a rural paradise, with clean air, clean water and views of the woods and lake and mountains that almost broke my heart each time I climbed out of bed, stiff with old dreams and old scars. The long days were filled with work and activities I'd never had time for. Cutting old brush and trimming dead branches. Planting annuals. Clearing my tiny beach of leaves and other debris. Filling bird feeders. And during the long evenings on the front porch or on the dock, I tackled thick history books.

But one night after dinner—I surprised myself at how much I enjoyed cooking—I was out on the dock, sitting in a Fifties-era web lawn chair, a glass of red wine in my hand and a history of the Apollo space program in my lap. Along the shoreline of Lake Marie, I could see the lights of the cottages and other homes. Every night there were fewer and fewer lights, as more of the summer people boarded up their places and headed back to suburbia.

I was enjoying my wine and the book and the slight breeze, but there was also a distraction: three high-powered speedboats, racing around on the lake and tossing up great spray and noise. They were dragging people along in inner tubes, and it was hard to concentrate on my book. After a while the engines slowed and I was hoping the boats would head back to their docks, but they drifted together and ropes were exchanged, and soon they became a large raft. A couple of grills were set up and there were more hoots and yells, and then a sound system kicked in, with rock music and a heavy bass that echoed among the hills.

It was then too dark to read and I'd lost interest in the wine. I was sitting there, arms folded tight against my chest, trying hard to breathe. The noise got louder and I gave up and retreated into the house, where the heavy thump-thump of the bass followed me in. If I'd had a boat I could have gone out and asked them politely to turn it down, but that would have meant talking with people and putting myself in the way, and I didn't want to do that.

Instead, I went upstairs to my bedroom and shut the door and windows. Still, that thump-thump shook the beams of the house. I lay down with a pillow wrapped about my head and tried not to think of what was in the basement.

Later that night I got up for a drink of water, and there was still noise and music. I walked out onto the porch and could see movement on the lake and hear laughter. On a tree near the dock was a spotlight that the previous owners had installed and which I had rarely used. I flipped on the switch. Some shouts and shrieks. Two powerboats, tied together, had drifted close to my shore. The light caught a young muscular man with a fierce black mustache standing on the stern of his powerboat and urinating into the lake. His half a dozen companions, male and female, yelled and cursed in my direction. The boats started up and two men and a young woman stumbled to the side of one and dropped their bathing suits, exposing their buttocks. A couple others gave me a one-fingered salute, and there was a shower of bottles and cans tossed over the side as they sped away.

I spent the next hour on the porch, staring into the darkness.

The next day I made two phone calls, to the town hall and the police department of Nansen. I made gentle and polite inquiries and got the same answers from each office. There was no local or state law about boats coming to within a certain distance of shore. There was no law forbidding boats from mooring together. Nansen being such a small town, there was also no noise ordinance.

Home sweet home.

On my next visit Ron was wearing a bow tie, and we discussed necktie fashions before we got into the business at hand. He said, "Still having sleeping problems?"

I smiled. "No, not at all."

"Really?"

"It's fall," I said. "The tourists have gone home, most of the cottages along the lake have been boarded up and nobody takes out boats anymore. It's so quiet at night I can hear the house creak and settle."

"That's good, that's really good," Ron said, and I changed the subject. A half hour later, I was heading back to Nansen, thinking about my latest white lie. Well, it wasn't really a lie. More of an oversight.

I hadn't told Ron about the hang-up phone calls. Or how trash had twice been dumped in my driveway. Or how a week ago, when I was shopping, I had come back to find a bullet hole through one of my windows. Maybe it had been a hunting accident. Hunting season hadn't started, but I knew that for some of the workingmen in this town, it didn't matter when the state allowed them to do their shooting.

I had cleaned up the driveway, shrugged off the phone calls and cut away brush and saplings around the house, to eliminate any hiding spots for . . . hunters.

Still, I could sit out on the dock, a blanket around my legs and a mug of tea in my hand, watching the sun set in the distance, the reddish pink highlighting the strong yellows, oranges and reds of the fall foliage. The water was a slate gray, and though I missed the loons, the smell of the leaves and the tang of woodsmoke from my chimney seemed to settle in just fine.

As it grew colder, I began to go into town for breakfast every few days. The center of Nansen could be featured in a documentary on New Hampshire small towns. Around the green common with its Civil War statue are a bank, a real estate office, a hardware store, two gas stations, a general store and a small strip of service places with everything from a plumber to video rentals and Gretchen's Kitchen. At Gretchen's I read the paper while letting the mornings drift by. I listened to the old-timers at the counter pontificate on the ills of the state, nation and world, and watched harried workers fly in to grab a quick meal. Eventually, a waitress named Sandy took some interest in me.

She was about 20 years younger than I, with raven hair, a wide smile and a pleasing body that filled out her regulation pink uniform. After a couple weeks of flirting and generous tips on my part, I asked her out, and when she said yes, I went to my pickup truck and burst out laughing. A real date. I couldn't remember the last time I had had a real date.

The first date was dinner a couple of towns over, in Montcalm, the second was dinner and a movie outside Manchester and the third was dinner at my house, which was supposed to end with a rented movie in the living room but instead ended up in the bedroom. Along the way I learned that Sandy had always lived in Nansen, was divorced with two young boys and was saving her money so she could go back to school and become a legal aide. "If you think I'm going to keep slinging hash and waiting for Billy to send his support check, then you're a damn fool," she said on our first date.

After a bedroom interlude that surprised me with its intensity, we sat on the enclosed porch. I opened a window for Sandy, who needed a smoke. The house was warm and I had on a pair of shorts; she had wrapped a towel around her torso. I sprawled in an easy chair while she sat on the couch, feet in my lap. Both of us had glasses of wine and I felt comfortable and tingling. Sandy glanced at me as she worked on her cigarette. I'd left the lights off and lit a couple of candles, and in the hazy yellow light, I could see the small tattoo of a unicorn on her right shoulder.

Sandy looked at me and asked, "What were you doing when you was in the government?"

"Traveled a lot and ate bad food."

"No, really," she said. "I want a straight answer."

Well, I thought, as straight as I can be. I said, "I was a consultant, to foreign armies. Sometimes they needed help with certain weapons or training techniques. That was my job."

"Were you good?"

Too good. I thought. "I did all right."

"You've got a few scars there."

"That I do."

She shrugged, took a lazy puff off her cigarette. "I've seen worse."

I wasn't sure where this was headed. Then she said, "When are you going to be leaving?"

Confused, I asked her, "You mean, tonight?"

"No," she said. "I mean, when are you leaving Nansen and going back home?"

I looked around the porch and said, "This is my home."

She gave me a slight smile, like a teacher correcting a fumbling but eager student. "No, it's not. This place was built by the Gerrish family. It's the Gerrish place. You're from away, and this ain't your home."

I tried to smile, though my mood was slipping. "Well, I beg to disagree."

She said nothing for a moment, just studied the trail of smoke from her cigarette. Then she said, "Some people in town don't like you. They think you're uppity, a guy that don't belong here."

I began to find it quite cool on the porch. "What kind of people?"

"The Garr brothers. Jerry Tompkins. Kit Broderick. A few others. Guys in town. They don't particularly like you."

"I don't particularly care," I shot back.

A small shrug as she stubbed out her cigarette. "You will."

The night crumbled some more after that, and the next morning, while sitting in the corner at Gretchen's, I was ignored by Sandy. One of the older waitresses served me, and my coffee arrived in a cup stained with lipstick, the bacon was charred black and the eggs were cold. I got the message. I started making breakfast at home, sitting alone on the porch, watching the leaves fall and days grow shorter.

I wondered if Sandy was on her own or if she had been scouting out enemy territory on someone's behalf.

At my December visit, I surprised myself by telling Ron about something that had been bothering me.

"It's the snow," I said, leaning forward, hands clasped between my legs. "It's going to start snowing soon. And I've always hated the snow, especially since. . . ."

"Since when?"

"Since something I did once," I said. "In Serbia."

"Go on," he said, fingers making a tent in front of his face.

"I'm not sure I can."

Ron tilted his head quizzically. "You know I have the clearances."

I cleared my throat, my eyes burning a bit. "I know. It's just that it's . . . Ever see blood on snow, at night?"

I had his attention. "No," he said, "no, I haven't."

"It steams at first, since it's so warm," I said. "And then it gets real dark, almost black. Dark snow, if you can believe it. It's something that stays with you, always."

He looked steadily at me for a moment, then said, "Do you want to talk about it some more?"

"No."

I spent all of one gray afternoon in my office cubbyhole, trying to get a new computer up and running. When at last I went downstairs for a quick drink, I looked outside and there they were, big snowflakes lazily drifting to the ground. Forgetting about the drink, I went out to the porch and looked at the pure whiteness of everything, of the snow covering the bare limbs, the shrubbery and the frozen lake. I stood there and hugged myself, admiring the softly accumulating blanket of white and feeling lucky.

Two days after the snowstorm I was out on the frozen waters of Lake Marie, breathing hard and sweating and enjoying every second of it. The day before I had driven into Manchester to a sporting goods store and had come out with a pair of cross-country skis. The air was crisp and still, and the sky was a blue so deep I half-expected to see brush strokes. From the lake, I looked back at my home and liked what I saw. The white paint and plain construction made me smile for no particular reason. I heard not a single sound, except for the faint drone of a distant airplane. Before me someone had placed signs and orange ropes in the snow, covering an oval area at the center of the lake. Each sign said the same thing: DANGER! THIN ICE! I remembered the old-timers at Gretchen's Kitchen telling a story about a hidden spring coming up through the lake bottom, or some damn thing, that made ice at the center of the lake thin, even in the coldest weather. I got cold and it was time to go home.

About halfway back to the house is where it happened.

At first it was a quiet sound, and I thought that it was another air-plane. Then the noise got louder and louder, and separated, becoming distinct. Snowmobiles, several of them. I turned and they came speed-ing out of the woods, tossing up great rooster tails of snow and ice. They were headed straight for me. I turned away and kept up a steady pace, trying to ignore the growing loudness of the approaching engines. An itchy feeling crawled up my spine to the base of my head, and the noise exploded in pitch as they raced by me.

Even over the loudness of the engines I could make out the yells as the snowmobiles roared by, hurling snow in my direction. There were two people to each machine and they didn't look human. Each was dressed in a bulky jumpsuit, heavy boots and a padded helmet. They raced by and, sure enough, circled around and came back at me. This time I flinched. This time, too, a couple of empty beer cans were thrown my way.

By the third pass, I was getting closer to my house. I thought it was almost over when one of the snowmobiles broke free from the pack and raced across about 50 feet in front of me. The driver turned so that the machine was blocking me and sat there, racing the throttle. Then he pulled off his helmet, showing an angry face and thick mustache, and I recognized him as the man on the powerboat a few months earlier. He handed his helmet to his passenger, stepped off the snowmobile and unzipped his jumpsuit. It took only a moment as he marked the snow in a long, steaming stream, and there was laughter from the others as he got back on the machine and sped away. I skied over the soiled snow and took my time climbing up the snow-covered shore. I entered my home, carrying my skis and poles like weapons over my shoulder.

That night, and every night afterward, they came back, breaking the winter stillness with the throbbing sounds of engines, laughter, drunken shouts and music from portable stereos. Each morning I cleared away their debris and scuffed fresh snow over the stains. In the quiet of my house, I found myself constantly on edge, listening, waiting for the noise to suddenly return and break up the day. Phone calls to the police department and town hall confirmed what I already knew: Except for maybe littering, no ordinances or laws were being broken.

On one particularly loud night, I broke a promise to myself and went to the tiny, damp cellar to unlock the green metal case holding a pistol-shaped device. I went back upstairs to the enclosed porch, and with the lights off, I switched on the night-vision scope and looked at the scene below me. Six snowmobiles were parked in a circle on the snow-covered ice, and in the center, a fire had been made. Figures stumbled around in the snow, talking and laughing. Stereos had been set up on the seats of two of the snowmobiles, and the loud music with its bass thump-thump-thump echoed across the flat ice. Lake Marie is one of the largest bodies of water in this part of the country, but the camp was set up right below my windows.

I watched for a while as they partied. Two of the black-suited figures started wrestling in the snow. More shouts and laughter, and then the fight broke up and someone turned the stereos even louder. Thump-thump-thump.

I switched off the night scope, returned it to its case in the cellar and went to bed. Even with foam rubber plugs in my ears, the bass noise reverberated inside my skull. I put the pillow across my face and tried to ignore the sure knowledge that this would continue all winter, the noise and the littering and the aggravation, and when the spring came, they would turn in their snowmobiles for boats, and they'd be back, all summer long.

Thump-thump-thump.

★   ★   ★

At the next session with Ron, we talked about the weather until he pierced me with his gaze and said, "Tell me what's wrong."

I went through half a dozen rehearsals of what to tell him, and then skated to the edge of the truth and said, "I'm having a hard time adjusting, that's all."

"Adjusting to what?"

"To my home," I said, my hands clasped before me. "I never thought I would say this, but I'm really beginning to get settled, for the first time in my life. You ever been in the military, Ron?"

"No, but I know—"

I held up my hand. "Yes, I know what you're going to say. You've worked as a consultant, but you've never been one of us, Ron. Never. You can't know what it's like, constantly being ordered to uproot yourself and go halfway across the world to a new place with a different language, customs and weather, all within a week. You never settle in, never really get into a place you call home."

He swiveled a bit in his black leather chair. "But that's different now?"

"It sure is," I said.

There was a pause as we looked at each other, and Ron said, "But something is going on."

"Something is."

"Tell me."

And then I knew I wouldn't. A fire wall had already been set up between Ron and the details of what was going on back at my home. If I let him know what was really happening, I knew that he would make a report, and within the week I'd be ordered to go somewhere else. If I'd been younger and not so dependent on a monthly check, I would have put up a fight.

But now, no more fighting. I looked past Ron and said, "An adjustment problem, I guess."

"Adjusting to civilian life?"

"More than that," I said. "Adjusting to Nansen. It's a great little town, but . . . I feel like an outsider."

"That's to be expected."

"Sure, but I still don't like it. I know it will take some time, but . . . well, I get the odd looks, the quiet little comments, the cold shoulders."

Ron seemed to choose his words carefully. "Is that proving to be a serious problem?"

Not even a moment of hesitation as I lied: "No, not at all."

"And what do you plan on doing?"

An innocent shrug. "Not much. Just try to fit in, try to be a good neighbor."

"That's all?"

I nodded firmly. "That's all."

It took a bit of research, but eventually I managed to put a name to the face of the mustached man who has pissed on my territory. Jerry Tompkins. Floor supervisor for a computer firm outside Manchester, married with three kids, an avid boater, snowmobiler, hunter and all-around guy. His family had been in Nansen for generations, and his dad was one of the three selectmen who ran the town. Using a couple of old skills, I tracked him down one dark afternoon and pulled my truck next to his in the snowy parking lot of a tavern on the outskirts of Nansen. The tavern was called Peter's Pub and its windows were barred and blacked out.

I stepped out of my truck and called to him as he walked to the entrance of the pub. He turned and glared at me. "What?"

"You're Jerry Tompkins, aren't you."

"Sure am," he said, hands in the pockets of his dark-green parka. "And you're the fella that's living up in the old Gerrish place."

"Yes, and I'd like to talk with you for a second."

His face was rough, like he had spent a lot of time outdoors in the wind and rain and an equal amount indoors, with cigarette smoke and loud country music. He rocked back on his heels with a little smile and said, "Go ahead. You got your second."

"Thanks," I said. "Tell you what, Jerry, I'm looking for something."

"And what's that?"

"I'm looking for a treaty."

He nodded, squinting his eyes. "What kind of treaty?"

"A peace treaty. Let's cut out the snowmobile parties on the lake by my place and the trash dumped in the driveway and the hang-up calls. Let's start fresh and just stay out of each other's way. What do you say? Then, this summer, you can all come over to my place for a cookout. I'll even supply the beer."

He rubbed at the bristles along his chin. "Seems like a one-sided deal. Not too sure what I get out of it."

"What's the point in what you're doing now?"

A furtive smile. "It suits me."

I felt like I was beginning to lose it. "You agree with the treaty, we all win."

"Still don't see what I get out of it," he said.

"That's the purpose of a peace treaty," I said. "You get peace."

"Feel pretty peaceful right now."

"That might change," I said, instantly regretting the words.

His eyes darkened. "Are you threatening me?"

A retreat, recalling my promise to myself when I'd come here. "No, not a threat, Jerry. What do you say?"

He turned and walked away, moving his head to keep me in view. "Your second got used up a long time ago, pal. And you better be out of this lot in another minute, or I'm going inside and coming out with a bunch of my friends. You won't like that."

No, I wouldn't, and it wouldn't be for the reason Jerry believed. If they did come out I'd be forced into old habits and old actions, and I'd promised myself I wouldn't do that. I couldn't.

"You got it," I said, backing away. "But remember, Jerry. Always."

"What's that?"

"The peace treaty," I said, going to the door of my pickup truck. "I offered."

Another visit to Ron, on a snowy day. The conversation meandered along, and I don't know what got into me, but I looked out the old mill windows and said, "What do people expect, anyway?"

"What do you mean?" he asked.

"You take a tough teenager from a small Ohio town, and you train him and train him and train him. You turn him into a very efficient hunter, a meat eater. Then, after 20 or 30 years, you say thank you very much and send him back to the world of quiet vegetarians, and you expect him to start eating cabbages and carrots with no fuss or muss. A hell of a thing, thinking you can expect him to put away his tools and skills."

"Maybe that's why we're here," he suggested.

"Oh, please," I said. "Do you think this makes a difference?"

"Does it make a difference to you?"

I kept looking out the window. "Too soon to tell, I'd say. Truth is, I wonder if this is meant to work, or is just meant to make some people feel less guilty. The people who did the hiring, training and discharging."

"What do you think?"

I turned to him. "I think for the amount of money you charge Uncle Sam, you ask too many damn questions."

★   ★   ★

Another night at two A.M. I was back outside, beside the porch, again with the night scope in my hands. They were back, and if anything, the music and the engines blared even louder. A fire burned merrily among the snowmobiles, and as the revelers pranced and hollered, I wondered if some base part of their brains was remembering thousand-year-old rituals. As I looked at their dancing and drinking figures, I kept thinking of the long case at the other end of the cellar. Nice heavy-duty assault rifle with another night-vision scope, this one with crosshairs. Scan and track. Put a crosshair across each one's chest. Feel the weight of a fully loaded clip in your hand. Know that with a silencer on the end of the rifle, you could quietly take out that crew in a fistful of seconds. Get your mind back into the realm of possibilities, of cartridges and windage and grains and velocities. How long could it take between the time you said go and the time you could say mission accomplished? Not long at all.

"No," I whispered, switching off the scope.

I stayed on the porch for another hour, and as my eyes adjusted, I saw more movements. I picked up the scope. A couple of snow machines moved in, each with shapes on the seats behind the drivers. They pulled up to the snowy bank and the people moved quickly, intent on their work. Trash bags were tossed on my land, about eight or nine, and to add a bit more fun, each bag had been slit several times with a knife so it could burst open and spew its contents when it hit the ground. A few more hoots and hollers and the snowmobiles growled away, leaving trash and the flickering fire behind. I watched the lights as the snowmobiles roared across the lake and finally disappeared, though their sound did not.

The night scope went back onto my lap. The rifle, I thought, could have stopped the fun right there with a couple of rounds through the engines. Highly illegal, but it would get their attention, right?

Right.

In my next session with Ron, I got to the point. "What kind of reports are you sending south?"

I think I might have surprised him. "Reports?"

"How I'm adjusting, that sort of thing."

He paused for a moment, and I knew there must be a lot of figuring going on behind those smiling eyes. "Just the usual things, that's all. That you're doing fine."

"Am I?"

"Seems so to me."

"Good." I waited for a moment, letting the words twist about on my tongue. "Then you can send them this message. I haven't been a hundred percent with you during these sessions, Ron. Guess it's not in my nature to be so open. But you can count on this. I won't lose it. I won't go into a gun shop and then take down a bunch of civilians. I'm not going to start hanging around 1600 Pennsylvania Avenue. I'm going to be all right."

He smiled. "I have never had any doubt."

"Sure you've had doubts," I said, smiling back. "But it's awfully polite of you to say otherwise."

On a bright Saturday, I tracked down the police chief of Nansen at one of the two service stations in town, Glen's Gas & Repair. His cruiser, ordinarily a dark blue, was now a ghostly shade of white from the salt used to keep the roads clear. I parked at the side of the garage, and walking by the service bays, I could sense that I was being watched. I saw three cars with their hoods up, and I also saw a familiar uniform: black snowmobile jumpsuits.

The chief was overweight and wearing a heavy blue jacket with a black Navy watch cap. His face was open and friendly, and he nodded in all the right places as I told him my story.

"Not much I can do, I'm afraid," he said, leaning against the door of his cruiser, one of two in the entire town. "I'd have to catch 'em in the act of trashing your place, and that means surveillance, and that means overtime hours, which I don't have."

"Surveillance would be a waste of time anyway," I replied. "These guys, they aren't thugs, right? For lack of a better phrase, they're good old boys, and they know everything that's going on in Nansen, and they'd know if you were setting up surveillance. And then they wouldn't show."

"You might think you're insulting me, but you're not," he said gently. "That's just the way things are done here. It's a good town and most of us get along, and I'm not kept that busy, not at all."

"I appreciate that, but you should also appreciate my problem," I said. "I live here and pay taxes, and people are harassing me. I'm looking for some assistance, that's all, and a suggestion of what I can do."

"You could move," the chief said, raising his coffee cup.

"Hell of a suggestion."

"Best one I can come up with. Look, friend, you're new here, you've got no family, no ties. You're asking me to take on some prominent families just because you don't get along with them. So why don't you move on? Find someplace smaller, hell, even someplace bigger, where you don't stand out so much. But face it, it's not going to get any easier."

"Real nice folks," I said, letting an edge of bitterness into my voice.

That didn't seem to bother the chief. "That they are. They work hard and play hard, and they pay taxes, too, and they look out for one another. I know they look like hell-raisers to you, but they're more than that. They're part of the community. Why, just next week, a bunch of them are going on a midnight snow run across the lake and into the mountains, raising money for the children's camp up at Lake Montcalm. People who don't care wouldn't do that."

"I just wish they didn't care so much about me."

He shrugged and said, "Look, I'll see what I can do . . ." but the tone of his voice made it clear he wasn't going to do a damn thing.

The chief clambered into his cruiser and drove off, and as I walked past the bays of the service station, I heard snickers. I went around to my pickup truck and saw the source of the merriment.

My truck was resting heavily on four flat tires.

At night I woke up from cold and bloody dreams and let my thoughts drift into fantasies. By now I knew who all of them were, where all of them lived. I could go to their houses, every one of them, and bring them back and bind them in the basement of my home. I could tell them who I was and what I've done and what I can do, and I would ask them to leave me alone. That's it. Just give me peace and solitude and everything will be all right.

And they would hear me out and nod and agree, but I would know that I had to convince them. So I would go to Jerry Tompkins, the mustached one who enjoyed marking my territory, and to make my point, break a couple of his fingers, the popping noise echoing in the dark confines of the tiny basement.

Nice fantasies.

I asked Ron, "What's the point?"

He was comfortable in his chair, hands clasped over his little potbelly. "I'm sorry?"

"The point of our sessions."

His eyes were unflinching. "To help you adjust."

"Adjust to what?"

"To civilian life."

I shifted on the couch. "Let me get this. I work my entire life for this country, doing service for its civilians. I expose myself to death and injury every week, earning about a third of what I could be making in the private sector. And when I'm through, I have to adjust, I have to make allowances for civilians. But civilians, they don't have to do a damn thing. Is that right?"

"I'm afraid so."

"Hell of a deal."

He continued a steady gaze. "Only one you've got."

So here I am, in the smelly rubble that used to be my home. I make a few half-hearted attempts to turn the furniture back over and do some cleanup work, but I'm not in the mood. Old feelings and emotions are coursing through me, taking control. I take a few deep breaths and then I'm in the cellar, switching on the single lightbulb that hangs down from the rafters by a frayed black cord. As I maneuver among the packing cases, undoing combination locks, my shoulder strikes the lightbulb, causing it to swing back and forth, casting crazy shadows on the stone walls.

The night air is cool and crisp, and I shuffle through the snow around the house as I load the pickup truck, making three trips in all. I drive under the speed limit and halt completely at all stop signs as I go through the center of town. I drive around, wasting minutes and hours, listening to the radio. This late at night and being so far north, a lot of the stations that I can pick up are from Quebec, and there's a joyous lilt to the French-Canadian music and words that makes something inside me ache with longing.

When it's almost a new day, I drive down a street called Mast Road. Most towns around here have a Mast Road, where colonial surveyors marked tall pines that would eventually become masts for the Royal Navy. Tonight there are no surveyors, just the night air and darkness and a skinny rabbit racing across the cracked asphalt. When I'm near the target, I switch off the lights and engine and let the truck glide the last few hundred feet or so. I pull up across from a darkened house. A pickup truck and a Subaru station wagon are in the driveway. Gray smoke is wafting up from the chimney.

I roll down the window, the cold air washing over me like a wave of water. I pause, remembering what has gone on these past weeks, and then I get to work.

The night scope comes up and clicks into action, and the name on the mailbox is clear enough in the sharp green light. TOMPKINS, in silver and black stick-on letters. I scan the two-story Cape Cod, checking out the surroundings. There's an attached garage to the right and a sunroom to the left. There is a front door and two other doors in a breezeway that runs from the garage to the house. There are no rear doors.

I let the night scope rest on my lap as I reach toward my weapons. The first is a grenade launcher, with a handful of white phosphorus rounds clustered on the seat next to it like a gathering of metal eggs. Next to the grenade launcher is a 9mm Uzi, with an extended wooden stock for easier use. Another night-vision scope with crosshairs is attached to the Uzi.

Another series of deep breaths. Easy enough plan. Pop a white phosphorus round into the breezeway and another into the sunroom. In a minute or two both ends of the house are on fire. Our snowmobiler friend and his family wake up and, groggy from sleep and the fire and the noise, stumble out the front door onto the snow-covered lawn.

With the Uzi in my hand and the crosshairs on a certain face, a face with a mustache, I take care of business and drive to the next house.

I pick up the grenade launcher and rest the barrel on the open window. It's cold. I rub my legs together and look outside at the stars. The wind comes up and snow blows across the road. I hear the low hoo-hoo-hoo of an owl.

I bring the grenade launcher up, resting the stock against my cheek. I aim. I wait.

It's very cold.

The weapon begins trembling in my hands and I let it drop to the front seat.

I sit on my hands, trying to warm them while the cold breeze blows. Idiot. Do this and how long before you're in jail, and then on trial before a jury of friends or relatives of those fine citizens you gun down tonight?

I start up the truck and let the heater sigh itself on, and then I roll up the window and slowly drive away, lights still off.

"Fool," I say to myself, "remember who you are." And with the truck's lights now on, I drive home. To what's left of it.

Days later, there's a fresh smell to the air in my house, for I've done a lot of cleaning and painting, trying not only to bring everything back to where it was but also to spruce up the place. The only real problem has been in the main room, where the words GO HOME were marked in bright red on the white plaster wall. It took me three coats to cover that up, and of course I ended up doing the entire room.

The house is dark and it's late. I'm waiting on the porch with a glass of wine in my hand, watching a light snow fall on Lake Marie. Every light in the house is off and the only illumination comes from the fireplace, which needs more wood.

But I'm content to dawdle. I'm finally at peace after these difficult weeks in Nansen. Finally, I'm beginning to remember who I really am.

I sip my wine, waiting, and then comes the sound of the snowmobiles. I see their wavering dots of light racing across the lake, doing their bit for charity. How wonderful. I raise my glass in salute, the noise of the snowmobiles getting louder as they head across the lake in a straight line.

I put the wineglass down, walk into the living room and toss the last few pieces of wood onto the fire. The sudden heat warms my face in a pleasant glow. The wood isn't firewood, though. It's been shaped and painted by man, and as the flames leap up and devour the lumber, I see the letters begin to fade: DANGER: THIN ICE!

I stroll back to the porch, pick up the wineglass and wait.

Below me, on the peaceful ice of Lake Marie, my new home for my new life, the headlights go by.

And then, one by one, they blink out, and the silence is wonderful.

Mark Twain was the pseudonym for Samuel Langhorne Clemens (1835–1910), who is widely regarded as one of America's greatest authors. His biting satire brought to light the social injustices of his times, such as racism and slavery. His best-known works include The Adventures of Tom Sawyer, The Adventures of Huckleberry Finn, *and* A Connecticut Yankee in King Arthur's Court. *In the following story he takes on the idea of small-town friendliness and unravels the myth as only he can.*

The Man That Corrupted Hadleyburg

Mark Twain

I

It was many years ago. Hadleyburg was the most honest and upright town in all the region round about. It had kept that reputation unsmirched during three generations, and was prouder of it than of any other of its possessions. It was so proud of it, and so anxious to insure its perpetuation, that it began to teach the principles of honest dealing to its babies in the cradle, and made the like teachings the staple of their culture thenceforward through all the years devoted to their education. Also, throughout the formative years temptations were kept out of the way of the young people, so that their honesty could have every chance to harden and solidify, and become a part of their very bone. The neighboring towns were jealous of this honorable supremacy, and affected to sneer at Hadleyburg's pride in it and call it vanity; but all the same they were obliged to acknowledge that Hadleyburg was in reality an incorruptible town; and if pressed they would also acknowledge that the mere fact that a young man hailed from Hadleyburg was all the recommendation he needed when he went forth from his natal town to seek for responsible employment.

But at last, in the drift of time, Hadleyburg had the ill luck to offend a passing stranger—possibly without knowing it, certainly without caring, for Hadleyburg was sufficient unto itself, and cared not a rap for strangers or their opinions. Still, it would have been well to make an exception in this one's case, for he was a bitter man and revengeful. All through his wanderings during a whole year he kept his injury in mind, and gave all his leisure moments to trying to invent a compensating satisfaction for it. He contrived many plans, and all of them were good, but none of them was quite sweeping enough; the poorest of them would hurt a great many individuals, but what he wanted was a plan which would comprehend the entire town, and not let so much as one person escape unhurt. At last he had a fortunate idea, and when it fell into his brain it lit up his whole head with an evil joy. He began to form a plan at once, saying to himself, "That is the thing to do—I will corrupt the town."

Six months later he went to Hadleyburg, and arrived in a buggy at the house of the old cashier of the bank about ten at night. He got a sack out of the buggy, shouldered it, and staggered with it through the cottage yard, and knocked at the door. A woman's voice said "Come in," and he entered, and set his sack behind the stove in the parlor, saying politely to the old lady who sat reading the *Missionary Herald* by the lamp:

"Pray keep your seat, madam, I will not disturb you. There—now it is pretty well concealed; one would hardly know it was there. Can I see your husband a moment, madam?"

No, he was gone to Brixton, and might not return before morning.

"Very well, madam, it is no matter. I merely wanted to leave that sack in his care, to be delivered to the rightful owner when he shall be found. I am a stranger; he does not know me; I am merely passing through the town to-night to discharge a matter which has been long in my mind. My errand is now completed, and I go pleased and a little proud, and you will never see me again. There is a paper attached to the sack which will explain everything. Good-night, madam."

The old lady was afraid of the mysterious big stranger, and was glad to see him go. But her curiosity was roused, and she went straight to the sack and brought away the paper. It began as follows:

"TO BE PUBLISHED: or, the right man sought out by private inquiry—either will answer. This sack contains gold coin weighing a hundred and sixty pounds four ounces—"

"Mercy on us, and the door not locked!"

Mrs. Richards flew to it all in a tremble and locked it, then pulled down the window-shades and stood frightened, worried, and wondering if there was anything else she could do toward making herself and the money more safe. She listened awhile for burglars, then surrendered to curiosity and went back to the lamp and finished reading the paper:

> "I am a foreigner, and am presently going back to my own country, to remain there permanently. I am grateful to America for what I have received at her hands during my long stay under her flag; and to one of her citizens— a citizen of Hadleyburg—I am especially grateful for a great kindness done me a year or two ago. Two great kindnesses, in fact. I will explain. I was a gambler. I say I WAS. I was a ruined gambler. I arrived in this village at night, hungry and without a penny. I asked for help—in the dark; I was ashamed to beg in the light. I begged of the right man. He gave me twenty dollars—that is to say, he gave me life, as I considered it. He also gave me a fortune; for out of that money I have made myself rich at the gaming-table. And finally, a remark which he made to me has remained with me to this day, and has at last conquered me; and in conquering has saved the remnant of my morals: I shall gamble no more. Now I have no idea who that man was, but I want him found, and I want him to have this money, to give away, throw away, or keep, as he pleases. It is merely my way of testifying my gratitude to him. If I could stay, I would find him myself; but no matter, he will be found. This is an honest town, an incorruptible town, and I know I can trust it without fear. This man can be identified by the remark which he made to me; I feel persuaded that he will remember it.
>
> "And now my plan is this: If you prefer to conduct the inquiry privately, do so. Tell the contents of this present writing to any one who is likely to be the right man. If he shall answer, 'I am the man; the remark I made was so-and-so,' apply the test—to wit: open the sack, and in it you will find a sealed envelope containing that remark. If the remark mentioned by the candidate tallies with it, give him the money, and ask no further questions, for he is certainly the right man.
>
> "But if you shall prefer a public inquiry, then publish this present writing in the local paper—with these instructions added, to wit: Thirty days from now, let the candidate appear at the town-hall at eight in the evening (Friday), and hand his remark, in a sealed envelope, to the Rev. Mr. Burgess (if he will be kind enough to act); and let Mr. Burgess there and then destroy the seals of the sack, open it, and see if the remark is correct; if correct, let the money be delivered, with my sincere gratitude, to my benefactor thus identified."

Mrs. Richards sat down, gently quivering with excitement, and was soon lost in thinkings—after this pattern: "What a strange thing it is! . . . And what a fortune for that kind man who set his bread afloat upon the waters! . . . If it had only been my husband that did it! . . . for we are so poor, so old and poor! . . ." Then, with a sigh—"But it was not my Edward; no, it was not he that gave a stranger twenty dollars. It is a pity, too; I see it now . . ." Then, with a shudder—"But it is *gambler's* money! the wages of sin: we couldn't take it; we couldn't touch it. I don't like to be near it; it seems a defilement." She moved to a farther chair . . . "I wish Edward would come, and take it to the bank; a burglar might come at any moment; it is dreadful to be here all alone with it."

At eleven Mr. Richards arrived, and while his wife was saying, "I am *so* glad you've come!" he was saying, "I'm so tired—tired clear out; it is dreadful to be poor, and have to make these dismal journeys at my time of life. Always at the grind, grind, grind, on a salary—another man's slave, and he sitting at home in his slippers, rich and comfortable."

"I am so sorry for you, Edward, you know that; but be comforted: we have our livelihood; we have our good name—"

"Yes, Mary, and that is everything. Don't mind my talk—it's just a moment's irritation and doesn't mean anything. Kiss me—there, it's all gone now, and I am not complaining any more. What have you been getting? What's in the sack?"

Then his wife told him the great secret. It dazed him for a moment; then he said:

"It weighs a hundred and sixty pounds? Why, Mary, it's forty thousand dollars—think of it—a whole fortune! Not ten men in this village are worth that much. Give me the paper."

He skimmed through it and said:

"Isn't it an adventure! Why, it's a romance; it's like the impossible things one reads about in books, and never sees in life." He was well stirred up now, cheerful, even gleeful. He tapped his old wife on the cheek, and said, humorously, "Why, we're rich, Mary, rich; all we've got to do is to bury the money and burn the papers. If the gambler ever comes to inquire, we'll merely look coldly upon him and say: 'What is this nonsense you are talking? We have never heard of you and your sack of gold before'; and then he would look foolish, and—"

"And in the meantime, while you are running on with your jokes, the money is still here, and it is fast getting along toward burglar-time."

"True. Very well, what shall we do—make the inquiry private? No, not that: it would spoil the romance. The public method is better. Think what a noise it will make! And it will make all the other towns jealous; for no stranger would trust such a thing to any town but Hadleyburg, and they know it. It's a great card for us. I must get to the printing-office, now, or I shall be too late."

"But stop—stop—don't leave me here alone with it, Edward!"

But he was gone. For only a little while, however. Not far from his own house he met the editor-proprietor of the paper, and gave him the document, and said, "Here is a good thing for you, Cox—put it in!"

"It may be too late, Mr. Richards, but I'll see."

At home again he and his wife sat down to talk the charming mystery over; they were in no condition for sleep. The first question was, "Who could the citizen have been who gave the stranger the twenty dollars?" It seemed a simple one; both answered it in the same breath—

"Barclay Goodson."

"Yes," said Richards, "he would have done it, and it would have been like him, but there's not another in the town."

"Everybody will grant that, Edward—grant it privately, anyway. For six months, now, the village has been its own proper self once more—honest, narrow, self-righteous, and stingy."

"It's what he always called it, to the day of his death—said it right out publicly, too."

"Yes, and he was hated for it."

"Oh, of course; but he didn't care. I reckon he was the best-hated man among us, except the Reverend Burgess."

"Well, Burgess deserves it—he will never get another congregation here. Mean as the town is, it knows how to estimate *him*. Edward, doesn't it seem odd that the stranger should appoint Burgess to deliver the money?"

"Well, yes—it does. That is—that is—"

"Why so much that-*is*-ing? Would *you* select him?"

"Mary, maybe the stranger knows him better than this village does."

"Much *that* would help Burgess!"

The husband seemed perplexed for an answer; the wife kept a steady eye upon him, and waited. Finally Richards said, with the hesitancy of one who is making a statement which is likely to encounter doubt,

"Mary, Burgess is not a bad man."

His wife was certainly surprised.

"Nonsense!" she exclaimed.

"He is not a bad man. I know. The whole of his unpopularity had its foundation in that one thing—the thing that made so much noise."

"That 'one thing,' indeed! As if that 'one thing' wasn't enough, all by itself."

"Plenty. Plenty. Only he wasn't guilty of it."

"How you talk! Not guilty of it! Everybody knows he *was* guilty."

"Mary, I give you my word—he was innocent."

"I can't believe it, and I don't. How do you know?"

"It is a confession. I am ashamed, but I will make it. I was the only man who knew he was innocent. I could have saved him, and—and—well, you know how the town was wrought up—I hadn't the pluck to do it. It would have turned everybody against me. I felt mean, ever so mean; but I didn't dare; I hadn't the manliness to face that."

Mary looked troubled, and for a while was silent. Then she said, stammeringly:

"I—I don't think it would have done for you to—to—One mustn't—er—public opinion—one has to be so careful—so—" It was a difficult road, and she got mired; but after a little she got started again. "It was a great pity, but—Why, we couldn't afford it, Edward—we couldn't indeed. Oh, I wouldn't have had you do it for anything!"

"It would have lost us the good-will of so many people, Mary; and then—and then—"

"What troubles me now is, what *he* thinks of us, Edward."

"He? *He* doesn't suspect that I could have saved him."

"Oh," exclaimed the wife, in a tone of relief, "I am glad of that. As long as he doesn't know that you could have saved him, he—he—well, that makes it a great deal better. Why, I might have known he didn't know, because he is always trying to be friendly with us, as little encouragement as we give him. More than once people have twitted me with it. There's the Wilsons, and the Wilcoxes, and the Harknesses, they have a mean pleasure in saying, '*Your friend* Burgess,' because they know it pesters me. I wish he wouldn't persist in liking us so; I can't think why he keeps it up."

"I can explain it. It's another confession. When the thing was new and hot, and the town made a plan to ride him on a rail, my conscience hurt me so that I couldn't stand it, and I went privately and gave him notice, and he got out of the town and staid out till it was safe to come back."

"Edward! If the town had found it out—"

"*Don't!* It scares me yet, to think of it. I repented of it the minute it was done; and I was even afraid to tell you, lest your face might betray it to somebody. I didn't sleep any that night, for worrying. But after a few days I saw that no one was going to suspect me, and after that I got to feeling glad I did it. And I feel glad yet, Mary—glad through and through."

"So do I, now, for it would have been a dreadful way to treat him. Yes, I'm glad; for really you did owe him that, you know. But, Edward, suppose it should come out yet, some day!"

"It won't."

"Why?"

"Because everybody thinks it was Goodson."

"Of course they would!"

"Certainly. And of course *he* didn't care. They persuaded poor old Sawlsberry to go and charge it on him, and he went blustering over there and did it. Goodson looked him over, like as if he was hunting for a place on him that he could despise the most, then he says, 'So you are the Committee of Inquiry, are you?' Sawlsberry said that was about what he was. 'Hm. Do they require particulars, or do you reckon a kind of a *general* answer will do?' 'If they require particulars, I will come back, Mr. Goodson; I will take the general answer first,' 'Very well, then, tell them to go to hell—I reckon that's general enough. And I'll give you some advice, Sawlsberry; when you come back for the particulars, fetch a basket to carry the relics of yourself home in.'"

"Just like Goodson; it's got all the marks. He had only one vanity: he thought he could give advice better than any other person."

"It settled the business, and saved us, Mary. The subject was dropped."

"Bless you, I'm not doubting *that.*"

Then they took up the gold-sack mystery again, with strong interest. Soon the conversation began to suffer breaks—interruptions caused by absorbed thinkings. The breaks grew more and more frequent. At last Richards lost himself wholly in thought. He sat long, gazing vacantly at the floor, and by and by he began to punctuate his thoughts with little nervous movements of his hands that seemed to indicate vexation. Meantime his wife too had relapsed into a thoughtful silence, and her movements were beginning to show a troubled discomfort. Finally Richards got up and strode aimlessly about the room, plowing his hands through his hair, much as a somnambulist might do who was having a bad dream. Then he seemed to arrive at a definite purpose; and without a word he put on his hat and passed quickly out of the house. His wife sat brooding, with a drawn face, and did not seem to be aware that she was alone. Now and then she murmured, "Lead us not into t— . . . but—but—we are so poor, so poor! . . . Lead us not into . . . Ah, who would be hurt by it?—and no one would ever know . . . Lead us . . ." The voice died out in mumblings. After a little she glanced up and muttered in a half-frightened, half-glad way—

"He is gone! But, oh dear, he may be too late—too late . . . Maybe not—maybe there is still time." She rose and stood thinking, nervously clasping and unclasping her hands. A slight shudder shook her frame, and she said, out of a dry throat, "God forgive me—it's awful to think such things—but . . . Lord, how we are made—how strangely we are made!"

She turned the light low, and slipped stealthily over and kneeled down by the sack and felt of its ridgy sides with her hands, and fondled them lovingly; and there was a gloating light in her poor old eyes. She fell into fits of absence; and came half out of them at times to mutter, "If we had only waited!—oh, if we had only waited a little, and not been in such a hurry!"

Meantime Cox had gone home from his office and told his wife all about the strange things that had happened, and they had talked it over eagerly, and guessed that the late Goodson was the only man in the town who could have helped a suffering stranger with so noble a sum as twenty dollars. Then there was a pause, and the two became thoughtful and silent. And by and by nervous and fidgety. At last the wife said, as if to herself,

"Nobody knows this secret but the Richardses . . . and us . . . nobody."

The husband came out of his thinkings with a slight start, and gazed wistfully at his wife, whose face was become very pale; then he hesitatingly rose, and glanced furtively at his hat, then at his wife—a sort of mute inquiry. Mrs. Cox swallowed once or twice, with her hand at her throat, then in place of speech she nodded her head. In a moment she was alone, and mumbling to herself.

And now Richards and Cox were hurrying through the deserted streets, from opposite directions. They met, panting, at the foot of the printing-office stairs; by the night-light there they read each other's face. Cox whispered,

"Nobody knows about this but us?"

The whispered answer was,

"Not a soul—on honor, not a soul!"

"If it isn't too late to—"

The men were starting up-stairs; at this moment they were overtaken by a boy, and Cox asked,

"Is that you, Johnny?"

"Yes, sir."

"You needn't ship the early mail—nor *any* mail; wait till I tell you."

"It's already gone, sir."

"Gone?" It had the sound of an unspeakable disappointment in it.

"Yes, sir. Time-table for Brixton and all the towns beyond changed today, sir—had to get the papers in twenty minutes earlier than common. I had to rush; if I had been two minutes later—"

The men turned and walked slowly away, not waiting to hear the rest. Neither of them spoke during ten minutes; then Cox said, in a vexed tone,

"What possessed you to be in such a hurry, I can't make out."

The answer was humble enough:

"I see it now, but somehow I never thought, you know, until it was too late. But the next time—"

"Next time be hanged! It won't come in a thousand years."

Then the friends separated without a good-night, and dragged themselves home with the gait of mortally stricken men. At their homes their wives sprang up with an eager "Well?"—then saw the answer with their eyes and sank down sorrowing, without waiting for it to come in words. In both houses a discussion followed of a heated sort—a new thing; there had been discussions before, but not heated ones, not ungentle ones. The discussions tonight were a sort of seeming plagiarisms of each other. Mrs. Richards said,

"If you had only waited, Edward—if you had only stopped to think; but no, you must run straight to the printing-office and spread it all over the world."

"It *said* publish it."

"That is nothing; it also said do it privately, if you liked. There, now—is that true, or not?"

"Why, yes—yes, it is true; but when I thought what a stir it would make, and what a compliment it was to Hadleyburg that a stranger should trust it so—"

"Oh, certainly, I know all that; but if you had only stopped to think, you would have seen that you *couldn't* find the right man, because he is in his grave, and hasn't left chick nor child nor relation behind him; and as long as the money went to somebody that awfully needed it, and nobody would be hurt by it, and—and—"

She broke down crying. Her husband tried to think of some comforting thing to say, and presently came out with this:

"But after all, Mary, it must be for the best—it *must* be; we know that. And we must remember that it was so ordered—"

"Ordered! Oh, everything's *ordered,* when a person has to find some way out when he has been stupid. Just the same, it was *ordered* that the money should come to us in this special way, and it was you that must take it on yourself to go meddling with the designs of Providence—and who gave you the right? It was wicked, that is what it was—just blasphemous presumption, and no more becoming to a meek and humble professor of—"

"But, Mary, you know how we have been trained all our lives long, like the whole village, till it is absolutely second nature to us to stop not a single moment to think when there's an honest thing to be done—"

"Oh, I know it, I know it—it's been one everlasting training and training and training in honesty—honesty shielded, from the very cradle, against every possible temptation, and so it's *artificial* honesty, and weak as water when temptation comes, as we have seen this night. God knows I never had shade nor shadow of a doubt of my petrified and indestructible honesty until now—and now, under the very first big and real temptation, I—Edward, it is my belief that this town's honesty is as rotten as mine is; as rotten as yours is. It is a mean town, a hard, stingy town, and hasn't a virtue in the world but this honesty it is so celebrated for and so conceited about; and so help me, I do believe that if ever the day comes that its honesty falls under great temptation, its grand reputation will go to ruin like a house of cards. There, now, I've made confession, and I feel better; I am a humbug, and I've been one all my life, without knowing it. Let no man call me honest again—I will not have it."

"I—well, Mary, I feel a good deal as you do; I certainly do. It seems strange, too, so strange. I never could have believed it—never."

A long silence followed; both were sunk in thought. At last the wife looked up and said,

"I know what you are thinking, Edward."

Richards had the embarrassed look of a person who is caught.

"I am ashamed to confess it, Mary, but—"

"It's no matter, Edward, I was thinking the same question myself."

"I hope so. State it."

"You were thinking, if a body could only guess out *what the remark was* that Goodson made to the stranger.

"It's perfectly true. I feel guilty and ashamed. And you?"

"I'm past it. Let us make a pallet here, we've got to stand watch till the bank vault opens in the morning and admits the sack . . . Oh dear, oh dear—if we hadn't made the mistake!"

The pallet was made, and Mary said:

"The open sesame—what could it have been? I do wonder what that remark could have been? But come; we will get to bed now."

"And sleep?"

"No: think."

"Yes, think."

By this time the Coxes too had completed their spat and their reconciliation, and were turning in—to think, to think, and toss, and fret, and worry over what the remark could possibly have been which Goodson made to the stranded derelict; that golden remark; that remark worth forty thousand dollars, cash.

The reason that the village telegraph office was open later than usual that night was this: The foreman of Cox's paper was the local representative of the Associated Press. One might say its honorary representative, for it wasn't four times a year that he could furnish thirty words that would be accepted. But this time it was different. His dispatch stating what he had caught got an instant answer:

Send the whole thing—all the details—twelve hundred words.

A colossal order! the foreman filled the bill; and he was the proudest man in the State. By breakfast-time the next morning the name of Hadleyburg the Incorruptible was on every lip in America, from Montreal to the Gulf, from the glaciers of Alaska to the orange-groves of Florida; and millions and millions of people were discussing the stranger and his money-sack, and wondering if the right man would be found, and hoping some more news about the matter would come soon—right away.

II

Hadleyburg village woke up world-celebrated—astonished—happy—vain. Vain beyond imagination. Its nineteen principal citizens and their wives went about shaking hands with each other, and beaming, and smiling, and congratulating, and saying *this* thing adds a new word to the dictionary—*Hadleyburg,* synonym for *incorruptible*—destined to live in dictionaries forever! And the minor and unimportant citizens and their wives went around acting in much the same way. Everybody ran to the bank to see the gold-sack; and before noon grieved and envious crowds began to flock in from Brixton and all neighboring towns; and that afternoon and next day reporters began to arrive from everywhere to verify the sack and its history and write the whole thing up anew, and make dashing free-hand pictures of the sack, and of Richárds's house, and the bank, and the Presbyterian church, and the Baptist church, and the public square, and the town-hall where the test would be applied and the money delivered; and damnable portraits of the Richardses, and Pinkerton the banker, and Cox, and the foreman, and Reverend Burgess, and the postmaster—and even of Jack Halliday, who was the loafing, good-natured, no-account, irreverent fisherman, hunter, boys' friend, stray-dogs' friend, typical "Sam Lawson" of the town. The little mean, smirking, oily Pinkerton showed the sack to all comers, and rubbed his sleek palms together pleasantly, and enlarged upon the town's fine old reputation for honesty and upon this wonderful endorsement of it, and hoped and believed that the example would now spread far and wide over the American world, and be epoch-making in the matter of moral regeneration. And so on, and so on.

By the end of the week things had quieted down again; the wild intoxication of pride and joy had sobered to a soft, sweet, silent delight—a sort of deep, nameless, unutterable content. All faces bore a look of peaceful, holy happiness.

Then a change came. It was a gradual change; so gradual that its beginnings were hardly noticed; maybe were not noticed at all, except by Jack Halliday, who always noticed everything; and always made fun of it, too, no matter what it was. He began to throw out chaffing remarks about people not looking quite so happy as they did a day or two ago; and next he claimed that the new aspect was deepening to positive sadness; next, that it was taking on a sick look; and finally he said that everybody was become so moody, thoughtful, and absent-minded that he could rob the meanest man in town of a cent out of the bottom of his breeches pocket and not disturb his revery.

At this stage—or at about this stage—a saying like this was dropped at bedtime—with a sigh, usually—by the head of each of the nineteen principal households: "Ah, what *could* have been the remark that Goodson made?"

And straightway—with a shudder—came this, from the man's wife:

"Oh, *don't!* What horrible thing are you mulling in your mind? Put it away from you, for God's sake!"

But that question was wrung from those men again the next night—and got the same retort. But weaker.

And the third night the men uttered the question yet again—with anguish, and absently. This time—and the following night—the wives fidgeted feebly, and tried to say something. But didn't.

And the night after that they found their tongues and responded—longingly.

"Oh, if we *could* only guess!"

Halliday's comments grew daily more and more sparklingly disagreeable and disparaging. He went diligently about, laughing at the town, individually and in mass. But his laugh was the only one left in the village: it fell upon a hollow and mournful vacancy and emptiness. Not even a smile was findable anywhere. Halliday carried a cigar-box around on a tripod, playing that it was a camera, and halted all passers and aimed the thing and said, "Ready!—now look pleasant, please," but not even this capital joke could surprise the dreary faces into any softening.

So three weeks passed—one week was left. It was Saturday evening—after supper. Instead of the aforetime Saturday-evening flutter and bustle and shopping and larking, the streets were empty and desolate. Richards and his old wife sat apart in their little parlor—miserable and thinking. This was become their evening habit now: the lifelong habit which had preceded it, of reading, knitting, and contented chat, or receiving or paying neighborly calls, was dead and gone and forgotten, ages ago—two or three weeks ago; nobody talked now, nobody read, nobody visited—the whole village sat at home, sighing, worrying, silent. Trying to guess out that remark.

The postman left a letter. Richards glanced listlessly at the superscription and the postmark—unfamiliar, both—and tossed the letter on the table and resumed his might-have-beens and his hopeless dull miseries where he had left them off. Two or three hours later his wife got wearily up and was going away to bed without a good-night—custom now—but she stopped near the letter and eyed it awhile with a dead interest, then broke it open, and began to skim it over. Richards, sitting there with his chair tilted back against the wall and his chin between his knees, heard something fall. It was his wife. He sprang to her side, but she cried out:

"Leave me alone, I am too happy. Read the letter—read it!"

He did. He devoured it, his brain reeling. The letter was from a distant State, and it said:

"I am a stranger to you, but no matter: I have something to tell. I have just arrived home from Mexico, and learned about that episode. Of course you do not know who made that remark, but I know, and I am the only

person living who does know. It was GOODSON. *I knew him well, many years ago. I passed through your village that very night, and was his guest till the midnight train came along. I overheard him make that remark to the stranger in the dark—it was in Hale Alley. He and I talked of it the rest of the way home, and while smoking in his house. He mentioned many of your villagers in the course of his talk—most of them in a very uncomplimentary way, but two or three favorably; among these latter yourself. I say 'favorably'—nothing stronger. I remember his saying he did not actually* LIKE *any person in the town—not one; but that you—I* THINK *he said you—am almost sure—had done him a very great service once, possibly without knowing the full value of it, and he wished he had a fortune, he would leave it to you when he died, and a curse apiece for the rest of the citizens. Now, then, if it was you that did him that service, you are his legitimate heir, and entitled to the sack of gold. I know that I can trust to your honor and honesty, for in a citizen of Hadleyburg these virtues are an unfailing inheritance, and so I am going to reveal to you the remark, well satisfied that if you are not the right man you will seek and find the right one and see that poor Goodson's debt of gratitude for the service referred to is paid. This is the remark: 'YOU ARE FAR FROM BEING A BAD MAN: GO AND REFORM.'*

"Howard L. Stephenson."

"Oh, Edward, the money is ours, and I am so grateful, *oh,* so grateful—kiss me, dear, it's forever since we kissed—and we needed it so—the money—and now you are free of Pinkerton and his bank, and nobody's slave any more; it seems to me I could fly for joy."

It was a happy half-hour that the couple spent there on the settee caressing each other; it was the old days come again—days that had begun with their courtship and lasted without a break till the stranger brought the deadly money. By and by the wife said:

"Oh, Edward, how lucky it was you did him that grand service, poor Goodson! I never liked him, but I love him now. And it was fine and beautiful of you never to mention it or brag about it." Then, with a touch of reproach, "But you ought to have told *me,* Edward, you ought to have told your wife, you know."

"Well, I—er—well, Mary, you see—"

"Now stop hemming and hawing, and tell me about it, Edward. I always loved you, and now I'm proud of you. Everybody believes there was only one good generous soul in this village, and now it turns out that you—Edward, why don't you tell me?"

"Well—er—er—Why, Mary, I can't!"

"You *can't? Why* can't you?"

"You see, he—well, he—he made me promise I wouldn't."

The wife looked him over, and said, very slowly,

"Made—you—promise? Edward, what do you tell me that for?"

"Mary, do you think I would lie?"

She was troubled and silent for a moment, then she laid her hand within his and said:

"No . . . no. We have wandered far enough from our bearings—God spare us that! In all your life you have never uttered a lie. But now—now that the foundations of things seem to be crumbling from under us, we—we—" She lost her voice for a moment, then said, brokenly, "lead us not into temptation . . . I think you made the promise, Edward. Let it rest so. Let us keep away from that ground. Now—that is all gone by; let us be happy again; it is no time for clouds."

Edward found it something of an effort to comply, for his mind kept wandering—trying to remember what the service was that he had done Goodson.

The couple lay awake the most of the night, Mary happy and busy, Edward busy but not so happy. Mary was planning what she would do with the money. Edward was trying to recall that service. At first his conscience was sore on account of the lie he had told Mary—if it was a lie. After much reflection—suppose it *was* a lie? What then? Was it such a great matter? Aren't we always *acting* lies? Then why not *tell* them? Look at Mary—look what she had done. While he was hurrying off on his honest errand, what was she doing? Lamenting because the papers hadn't been destroyed and the money kept! Is theft better than lying?

That point lost its sting—the lie dropped into the background and left comfort behind it. The next point came to the front: *Had* he rendered that service? Well, here was Goodson's own evidence as reported in Stephenson's letter, there could be no better evidence than that—it was even *proof* that he had rendered it. Of course. So that point was settled . . . No, not quite. He recalled with a wince that his unknown Mr. Stephenson was just a trifle unsure as to whether the performer of it was Richards or some other—and, oh dear, he had put Richards on his honor! He must himself decide whither that money must go—and Mr. Stephenson was not doubting that if he was the wrong man he would go honorably and find the right one. Oh, it was odious to put a man in such a situation—ah, why couldn't Stephenson have left out that doubt! What did he want to intrude that for?

Further reflection. How did it happen that *Richards's* name remained in Stephenson's mind as indicating the right man, and not some other man's name? That looked good. Yes, that looked very good. In fact, it went on looking better and better, straight along—until by and by it grew into positive *proof.* And then Richards put the matter at once out of his mind, for he had a private instinct that a proof once established is better left so.

He was feeling reasonably comfortable now, but there was still one other detail that kept pushing itself on his notice: of course he had done that service—that was settled; but what *was* that service? He must recall it—he would not go to sleep till he had recalled it; it would make his peace of mind perfect. And so he thought and thought. He thought of a dozen things—possible services, even probable services—but none of them seemed adequate, none of them seemed large enough, none of them seemed worth the money—worth the fortune Goodson had wished he could leave in his will. And besides, he couldn't remember having done them, anyway. Now, then—now, then—what *kind* of a service would it be that would make a man so inordinately grateful? Ah—the saving of his soul! That must be it. Yes, he could remember, now, how he once set himself the task of converting Goodson, and labored at it as much as—he was going to say three months; but upon closer examination it shrunk to a month, then to a week, then to a day, then to nothing. Yes, he remembered now, and with unwelcome vividness, that Goodson had told him to go to thunder and mind his own business—*he* wasn't hankering to follow Hadleyburg to heaven!

So that solution was a failure—he hadn't saved Goodson's soul. Richards was discouraged. Then after a little came another idea: had he saved Goodson's property? No, that wouldn't do—he hadn't any. His life? That is it! Of course. Why, he might have thought of it before. This time he was on the right track, sure. His imagination-mill was hard at work in a minute, now.

Thereafter during a stretch of two exhausting hours he was busy saving Goodson's life. He saved it in all kinds of difficult and perilous ways. In every case he got it saved satisfactorily up to a certain point; then, just as he was beginning to get well persuaded that it had really happened, a troublesome detail would turn up which made the whole thing impossible. As in the matter of drowning, for instance. In that case he had swum out and tugged Goodson ashore in an unconscious state with a great crowd looking on and applauding, but when he had got it all thought out and was just beginning to remember all about it, a whole swarm of disqualifying details arrived on the ground; the town would have known of the circumstance, Mary would have known of it, it would glare like a limelight in his own memory instead of being an inconspicuous service which he had possibly rendered "without knowing its full value." And at this point he remembered that he couldn't swim, anyway.

Ah—*there* was a point which he had been overlooking from the start: it had to be a service which he had rendered "possibly without knowing the full value of it." Why, really, that ought to be an easy hunt—much easier than those others. And sure enough, by and by he found it. Goodson, years and years ago, came near marrying a very sweet and pretty girl, named Nancy Hewitt, but in some way or other the match had been broken off; the girl died; Goodson remained a bachelor, and by and by became a soured one and a frank despiser of the human species. Soon after the girl's death the village found out, or thought it had found out, that she carried a spoonful of negro blood in her veins. Richards worked at these details a good while, and in the end he thought he remembered things concerning them which must have gotten mislaid in his memory through long neglect. He seemed to dimly remember that it was *he* that found out about the negro blood; that it was he that told the village; that the village told Goodson where they got it; that he thus saved Goodson from marrying the tainted girl; that he had done him this great service "without knowing the full value of it," in fact without knowing that he *was* doing it; but that Goodson knew the value of it, and what a narrow escape he had had, and so went to his grave grateful to his benefactor and wishing he had a fortune to leave him. It was all clear and simple now, and the more he went over it the more luminous and certain it grew; and at last, when he nestled to sleep satisfied and happy, he remembered the whole thing just as if it had been yesterday. In fact, he dimly remembered Goodson's *telling* him his gratitude once. Meantime Mary had spent six thousand dollars on a new house for herself and a pair of slippers for her pastor, and then had fallen peacefully to rest.

That same Saturday evening the postman had delivered a letter to each of the other principal citizens—nineteen letters in all. No two of the envelopes were alike, and no two of the superscriptions were in the same hand, but the letters inside were just like each other in every detail but one. They were exact copies of the letter received by Richards—handwriting and all—and were all signed by Stephenson, but in place of Richards's name each receiver's own name appeared.

All night long eighteen principal citizens did what their caste-brother Richards was doing at the same time—they put in their energies trying to remember what notable service it was that they had unconsciously done Barclay Goodson. In no case was it a holiday job; still they succeeded.

And while they were at this work, which was difficult, their wives put in the night spending the money, which was easy. During that one night the nineteen wives spent an average of seven thousand dollars each out of the forty thousand in the sack—a hundred and thirty-three thousand altogether.

Next day there was a surprise for Jack Halliday. He noticed that the faces of the nineteen chief citizens and their wives bore that expression of peaceful and holy happiness again. He could not understand it, neither was he able to invent any remarks about it that could damage it or disturb it. And so it was his turn to be dissatisfied with life. His private guesses at the reasons for the happiness failed in all instances, upon examination. When he met Mrs. Wilcox and noticed the placid ecstasy in her face, he said to himself, "Her cat has had kittens"—and went and asked the cook: but it was not so; the cook had detected the happiness, but did not know the cause. When Halliday found the duplicate ecstasy in the face of "Shadbelly" Billson (village nickname), he was sure some neighbor of Billson's had broken his leg, but inquiry showed that this had not happened. The subdued ecstasy in Gregory Yates's face could mean but one thing—he was a mother-in-law short: it was another mistake. "And Pinkerton—Pinkerton—he has collected ten cents that he thought he was going to lose." And so on, and so on. In some cases the guesses had to remain in doubt, in the others they proved distinct errors. In the end Halliday said to himself, "Anyway it foots up that there's nineteen Hadleyburg families temporarily in heaven: I don't know how it happened; I only know Providence is off duty today."

An architect and builder from the next State had lately ventured to set up a small business in this unpromising village, and his sign had now been hanging out a week. Not a customer yet; he was a discouraged man, and sorry he had come. But his weather changed suddenly now. First one and then another chief citizen's wife said to him privately:

"Come to my house Monday week—but say nothing about it for the present. We think of building."

He got eleven invitations that day. That night he wrote his daughter and broke off her match with her student. He said she could marry a mile higher than that.

Pinkerton the banker and two or three other well-to-do men planned country-seats—but waited. That kind don't count their chickens until they are hatched.

The Wilsons devised a grand new thing—a fancy-dress ball. They made no actual promises, but told all their acquaintanceship in confidence that they were thinking the matter over and thought they should give it—"and if we do, you will be invited, of course." People were surprised, and said, one to another, "Why they are crazy, those poor Wilsons, they can't afford it." Several among the nineteen said privately to their husbands, "It is a good idea: we will keep still till their cheap thing is over, then *we* will give one that will make it sick."

The days drifted along, and the bill of future squanderings rose higher and higher, wilder and wilder, more and more foolish and reckless. It began to look as if every member of the nineteen would not only spend his whole forty thousand dollars before receiving-day, but be actually in debt by the time he got the money. In some cases lightheaded people did not stop with planning to spend, they really spent—on credit. They bought land, mortgages, farms, speculative stocks, fine clothes, horses, and various other things, paid down the bonus, and made themselves liable for the rest—at ten days. Presently the sober second thought came, and Halliday noticed that a ghastly anxiety was beginning to show up in a good many faces. Again he was puzzled, and didn't know what to make of it. "The Wilcox kittens aren't dead, for they weren't born; nobody's broken a leg; there's no shrinkage in mother-in-laws; *nothing* has happened—it is an unsolvable mystery."

There was another puzzled man, too—the Rev. Mr. Burgess. For days, wherever he went, people seemed to follow him or to be watching out for him; and if he ever found himself in a retired spot, a member of the nineteen would be sure to appear, thrust an envelope privately into his hand, whisper "To be opened at the town-hall Friday evening," then vanish away like a guilty thing. He was expecting that there might be one claimant for the sack— doubtful, however, Goodson being dead—but it never occurred to him that all this crowd might be claimants. When the great Friday came at last, he found that he had nineteen envelopes.

III

The town-hall had never looked finer. The platform at the end of it was backed by a showy draping of flags; at intervals along the walls were festoons of flags; the gallery fronts were clothed in flags; the supporting columns were swathed in flags; all this was to impress the stranger, for he would be there in considerable force, and in a large degree he would be connected with the press. The house was full. The 412 fixed seats were occupied; also the 68 extra chairs which had been packed into the aisles; the steps of the platform were occupied; some distinguished strangers were given seats on the platform; at the horseshoe of tables which fenced the front and sides of the platform sat a strong force of special correspondents who had come from everywhere. It was the best-dressed house the town had ever produced. There were some tolerably expensive toilets there, and in several cases the ladies who wore them had the look of being unfamiliar with that kind of clothes. At least the town thought they had that look, but the notion could have arisen from the town's knowledge of the fact that these ladies had never inhabited such clothes before.

The gold-sack stood on a little table at the front of the platform where all the house could see it. The bulk of the house gazed at it with a burning interest, a mouth-watering interest, a wistful and pathetic interest; a minority of nineteen couples gazed at it tenderly, lovingly, proprietarily, and the male half of this minority kept saying over to themselves the moving little impromptu speeches of thankfulness for the audience's applause and congratulations which they were presently going to get up and deliver. Every now and then one of these got a piece of paper out of his vest pocket and privately glanced at it to refresh his memory.

Of course there was a buzz of conversation going on—there always is; but at last when the Rev. Mr. Burgess rose and laid his hand on the sack he could hear his microbes gnaw, the place was so still. He related the curious history of the sack, then went on to speak in warm terms of Hadleyburg's old and well-earned reputation for spotless honesty, and of the town's pride in this reputation. He said that this reputation was a treasure of priceless value; that under Providence its value had now become inestimably enhanced, for the recent episode had spread this fame far and wide, and thus had focused the eyes of the American world upon this village, and made its name for all time, as he hoped and believed, a synonym for commercial incorruptibility. [*Applause.*] "And who is to be the guardian of this noble treasure—the community as a whole? No! The responsibility is individual, not communal. From this day forth each and every one of you is in his own person its special guardian, and individually responsible that no harm shall come of it. Do you—does each of you—accept this great trust? [*Tumultuous assent.*] Then all is well. Transmit it to your children and to your children's children. Today your purity is beyond reproach—see to it that it shall remain so. Today there is not a person in your community who could be beguiled to touch a penny not his own—see to it that you abide in this grace. [*"We will! We will!"*] This is not the place to make comparisons between ourselves and other communities—some of them ungracious toward us; they have their ways, we have ours; let us be content. [*Applause.*] I am done. Under my hand, my friends, rests a stranger's eloquent recognition of what we are; through him the world will always henceforth know what we are. We do not know who he is, but in your name I utter your gratitude, and ask you to raise your voices in endorsement."

The house rose in a body and made the walls quake with the thunders of its thankfulness for the space of a long minute. Then it sat down, and Mr. Burgess took an envelope out of his pocket. The house held its breath while he slit the envelope open and took from it a slip of paper. He reads it contents—slowly and impressively—the audience listening with tranced attention to this magic document, each of whose words stood for an ingot of gold:

"'*The remark which I made to the distressed stranger was this: "You are very far from being a bad man; go, and reform."*'" Then he continued:

"We shall know in a moment now whether the remark here quoted corresponds with the one concealed in the sack; and if that shall prove to be so—and it undoubtedly will—this sack of gold belongs to a fellow citizen who will henceforth stand before the nation as a symbol of the special virtue which has made our town famous throughout the land—Mr. Billson!"

The house had gotten itself all ready to burst into the proper tornado of applause; but instead of doing it, it seemed stricken with a paralysis; there was a deep hush for a moment or two, then a wave of whispered murmurs swept the place—of about this tenor: *"Billson!* oh, come, this is *too* thin! Twenty dollars to a stranger—or anybody—*Billson!* tell it to the marines!" And now at this point the house caught its breath all of a sudden in a new access of astonishment, for it discovered that whereas in one part of the hall Deacon Billson was standing up with his head meekly bowed, in another part of it Lawyer Wilson was doing the same. There was a wondering silence now for a while.

Everybody was puzzled, and nineteen couples were surprised and indignant.

Billson and Wilson turned and stared at each other. Billson asked, bitingly,

"Why do *you* rise, Mr. Wilson?"

"Because I have a right to. Perhaps you will be good enough to explain to the house why *you* rise?"

"With great pleasure. Because I wrote that paper."

"It is an impudent falsity! I wrote it myself."

It was Burgess's turn to be paralyzed. He stood looking vacantly at first one of the men and then the other, and did not seem to know what to do. The house was stupefied. Lawyer Wilson spoke up, now, and said,

"I ask the Chair to read the name signed to that paper."

That brought the Chair to itself, and it read out the name,

"'John Wharton *Billson.*'"

"There!" shouted Billson, "what have you got to say for yourself, now? And what kind of apology are you going to make to me and to this insulted house for the imposture which you have attempted to play here?"

"No apologies are due, sir; and as for the rest of it, I publicly charge you with pilfering my note from Mr. Burgess and substituting a copy of it signed with your own name. There is no other way by which you could have gotten hold of the test-remark; I alone, of living men, possessed the secret of its wording."

There was likely to be a scandalous state of things if this went on; everybody noticed with distress that the short-hand scribes were scribbling like mad; many people were crying "Chair, Chair! Order! Order!" Burgess rapped with his gavel, and said:

"Let us not forget the proprieties due. There has evidently been a mistake somewhere, but surely that is all. If Mr. Wilson gave me an envelope—and I remember now that he did—I still have it."

He took one out of his pocket, opened it, glanced at it, looked surprised and worried, and stood silent a few moments. Then he waved his hand in a wandering and mechanical way, and made an effort or two to say something, then gave it up, despondently. Several voices cried out:

"Read it! Read it! What is it?"

So he began in a dazed and sleep-walker fashion:

"'*The remark which I made to the unhappy stranger was this: "You are far from being a bad man.* [The house gazed at him, marveling.] *Go, and reform."*' [*Murmurs:* "Amazing! What can this mean?"] This one," said the Chair, "is signed Thurlow G. Wilson."

"There!" cried Wilson, "I reckon that settles it! I knew perfectly well my note was purloined."

"Purloined!" retorted Billson. "I'll let you know that neither you nor any man of your kidney must venture to—"

The Chair. "Order, gentlemen, order! Take your seats, both of you, please."

They obeyed, shaking their heads and grumbling angrily. The house was profoundly puzzled; it did not know what to do with this curious emergency. Presently Thompson got up. Thompson was the hatter. He would have liked to be a Nineteener; but such was not for him: his stock of hats was not considerable enough for the position. He said:

"Mr. Chairman, if I may be permitted to make a suggestion, can both of these gentlemen be right? I put it to you, sir, can both have happened to say the very same words to the stranger? It seems to me—"

The tanner got up and interrupted him. The tanner was a disgruntled man; he believed himself entitled to be a Nineteener, but he couldn't get recognition. It made him a little unpleasant in his ways and speech. Said he:

"Sho, *that's* not the point! *That* could happen—twice in a hundred years—but not the other thing. *Neither* of them gave the twenty dollars!"

[*A ripple of applause.*]

Billson. "I did!"

Wilson. "I did!"

Then each accused the other of pilfering.

The Chair. "Order! Sit down, if you please—both of you. Neither of the notes has been out of my possession at any moment."

A Voice. "Good—that settles *that!*"

The Tanner. "Mr. Chairman, one thing is now plain: one of these men has been eavesdropping under the other one's bed, and filching family secrets. If it is not unparliamentary to suggest it, I will remark that both are equal to it. [*The Chair.* "Order! order!"] I withdraw the remark, sir, and will confine myself to suggesting that *if* one of them has overheard the other reveal the test-remark to his wife, we shall catch him now."

A Voice. "How?"

The Tanner. "Easily. The two have not quoted the remark in exactly the same words. You would have noticed that, if there hadn't been a considerable stretch of time and an exciting quarrel inserted between the two readings."

A Voice. "Name the difference."

The Tanner. "The word *very* is in Billson's note, and not in the other."

Many Voices. "That's so—he's right!"

The Tanner. "And so, if the Chair will examine the test-remark in the sack, we shall know which of these two frauds— [*The Chair.* "Order!"]—which of these two adventurers—[*The Chair.* "Order! order!"]—which of these two gentlemen—[*laughter and applause*]—is entitled to wear the belt as being the first dishonest blatherskite ever bred in this town—which he has dishonored, and which will be a sultry place for him from now out!" [*Vigorous applause.*]

Many Voices. "Open it!—open the sack!"

Mr. Burgess made a slit in the sack, slid his hand in and brought out an envelope. In it were a couple of folded notes. He said:

"One of these is marked, 'Not to be examined until all written communications which have been addressed to the Chair—if any— shall have been read.' The other is marked '*The Test.*' Allow me. It is worded—to wit:

"'I do not require that the first half of the remark which was made to me by my benefactor shall be quoted with exactness, for it was not striking, and could be forgotten; but its closing fifteen words are quite striking, and I think easily rememberable; unless *these* shall be accurately reproduced, let the applicant be regarded as an imposter. My benefactor began by saying he seldom gave advice to any one, but that it always bore the hallmark of high value when he did give it. Then he said this—and it has never faded from my memory: *"You are far from being a bad man—"'"*

Fifty Voices. "That settles it—the money's Wilson's! Wilson! Wilson! Speech! Speech!"

People jumped up and crowded around Wilson, wringing his hand and congratulating fervently—meantime the Chair was hammering with the gavel and shouting:

"Order, gentlemen! Order! Order! Let me finish reading, please."
When quiet was restored, the reading was resumed—as follows:

" ' "*Go, and reform—or, mark my words—some day, for your sins, you will die and go to hell or Hadleyburg—*TRY AND MAKE IT THE FORMER*" ' "*

A ghastly silence followed. First an angry cloud began to settle darkly upon the faces of the citizenship; after a pause the cloud began to rise, and a tickled expression tried to take its place; tried so hard that it was only kept under with great and painful difficulty; the reporters, the Brixtonites, and other strangers bent their heads down and shielded their faces with their hands, and managed to hold in by main strength and heroic courtesy. At this most inopportune time burst upon the stillness the roar of a solitary voice—Jack Halliday's:

"*That's* got the hall-mark on it!"

Then the house let go, strangers and all. Even Mr. Burgess's gravity broke down presently, then the audience considered itself officially absolved from all restraint, and it made the most of its privilege. It was a good long laugh, and a tempestuously whole-hearted one, but it ceased at last—long enough for Mr. Burgess to try to resume, and for the people to get their eyes partially wiped; then it broke out again; and afterward yet again; then at last Mr. Burgess was able to get out these serious words:

"It is useless to try to disguise the fact—we find ourselves in the presence of a matter of grave import. It involves the honor of your town, it strikes at the town's good name. The difference of a single word between the test-remarks offered by Mr. Wilson and Mr. Billson was itself a serious thing, since it indicated that one or the other of these gentlemen had committed a theft—"

The two men were sitting limp, nerveless, crushed; but at these words both were electrified into movement, and started to get up—

"Sit down!" said the Chair, sharply, and they obeyed. "That, as I have said, was a serious thing. And it was—but for only one of them. But the matter has become graver; for the honor of *both* is now in formidable peril. Shall I go even further, and say in inextricable peril? *Both* left out the crucial fifteen words." He paused. During several moments he allowed the pervading stillness to gather and deepen its impressive effects, then added: "There would seem to be but one way whereby this could happen. I ask these gentlemen—Was there *collusion?—agreement!*"

A low murmur sifted through the house; its import was, "He's got them both."

Billson was not used to emergencies; he sat in a helpless collapse. But Wilson was a lawyer. He struggled to his feet, pale and worried, and said:

"I ask the indulgence of the house while I explain this most painful matter. I am sorry to say what I am about to say, since it must inflict irreparable injury upon Mr. Billson, whom I have always esteemed and respected until now, and in whose invulnerability to temptation I entirely believed—as did you all. But for the preservation of my *own* honor I must speak—and with frankness. I confess with shame—and I now beseech your pardon for it—that I said to the ruined stranger all of the words contained in the test-remark, including the disparaging fifteen. [*Sensation.*] When the late publication was made I recalled them, and resolved to claim the sack of coin, for by every right I was entitled to it. Now I will ask you to consider this point, and weigh it well: that stranger's gratitude to me that night knew no bounds; he said himself that he could find no words for it that were adequate, and that if he should ever be able he would repay me a thousand fold. Now, then, I ask you this: Could I expect—could I believe—could I even remotely imagine—that, feeling as I did, he would do so ungrateful a thing as to add those quite unnecessary fifteen words to his test?—set a trap for me?—expose me as a slanderer of my own town before my own people assembled in a public hall? It was preposterous; it was impossible. His test would contain only the kindly opening clause of my remark. Of that I had no shadow of doubt. You would have thought as I did. You would not have expected a base betrayal from one whom you had befriended and against whom you had committed no offense. And so, with perfect confidence, perfect trust, I wrote on a piece of paper the opening words—ending with 'Go, and reform,'— and signed it. When I was about to put it in an envelope I was called into my back office, and without thinking I left the paper lying open on my desk." He stopped, turned his head slowly toward Billson, waited a moment, then added: "I ask you to note this: when I returned, a little later, Mr. Billson was retiring by my street door." [*Sensation.*]

In a moment Billson was on his feet and shouting:

"It's a lie! It's an infamous lie!"

The Chair. "Be seated, sir! Mr. Wilson has the floor."

Billson's friends pulled him into his seat and quieted him, and Wilson went on:

"Those are the simple facts. My note was now lying in a different place on the table from where I had left it. I noticed that, but attached no importance to it, thinking a draught had blown it there. That Mr. Billson would read a private paper was a thing which could not occur to me; he was an honorable man, and he would be above that. If you will allow me to say it, I think his extra word *'very'* stands explained; it is attributable to a defect of memory. I was the only man in the world who could furnish here any detail of the test-remark—by *honorable* means. I have finished."

There is nothing in the world like a persuasive speech to fuddle the mental apparatus and upset the convictions and debauch the emotions of an audience not practiced in the tricks and elusions of oratory. Wilson sat down victorious. The house submerged him in tides of approving applause; friends swarmed to him and shook him by the hand and congratulated him, and Billson was shouted down and not allowed to say a word. The Chair hammered and hammered with its gavel, and kept shouting.

"But let us proceed, gentlemen, let us proceed!"

At last there was a measurable degree of quiet, and the hatter said:

"But what is there to proceed with, sir, but to deliver the money?"

Voices. "That's it! That's it! Come forward, Wilson!"

The Hatter. "I move three cheers for Mr. Wilson, Symbol of the special virtue which—"

The cheers burst forth before he could finish; and in the midst of them—and in the midst of the clamor of the gavel also—some enthusiasts mounted Wilson on a big friend's shoulder and were going to fetch him in triumph to the platform. The Chair's voice now rose above the noise—

"Order! To your places! You forget that there is still a document to read." When quiet had been restored he took up the document, and was going to read it, but laid it down again, saying, "I forgot; this is not to be read until all written communications received by me have first been read." He took an envelope out of his pocket, removed its enclosure, glanced at it—seemed astonished—held it out and gazed at it—stared at it.

Twenty or thirty voices cried out:

"What is it? Read it! read it!"

And he did—slowly, and wondering:

"'The remark which I made to the stranger—[*Voices.* "Hello! how's this?"]—was this: "You are far from being a bad man. [*Voices.* "Great Scott!"] Go, and reform.'" [*Voice.* "Oh, saw my leg off!"] Signed by Mr. Pinkerton the banker."

The pandemonium of delight which turned itself loose now was a sort to make the judicious weep. Those whose withers were unwrung laughed till the tears ran down; the reporters, in throes of laughter, set down disordered pot-hooks which would never in the world be decipherable; and a sleeping dog jumped up, scared out of its wits, and barked itself crazy at the turmoil. All manner of cries were scattered through the din: "We're getting rich—*two* Symbols of Incorruptibility!—without counting Billson!" "*Three!*—count Shadbelly in—we can't have too many!" "All right—Billson's elected!" "Alas, poor Wilson—victim of *two* thieves!"

A Powerful Voice. "Silence! The chair's fished up something more out of its pocket."

Voices. "Hurrah! Is it something fresh? Read it! read it! read!"

The Chair [reading]. "'The remark which I made,' etc.: "You are far from being a bad man. Go,'" etc. Signed, Gregory Yates.'"

Tornado of Voices. "Four symbols!" "'Rah for Yates!" "Fish again!"

The house was in a roaring humor now, and ready to get all the fun out of the occasion that might be in it. Several Nineteeners, looking pale and distressed, got up and began to work their way toward the aisles, but a score of shouts went up:

"The doors, the doors—close the doors; no Incorruptible shall leave this place! Sit down, everybody!"

The mandate was obeyed.

"Fish again! Read! read!"

The Chair fished again, and once more the familiar words began to fall from its lips—"'You are far from being a bad man—'"

"Name! name! What's his name?"

"'L. Ingoldsby Sargent.'"

"Five elected! Pile up the Symbols! Go on, go on!"

"'You are far from being a bad—'"

"Name! name!"

"'Nicholas Whitworth.'"

"Hooray! hooray! It's a symbolical day!"

Somebody wailed in, and began to sing this rhyme (leaving out "it's") to the lovely "Mikado" tune of "When a man's afraid, a beautiful maid—"; the audience joined in, with joy; then, just in time, somebody contributed another line—

And don't you this forget—

The house roared it out. A third line was at once furnished—

Corruptibles far from Hadleyburg are—

The house roared that one too. As the last note died, Jack Halliday's voice rose high and clear, freighted with a final line—

But the Symbols are here, you bet!

That was sung with booming enthusiasm. Then the happy house started in at the beginning and sang the four lines through twice, with immense swing and dash, and finished up with a crashing three-times-three and a tiger for "Hadleyburg the Incorruptible and all Symbols of it which we shall find worthy to receive the hall-mark tonight."

Then the shouting at the Chair began again, all over the place:

"Go on! go on! Read! read some more! Read all you've got!"

"That's it—go on! We are winning eternal celebrity!"

A dozen men got up now and began to protest. They said that this farce was the work of some abandoned joker, and was an insult to the whole community. Without a doubt these signatures were all forgeries—

"Sit down! sit down! Shut up! You are confessing. We'll find *your* names in the lot."

"Mr. Chairman, how many of those envelopes have you got?"

The Chair counted.

"Together with those that have already been examined, there are nineteen."

A storm of derisive applause broke out.

"Perhaps they all contain the secret. I move that you open them all and read every signature that is attached to a note of that sort—and read also the first eight words of the note."

"Second the motion!"

It was put and carried—uproariously. Then poor old Richards got up, and his wife rose and stood at his side. Her head bent down, so that none might see that she was crying. Her husband gave her his arm, and so supporting her, he began to speak in a quavering voice:

"My friends, you have known us two—Mary and me—all our lives, and I think you have liked us and respected us—"

The Chair interrupted him:

"Allow me. It is quite true—that which you are saying, Mr. Richards: this town *does* know you two; it *does* like you; it *does* respect you; more—it honors you and *loves* you—"

Halliday's voice rang out:

"That's the hall-marked truth, too! If the Chair is right, let the house speak up and say it. Rise! Now, then—hip! hip! hip!—all together!"

The house rose in mass, faced toward the old couple eagerly, filled the air with a snowstorm of waving handkerchiefs, and delivered the cheers with all its affectionate heart.

The Chair then continued:

"What I was going to say is this: We know your good heart, Mr. Richards, but this is not a time for the exercise of charity toward offenders. [*Shouts of "Right! right!"*] I see your generous purpose in your face, but I cannot allow you to plead for these men—"

"But I was going to—"

"Please take your seat, Mr. Richards. We must examine the rest of these notes—simple fairness to the men who have already been exposed requires this. As soon as that has been done—I give you my word for this—you shall be heard."

Many Voices. "Right!—the Chair is right—no interruption can be permitted at this stage! Go on!—the names! the names!—according to the terms of the motion!"

The old couple sat reluctantly down, and the husband whispered to the wife, "It is pitifully hard to have to wait; the shame will be greater than ever when they find we were only going to plead for *ourselves.*"

Straightway the jollity broke loose again with the reading of the names.

" 'You are far from being a bad man—' Signature, 'Robert. J. Titmarsh.'

" 'You are far from being a bad man—' Signature, 'Eliphalet Weeks.'

" 'You are far from being a bad man—' Signature, 'Oscar B. Wilder.' "

At this point the house lit upon the idea of taking the eight words out of the Chairman's hands. He was not unthankful for that. Thenceforward he held up each note in its turn, and waited. The house droned out the eight words in a massed and measured and musical deep volume of sound (with a daringly close resemblance to a well-known church chant)—"'You are f-a-r from being a b-a-a-d man.'" Then the Chair said, "Signature, 'Archibald Wilcox.'" And so on and so on, name after name, and everybody had an increasingly and gloriously good time except the wretched Nineteen. Now and then, when a particularly shining name was called, the house made the Chair wait while it changed the whole of the test-remark from the beginning to the closing words, "And go to hell or Hadleyburg—try and make it the for-or-m-e-r!" and in these special cases they added a grand and agonized and imposing "A-a-a-a-*men!*"

The list dwindled, dwindled, dwindled, poor old Richards keeping tally of the count, wincing when a name resembling his own was pronounced, and waiting in miserable suspense for the time to come when it would be his humiliating privilege to rise with Mary and finish his plea, which he was intending to word thus: ". . . for until now we have never done any wrong thing, but have gone our humble way unreproached. We are very poor, we are old, and have no chick nor child to help us; we were sorely tempted, and we fell. It was my purpose when I got up before to make confession and beg that my name might not be read out in this public place, for it seemed to us that we could not bear it; but I was prevented. It was just; it was our place to suffer with the rest. It has been hard for us. It is the first time we have ever heard our name fall from any one's lips—sullied. Be merciful—for the sake of the better days; make our shame as light to bear as in your charity you can." At this point in his revery Mary nudged him, perceiving that his mind was absent. The house was chanting, "You are f-a-r," etc.

"Be ready," Mary whispered. "Your name comes now; he has read eighteen."

The chant ended.

"Next! next! next!" came volleying from all over the house.

Burgess put his hand into his pocket. The old couple, trembling, began to rise. Burgess fumbled a moment, then said,

"I find I have read them all."

Faint with joy and surprise, the couple sank into their seats, and Mary whispered,

"Oh, bless God, we are saved!—he has lost ours—I wouldn't give this for a hundred of those sacks!"

The house burst out with its "Mikado" travesty, and sang it three times with ever-increasing enthusiasm, rising to its feet when it reached for the third time the closing line—

But the Symbols are here, you bet!

and finishing up with cheers and a tiger for "Hadleyburg purity and our eighteen immortal representatives of it."

Then Wingate, the saddler, got up and proposed cheers "for the cleanest man in town, the one solitary important citizen in it who didn't try to steal that money—Edward Richards."

They were given with great and moving heartiness; then somebody proposed that Richards be elected sole guardian and Symbol of the now Sacred Hadleyburg Tradition, with power and right to stand up and look the whole sarcastic world in the face.

Passed, by acclamation; then they sang the "Mikado" again, and ended it with,

And there's one Symbol left, you bet!

There was a pause; then—

A Voice. "Now, then, who's to get the sack?"

The Tanner [with bitter sarcasm]. "That's easy. The money has to be divided among the eighteen Incorruptibles. They gave the suffering stranger twenty dollars apiece—and that remark—each in his turn—it took twenty-two minutes for the procession to move past. Staked the stranger—total contribution, $360. All they want is just the loan back—and interest—forty thousand dollars altogether."

Many Voices [derisively]. "That's it! Divvy! divvy! Be kind to the poor—don't keep them waiting!"

The Chair. "Order! I now offer the stranger's remaining document. It says: 'If no claimant shall appear [*grand chorus of groans.*], I desire that you open the sack and count out the money to the principal citizens of your town, they to take it in trust [*cries of "Oh! Oh! Oh!"*], and use it in such ways as to them shall seem best for the propagation and preservation of your community's noble reputation for incorruptible honesty [*more cries*]—a reputation to which their names and their efforts will add a new and far-reaching lustre.' [*Enthusiastic outburst of sarcastic applause.*] That seems to be all. No—here is a postscript:

"'P.S.—CITIZENS OF HADLEYBURG: There *is* no test-remark—nobody made one. [*Great sensation.*] There wasn't any pauper stranger, nor any twenty-dollar contribution, nor any accompanying benediction and compliment—these are all inventions. [*General buzz and hum of astonishment and delight.*] Allow me to tell my story—it will take but a word or two. I passed through your town at a certain time, and received a deep offense which I had not earned. Any other man would have been content to kill one or two of you and call it square, but to me that would have been a trivial revenge, and inadequate; for the dead do not *suffer.* Besides, I could not kill you all—and, anyway, made as I am, even that would not have satisfied me. I wanted to damage every man in the place, and every woman—and not in their bodies or in their estate, but in their vanity—the place where feeble and foolish people are most vulnerable. So I disguised myself and came back and studied you. You were easy game. You had an old and lofty reputation for honesty, and naturally you were proud of it—it was your treasure of treasures, the very apple of your eye. As soon as I found out that you carefully and vigilantly kept yourselves and your children *out of temptation,* I knew how to proceed. Why, you simple creatures, the weakest of all weak things is a virtue which has not been tested in the fire. I laid a plan, and gathered a list of names. My project was to corrupt Hadleyburg the Incorruptible. My idea was to make liars and thieves of nearly half a hundred smirchless men and women who had never in their lives uttered a lie or stolen a penny. I was afraid of Goodson. He was neither born nor reared in Hadleyburg. I was afraid that if I started to operate my scheme by getting my letter laid before you, you would say to yourselves, "Goodson is the only man among us who would give away twenty dollars to a poor devil"—and then you might not bite at my bait. But Heaven took Goodson; then I knew I was safe, and I set my trap and baited it. It may be that I shall not catch all the men to whom

I mailed the pretended test secret, but I shall catch the most of them, if I know Hadleyburg nature. [*Voices.* "Right—he got every last one of them."] I believe they will even steal ostensible *gamble*-money, rather than miss, poor, tempted, and mistrained fellows. I am hoping to eternally and everlastingly squelch your vanity and give Hadleyburg a new reknown— one that will *stick*—and spread far. If I have succeeded, open the sack and summon the Committee on Propagation and Preservation of the Hadley- burg Reputation.'"

A *Cyclone of Voices.* "Open it! Open it! The Eighteen to the front! Committee on Propagation of the Tradition! Forward—the Incorrupt- ibles!"

The Chair ripped the sack wide, and gathered up a handful of bright, broad, yellow coins, shook them together, then examined them—

"Friends, they are only gilded disks of lead!"

There was a crashing outbreak of delight over this news, and when the noise had subsided, the tanner called out:

"By right of apparent seniority in this business, Mr. Wilson is Chair- man of the Committee on Propagation of the Tradition. I suggest that he step forward on behalf of his pals, and receive in trust the money."

A *Hundred Voices.* "Wilson! Wilson! Wilson! Speech! Speech!"

Wilson [in a voice trembling with anger]. "You will allow me to say, and without apologies for my language, *damn* the money!"

A *Voice.* "Oh, and him a Baptist!"

A *Voice.* "Seventeen Symbols left! Step up, gentlemen, and assume your trust!"

There was a pause—no response.

The Saddler. "Mr. Chairman, we've got *one* clean man left, anyway, out of the late aristocracy; and he needs money, and deserves it. I move that you appoint Jack Halliday to get up there and auction off that sack of gilt twenty-dollar pieces, and give the result to the right man—the man whom Hadleyburg delights to honor—Edward Richards."

This was received with great enthusiasm, the dog taking a hand again; the saddler started the bids at a dollar, the Brixton folk and Barnum's representative fought hard for it, the people cheered every jump that the bids made, the excitement climbed moment by moment higher and higher, the bidders got on their mettle and grew steadily more and more daring, more and more determined, the jumps went from a dollar up to five, then to ten, then to twenty, then fifty, then to a hundred, then—

At the beginning of the auction Richards whispered in distress to his wife: "O Mary, can we allow it? It—it—you see, it is an honor-reward, a testimonial to purity of character, and—and—can we allow it? Hadn't I better get up and—O Mary, what ought we to do?—what do you think we—[*Halliday's voice. "Fifteen I'm bid!—fifteen for the sack!—twenty!—ah, thanks!—thirty—thanks again! Thirty, thirty, thirty!—do I hear forty?—forty it is! Keep the ball rolling, gentlemen, keep it rolling!—fifty!—thanks, noble Roman! going at fifty, fifty, fifty!—seventy!—ninety!—splendid!—a hundred!—pile it up, pile it up!—hundred and twenty!—forty!—just in time!—hundred and fifty!—two hundred!—superb! Do I hear two h—thanks!—two hundred and fifty!—"*]

"It is another temptation, Edward—I'm all in a tremble—but, oh, we've escaped *one* temptation, and that ought to warn us to—[*"Six did I hear?—thanks!—six fifty, six f—* SEVEN *hundred!"*] And yet, Edward, when you think—nobody susp—[*"Eight hundred dollars!—hurrah!—make it nine!—Mr. Parsons, did I hear you say—thanks—nine!—this noble sack of virgin lead going at only nine hundred dollars, gilding and all—come! do I hear—a thousand!—gratefully yours!—did some one say eleven?—a sack which is going to be the most celebrated in the whole Uni—"*] O Edward (beginning to sob), "we are *so* poor!—but—but—do as you think best—do as you think best."

Edward fell—that is, he sat still; sat with a conscience which was not satisfied, but which was overpowered by circumstances.

Meantime a stranger, who looked like an amateur detective gotten up as an impossible English earl, had been watching the evening's proceedings with manifest interest, and with a contented expression in his face; and he had been privately commenting to himself. He was now soliloquizing somewhat like this: "None of the Eighteen are bidding; that is not satisfactory; I must change that—the dramatic unities require it; they must buy the sack they tried to steal; they must pay a heavy price, too—some of them are rich. And another thing, when I make a mistake in Hadleyburg nature the man that puts that error upon me is entitled to a high honorarium, and some one must pay it. This poor old Richards has brought my judgment to shame; he is an honest man:—I don't understand it, but I acknowledge it. Yes, he saw my deuces *and* with a straight flush, and by rights the pot is his. And it shall be a jack-pot, too, if I can manage it. He disappointed me, but let that pass."

He was watching the bidding. At a thousand, the market broke; the prices tumbled swiftly. He waited—and still watched. One competitor dropped out, then another, and another. He put in a bid or two, now. When the bids had sunk to ten dollars, he added a five; someone raised him a three; he waited a moment, then flung in a fifty-dollar jump, and the sack was his—at $1,282. The house broke out in cheers—then stopped; for he was on his feet, and had lifted his hand. He began to speak.

"I desire to say a word, and ask a favor. I am a speculator in rarities, and I have dealings with persons interested in numismatics all over the world. I can make a profit on this purchase, just as it stands; but there is a way, if I can get your approval, whereby I can make every one of these leaden twenty-dollar pieces worth its face in gold, and perhaps more. Grant me that approval, and I will give part of my gains to your Mr. Richards, whose invulnerable probity you have so justly and so cordially recognized to-night; his share shall be ten thousand dollars, and I will hand him the money to-morrow. [*Great applause from the house.* But the "invulnerable probity" made the Richardses blush prettily; however, it went for modesty, and did no harm.] If you will pass my proposition by a good majority—I would like a two-thirds vote—I will regard that as the town's consent, and that is all I ask. Rarities are always helped by any device which will rouse curiosity and compel remark. Now if I may have your permission to stamp upon the faces of each of these ostensible coins the names of the eighteen gentlemen who—"

Nine-tenths of the audience were on their feet in a moment—dog and all—and the proposition was carried with a whirlwind of approving applause and laughter.

They sat down, and all the Symbols except "Dr." Clay Harkness got up, violently protesting against the proposed outrage, and threatening to—

"I beg you not to threaten me," said the stranger, calmly. "I know my legal rights, and am not accustomed to being frightened at bluster." [*Applause.*] He sat down. "Dr." Harkness saw an opportunity here. He was one of the two very rich men of the place, and Pinkerton was the other. Harkness was proprietor of a mint; that is to say, a popular patent medicine. He was running for the Legislature on one ticket, and Pinkerton on the other. It was a close race and a hot one, and getting hotter every day. Both had strong appetites for money; each had bought a great tract of land, with a purpose; there was going to be a new railway, and each wanted to be in the Legislature and help locate the route to his own advantage; a single vote might make the decision, and with it two or three fortunes. The stake was large, and Harkness was a daring speculator. He was sitting close to the stranger. He leaned over while one or another of the other Symbols was entertaining the house with protests and appeals, and asked, in a whisper,

"What is your price for the sack?"

"Forty thousand dollars."

"I'll give you twenty."

"No."

"Twenty-five."

"No."

"Say thirty."

"The price is forty thousand dollars; not a penny less."

"All right, I'll give it. I will come to the hotel at ten in the morn-ing. I don't want it known; will see you privately."

"Very good." Then the stranger got up and said to the house:

"I find it late. The speeches of these gentlemen are not without merit, not without interest, not without grace; yet if I may be excused I will take my leave. I thank you for the great favor which you have shown me in granting my petition. I ask the Chair to keep the sack for me until to-morrow, and to hand these three five-hundred-dollar notes to Mr. Richards." They were passed up to the Chair. "At nine I will call for the sack, and at eleven will deliver the rest of the ten thousand to Mr. Richards in person, at his home. Good night."

Then he slipped out, and left the audience making a vast noise, which was composed of a mixture of cheers, the "Mikado" song, dog-disapproval, and the chant, "You are f-a-r from being a b-a-a-d man—a-a-a-a-men!"

IV

At home the Richardses had to endure congratulations and compli-ments until midnight. Then they were left to themselves. They looked a little sad, and they sat silent and thinking. Finally Mary sighed and said,

"Do you think we are to blame, Edward—*much* to blame?" and her eyes wandered to the accusing triplet of big bank notes lying on the table, where the congratulators had been gloating over them and rever-ently fingering them. Edward did not answer at once; then he brought out a sigh and said, hesitatingly:

"We—we couldn't help it, Mary. It—well, it was ordered. *All* things are."

Mary glanced up and looked at him steadily, but he didn't return the look. Presently she said:

"I thought congratulations and praises always tasted good. But—it seems to me, now—Edward?"

"Well?"

"Are you going to stay in the bank?"

"N-no."

"Resign?"

"In the morning—by note."

"It does seem best."

Richards bowed his head in his hands and muttered:

"Before, I was not afraid to let oceans of people's money pour through my hands, but—Mary, I am so tired, so tired—"

"We will go to bed."

At nine in the morning the stranger called for the sack and took it to the hotel in a cab. At ten Harkness had a talk with him privately. The stranger asked for and got five checks on a metropolitan bank—drawn to "Bearer,"—four for $1,500 each, and one for $34,000. He put one of the former in his pocketbook, and the remainder, representing $38,500, he put in an envelope, and with these he added a note, which he wrote after Harkness was gone. At eleven he called at the Richards house and knocked. Mrs. Richards peeped through the shutters, then went and received the envelope, and the stranger disappeared without a word. She came back flushed and a little unsteady on her legs, and gasped out:

"I am sure I recognized him! Last night it seemed to me that maybe I had seen him somewhere before."

"He is the man that brought the sack here?"

"I am almost sure of it."

"Then he is the ostensible Stephenson, too, and sold every important citizen in this town with his bogus secret. Now if he has sent checks instead of money, we are sold, too, after we thought we had escaped. I was beginning to feel fairly comfortable once more, after my night's rest, but the look of that envelope makes me sick. It isn't fat enough; $8,500 in even the largest bank notes makes more bulk than that."

"Edward, why do you object to checks?"

"Checks signed by Stephenson! I am resigned to take the $8,500 if it could come in bank notes—for it does seem that it was so ordered, Mary—but I have never had much courage, and I have not the pluck to try to market a check signed with that disastrous name. It would be a trap. That man tried to catch me, we escaped somehow or other; and now he is trying a new way. If it is checks—"

"Oh, Edward, it is *too* bad!" and she held up the checks and began to cry.

"Put them in the fire! quick! we mustn't be tempted. It is a trick to make the world laugh at *us,* along with the rest, and—Give them to *me,* since you can't do it!" He snatched them and tried to hold his grip till he could get to the stove; but he was human, he was a cashier, and he stopped a moment to make sure of the signature. Then he came near to fainting.

"Fan me, Mary, fan me! They are the same as gold!"

"Oh, how lovely, Edward! Why?"

"Signed by Harkness. What can the mystery of that be, Mary?"

"Edward, do you think—"

"Look here—look at this! Fifteen—fifteen—fifteen—thirty-four. Thirty-eight thousand five hundred! Mary, the sack isn't worth twelve dollars, and Harkness—apparently—has paid about par for it."

"And does it all come to us, do you think—instead of the ten thousand?"

"Why, it looks like it. And the checks are made to 'Bearer,' too."

"Is that good, Edward? What is it for?"

"A hint to collect them at some distant bank, I reckon. Perhaps Harkness doesn't want the matter known. What is that—a note?"

"Yes. It was with the checks."

It was in the "Stephenson" handwriting, but there was no signature. It said:

> "I am a disappointed man. Your honesty is beyond the reach of temptation. I had a different idea about it, but I wronged you in that and I beg pardon, and do it sincerely. I honor you—and that is sincere too. This town is not worthy to kiss the hem of your garment. Dear sir, I made a square bet with myself that there were nineteen debauchable men in your self-righteous community. I have lost. Take the whole pot, you are entitled to it."

Richards drew a deep sigh, and said:

"It seems written with fire—it burns so. Mary—I am miserable again."

"I, too. Ah, dear, I wish—"

"To think, Mary—he *believes* in me."

"If those beautiful words were deserved, Mary—and God knows I believed I deserved them once—I think I could give the forty thousand dollars for them. And I would put that paper away, as representing more than gold and jewels, and keep it always. But now—We could not live in the shadow of its accusing presence, Mary."

He put it in the fire.

A messenger arrived and delivered an envelope.

Richards took from it a note and read it; it was from Burgess.

You saved me in a difficult time. I saved you last night. It was at cost of a lie, but I made the sacrifice freely, and out of a grateful heart. None in this village knows so well as I know how brave and good and noble you are. At bottom you cannot respect me, knowing as you do of that matter of which I am accused, and by the general voice condemned; but I beg that you will at least believe that I am a grateful man; it will help me to bear my burden.

[Signed] Burgess

"Saved, once more. And on such terms!" He put the note in the fire. "I—I wish I were dead, Mary, I wish I were out of it all."

"Oh, these are bitter, bitter days, Edward. The stabs, through their very generosity, are so deep—and they come so fast!"

Three days before the election each of two thousand voters suddenly found himself in possession of a prized memento—one of the renowned bogus double-eagles. Around one of its faces was stamped these words: "THE REMARK I MADE TO THE POOR STRANGER WAS—" Around the other face was stamped these: "GO AND REFORM. [SIGNED] PINKERTON." Thus the entire remaining refuse of the renowned joke was emptied upon a single head, and with calamitous effect. It revived the recent vast laugh and concentrated it upon Pinkerton; and Harkness's election was a walkover.

Within twenty-four hours after the Richardses had received their checks their consciences were quieting down, discouraged; the old couple were learning to reconcile themselves to the sin which they had committed. But they were to learn, now, that a sin takes on new and real terrors when there seems a chance that it is going to be found out. This gives it a fresh and most substantial and important aspect. At church the morning sermon was of the usual pattern; it was the same old things said in the same old way; they had heard them a thousand times and found them innocuous, next to meaningless, and easy to sleep under; but now it was different: the sermon seemed to bristle with accusations; it seemed aimed straight and specially at people who were concealing deadly sins. After church they got away from the mob of congratulators as soon as they could, and hurried homeward, chilled to the bone at they did not know what—vague, shadowy, indefinite fears. And by chance they caught a glimpse of Mr. Burgess as he turned a corner. He paid no attention to their nod of recognition! He hadn't seen it; but they did not know that. What could his conduct mean? It might mean—it might mean—oh, a dozen dreadful things. Was it possible that he knew that Richards could have cleared him of guilt in that by gone time, and had been silently waiting for a chance to even up accounts? At home, in their distress they got to imagining that their servant might have been in the next room listening when Richards revealed the secret to his wife that he knew of Burgess's innocence; next, Richards began to imagine that he had heard the swish of a gown in there at that time; next, he was sure he *had* heard it. They would call Sarah in, on a pretext, and watch her face: if she had been betraying them to Mr. Burgess, it would show in her manner. They asked her some questions—questions which were so random and incoherent and seemingly purposeless that the girl felt sure that the old people's minds had been affected by their sudden good fortune; the sharp and watchful gaze which they bent upon her frightened her, and that completed the business. She blushed, she became nervous and confused, and to the old people these were plain signs of guilt—guilt of some fearful sort or other—without doubt she was a spy and a traitor. When they were alone again they began to piece many unrelated things together and get horrible results out of the combination. When things had got about to the worst, Richard was delivered of a sudden gasp, and his wife asked,

"Oh, what is it?—what is it?"

"The note—Burgess's note! Its language was sarcastic, I see it now." He quoted: "'At bottom you cannot respect me, *knowing,* as you do, of *that matter* of which I am accused'—oh, it is perfectly plain, now, God help me! He knows that I know! You see the ingenuity of the phrasing. It was a trap—and like a fool, I walked into it. And Mary—?"

"Oh, it is dreadful—I know what you are going to say—he didn't return your transcript of the pretended test-remark."

"No—kept it to destroy us with. Mary, he has exposed us to some already. I know it—I know it well. I saw it in a dozen faces after church. Ah, he wouldn't answer our nod of recognition—*he* knew what he had been doing!"

In the night the doctor was called. The news went around in the morning that the old couple were rather seriously ill—prostrated by the exhausting excitement growing out of their great windfall, the congratulations, and the late hours, the doctor said. The town was sincerely distressed; for these old people were about all it had left to be proud of, now.

Two days later the news was worse. The old couple were delirious, and were doing strange things. By witness of the nurses, Richards had exhibited checks—for $8,500? No—for an amazing sum—$38,500! What could be the explanation of this gigantic piece of luck?

The following day the nurses had more news—and wonderful. They had concluded to hide the checks, lest harm come to them; but when they searched they were gone from under the patient's pillow— vanished away. The patient said:

"Let the pillow alone; what do you want?"

"We thought it best that the checks—"

"You will never see them again—they are destroyed. They came from Satan. I saw the hell-brand on them, and I knew they were sent to betray me to sin." Then he fell to gabbling strange and dreadful things which were not clearly understandable, and which the doctor admonished them to keep to themselves.

Richards was right; the checks were never seen again.

A nurse must have talked in her sleep, for within two days the forbidden gabblings were the property of the town; and they were of a surprising sort. They seemed to indicate that Richards had been a claimant for the sack himself, and that Burgess had concealed that fact and then maliciously betrayed it.

Burgess was taxed with this and stoutly denied it. And he said it was not fair to attach weight to the chatter of a sick old man who was out of his mind. Still, suspicion was in the air, and there was much talk.

After a day or two it was reported that Mrs. Richards's delirious deliveries were getting to be duplicates of her husband's. Suspicion flamed up into conviction, now, and the town's pride in the purity of its one undiscredited important citizen began to dim down and flicker toward extinction.

Six days passed, then came more news. The old couple were dying. Richards's mind cleared in his latest hour, and he sent for Burgess. Burgess said:

"Let the room be cleared. I think he wishes to say something in privacy."

"No!" said Richards: "I want witnesses. I want you all to hear my confession, so that I may die a man, and not a dog. I was clean—artificially—like the rest; and like the rest I fell when temptation came. I signed a lie, and claimed the miserable sack. Mr. Burgess remembered that I had done him a service, and in gratitude (and ignorance) he suppressed my claim and saved me. You know the thing that was charged against Burgess years ago. My testimony, and mine alone, could have cleared him, and I was a coward, and left him to suffer disgrace—"

"No—no—Mr. Richards, you—"

"My servant betrayed my secret to him—"

"No one has betrayed anything to me—"

"—and then he did a natural and justifiable thing, he repented of the saving kindness he had done me, and he *exposed* me—as I deserved—"

"Never!—I make oath—"

"Out of my heart I forgive him."

Burgess's impassioned protestations fell upon deaf ears; the dying man passed away without knowing that once more he had done poor Burgess a wrong. The old wife died that night.

The last of the sacred Nineteen had fallen a prey to the fiendish sack; the town was stripped of the last rag of its ancient glory. Its mourning was not showy, but it was deep.

By act of the Legislature—upon prayer and petition—Hadleyburg was allowed to change its name to (never mind what—I will not give it away), and leave one word out of the motto that for many generations had graced the town's official seal.

It is an honest town once more, and the man will have to rise early that catches it napping again.

S. S. Rafferty combines history and crime in this next piece, a tale of mysterious lights along the Rhode Island coast. Able to seamlessly combine historical accuracy and a cunning crime, he is a frequent contributor to Ellery Queen's Mystery Magazine, *appearing there over a dozen times.*

The Rhode Island Lights

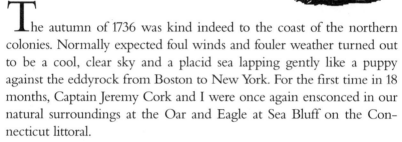

S. S. Rafferty

The autumn of 1736 was kind indeed to the coast of the northern colonies. Normally expected foul winds and fouler weather turned out to be a cool, clear sky and a placid sea lapping gently like a puppy against the eddyrock from Boston to New York. For the first time in 18 months, Captain Jeremy Cork and I were once again ensconced in our natural surroundings at the Oar and Eagle at Sea Bluff on the Connecticut littoral.

"Well, by jing," I said, opening the letters that had come by the post rider early that evening, "it appears that your social puzzles have produced some coin at last."

He was sitting at what he euphemistically calls his "work" table, absorbed in a newly arrived book from England. He looked up and grunted a slight note of interest.

"You remember Squire Delaney of the Rhode Island colony?"

"Of course, Oaks. We helped him in the Narragansett Pacer affair."

"Yes, well, he has seen fit to give your spermacite candle factory in Warwick a substantial contract. It's rather astounding, though. What could he possibly do with two-pound candles? My God, it says here, 'For delivery to the Pharos at Point Judith.' Could Delaney have fallen in with some pagan ritual?"

Cork closed the book and looked up at me with that smirk-a-mouth he uses when he is about to jape me. "Perhaps we ought to refuse the contract. We wouldn't want to be party to the Dark Arts, hey?"

Now there you have it. As Cork's financial yeoman, I am patiently building him an empire of holdings that may some day make him the richest man in the Americas. However, it is part of his sport to ignore my efforts and waste his time in the solution of crimes, which he calls "social puzzles." He has other unprofitable pastimes which are not mentionable in Christian company. This present piece of sarcasm about refusing the Delaney contract was a backhanded reminder that I once proposed the importation of shrunken heads from Spanish America. I said, give the public what it wants, but he was against it.

"I didn't say 'Dark Arts,' sir, you did. I was merely curious about the use of so large a candle, and in such quantity."

"Actually, Oaks, I am guilty of bad imagery. White Arts would have been a better choice."

I looked at him querulously, and he went on, "Even in the absence of all the information, we have the thread of the tapestry. Where does the good Squire live?"

"In the Rhode Island colony."

"More specifically, at Point Judith, does he not?"

"Yes, he owns his horse ranch, as he calls it, and everything in sight."

"And does not Point Judith's recent notoriety bring anything to mind?"

"Of course, the shipwrecks! Four, over the summer, I believe. Shifting sandbars and tricky shoals, the *Gazette* reported."

"And here we have a wealthy, public-spirited man ordering immense candles—"

"A lighthouse! He's building a lighthouse."

"Or Pharos, as mariners term it. But if he is now ordering his light source, I would guess that the Pharos is already built. Now that is something I want to see."

With *The Hawkers*, the ship he owns but never sails in, away to the Indies, we were forced to make the trip overland, and arrived at the Delaney ranch three days later.

I must point out here that our party also included Tunxis, a tame Quinnipiac, who serves as Cork's shadow and as my vexation. Although he speaks passable English, the Indian always talks to Cork in Injun jabber, and a three-day trip spent with two men laughing over incomprehensible jokes is not my recommendation for pleasant travel.

I once heard a back-stair rumor that Cork was related to the Quinnipiac by blood. I would have no truck with that notion. However, when observing Cork's demeanor once he entered the woods and wild, I admit to some doubts. He and Tunxis possess uncanny hearing, and I swear their sense of smell is even better than their eyesight. Perhaps it is these underlying animal instincts that give Cork his reputation as a detector.

In any case, I spent three days ahorse with two boys on a frolic with Nature.

In a previous visit to the Delaneys, I marveled at the luxury of their center-hall mansion. It had changed only of the better, now sprouting another wing. This annex, I assumed, was to accommodate the issue of the ever-fruitful Madame Delaney. As we were to learn later, the Delaneys, having produced seven brawny sons, were now one shy of matching that mark with females.

We arrived at dinnertime, but were not in peril of taking pot-luck. At the Delaney table it is always pot-wealth. There was the normal complement of cod chowder, steamed lobster and clams, and, of course, great hot bowls of succotash and pork. But, good wife that she was, Madame Delaney also served one of the original dishes for which she is justly famous. On this evening it was a platter of succulent squabs, which were as curious as they were delicious. Under Cork's prodding, she told us that they were spit-roasted and basted with a pungent, salty liquor used in China, called sauce of soy. I know little of the Chinese, but their bellies must be content. Since Tunxis refuses to eat or sleep under a roof, he took his repast outdoors.

Later we were sitting in the drawing room with clay bowls and mugs of Delaney's usquebaugh, a potent corn liquor of dark Scotch-Irish reputation, when I brought up a point that had bothered me since we arrived.

"When we turned into your property, Squire, I could see two towers far off the Point. Yet your order said a Pharos."

"Technical terminology, Oaks," Cork cut in. "One or several lights in one place are considered a unit, and referred to in the singular. I assume, Squire, that you have gone to the expense of two towers to give sailors a seamark that is clearly different from others along the coast."

"That and more," the Irishman said.

"Is it worth doubling the investment, just to be different?" I asked.

Cork refilled his bowl and said, "You'll have to forgive Oaks, Squire. He is a businessman, not a navigator."

"Nor am I, Captain, but mariners tell me it is worth the investment. Perhaps if you will explain it to Oaks, it will further clarify my own mind."

"Surely. Well, Oaks, you have certainly been at sea at night. It is something like waking up in a pitch-black room."

"I leave that to the helmsman," I said.

"And whom does he leave it to? Like an awakened man in a dark room, he can bump into things, not having a bearing on a fixed point. However, when our man at sea bumps into something, it is not a chair or a footstool, producing but a stubbed toe. No, my friend, his obstacle can be a reef or shoal, which can tear the bottom from his craft and send her under."

"What about stars?"

"Helpful in deep water but when near a landfall, you require well defined objects ashore. Most charts are not well defined. The sextant is only valuable in skilled hands, and then, of course, there are starless nights. But we are digressing into science. The Squire has put up two lights to tell all at sea who might be off course that the two lights are Point Judith and nowhere else, and I compliment him on his public spirit."

"Oh, that I could accept, it, Captain," said the Squire, with a moan. "But I cannot. The Pharos was built to protect my own good name, as well as the men at sea."

"Go on, man," the Captain said, squinting his eyes in interest.

"You might have read of the shipwrecks off these shores over the past year."

"Yes," I said, "the *Boston Weekly Gazette* mentioned them."

"But what they didn't mention was the ugly rumor that spread in these parts and which implied that I had somehow contrived to cause these wrecks for salvage rights."

"Did you salvage them?"

"Yes, Captain, the first one. But after the rumors I stopped. God help me, my eldest son is at this moment apprenticed to the master of a coaster. Would I be so callous?"

"Indeed not. But tell me, why do you carry the financial load alone? Other townships have raised Pharos with lotteries. Why not here?"

"The townspeople, like those everywhere, resent the wealthy, and feel they can't afford it. Those lottery-built lighthouses are near ports where a lighthouse tax is collectible. Such is not the case here. I bear the load, but alas, not out of public spirit."

"Tell me, Squire," Cork asked, "is there any suspicion that the wrecks might have been caused by foul play?"

"It's a perplexing question. The shoals off our shore are treacherous, and the sandbars seem to have shifted, so accident is highly possible. I have personally surveyed the surrounding waters at low tide, and I had a young fellow from Yale draw up some charts. When word got out that I was going to erect a lighthouse, a single one, all hell broke loose from here to Narragansett."

"But why?" I asked. "You would be protecting shipping by warning them away from underwater hazards."

"And away from Narragansett Bay, or so the dockmen up there claim. As Cork said, night navigation is tricky at best, and if my lone light was a beacon of danger, there was fear that a ship's master would steer a northerly parallel course to the light and end up in Buzzard's Bay, which would enrich New Bedford."

"That's nonsense," Cork growled, "and can be proved so."

"Captain, did you ever try to explain logic and reason to a group of more than three or four men? Especially on a technical subject?"

"Touché," Cork said, with a smile.

"Well, how do two lighthouses solve the problem?" I asked.

"The Yale student suggested it. Our charts show that a deep channel cuts through the shoals. If a means could be found to guide a ship through it at night, a master could safely change from a northerly course to a westerly line, go through the channel, and then swing northeast towards Narragansett."

"Aha." Cork slapped his knee and tossed his head back. "I should have seen it at once when I noticed that the two towers are not in parallel line. The second tower is set back, is it not?"

"Twenty-five feet."

"So you have not only a distinctive seamark, but a unique navigation aid. You present the sailor with a simple light-in-one sighting."

"That's precisely the term John Knox, the student, used."

Following this discussion was becoming as difficult as listening to Cork and Tunxis talk Injun. "Forgive me, gentlemen," I said, "but this is all beyond me."

"Shall I explain, Squire?"

"Pray do. I barely understand it myself."

"Probably because the academician likes to cloak his knowledge in long words. Actually, a light-in-one sighting is simple, but it is more easily demonstrated than explained. May I conduct an experiment for Oaks here so that he might understand?"

The Squire seemed delighted with the entertainment, and Cork set to it. "First, Oaks, you will go into that closet on the far wall. When you emerge, the room will be in darkness except for these two candles, which will be burning on the table to represent the two towers on the Point.

"Now, when you emerge from the closet, you will be facing north, and the floor area in front of you will be cleared of all furniture. This will represent the safety of deep water. Now, as you walk due north, keep your eye on the candles. At a certain point, you will see the two lights start to merge into one. It is no illusion, Oaks. The lights really aren't moving, *you* are. Now the trick is to get you to change to a westerly course. That would be to your left, and bring you forward without breaking your neck on the stools I will have scattered there to represent the shoals."

"Captain," I said suspiciously, "I don't mind barked shins, but a broken neck?"

"Have faith in the system, Oaks, as must the mariner. When the lights merge into one, you will turn to your left and proceed so through the aisle I will have made between the stools, to represent the deep channel. Now I have a question, Squire. Are the lanterns designed to emit light on a 180-degree radius?"

"Yes, that's the reason for the immense candles."

"To be sure. So when Oaks is safely through the aisle, he will again see two lights."

"Correct."

"Then you have nothing to fear, Oaks. Now into the closet while I scale the mathematics to fit our simplified situation in this room. Well, come, my boy, you will be just as safe as in your own bed."

On Cork's guarantee I left my dark closet and entered the room. The candles burned brightly on the table to my left, and I gingerly walked forward. I was amazed to see the candles appear to move, and when they merged into one, I turned left with some trepidation. To my surprise all went well, and when the candles were two again, I turned north again.

"Amazing," I said after the other tapers were lit and the furniture put back to rights.

"Well, you must appreciate that this was a crude example of how a light-in-one works," Cork said, taking some more usquebaugh. "This student, this Knox fellow, has obviously made precise calculations, to place the lights in their proper positions."

"He was at it for weeks, spending nights out in a skiff while my son Secundus and I lit fires from rude poles placed ashore at different angles and heights. Once we had the proper mathematics, we started construction. In the last three weeks of operation we personally have traversed the channel at least fifty times. Three ships' masters have also taken their crafts through successfully.

"Copies of the charts were sent to all the major ports to the south and the harbormasters have written back that they have made the information known to north-bound ships."

"And what of fog or heavy rain?" I asked.

"I am sorry to say that the lights are useless in foul weather, but we have tried to overcome that weakness by firing a star rocket every hour on the hour. At least it will be some warning, and will keep the taint of malicious rumor from my good name. Being accused of placing false lights to lure ships upon the rocks is a heinous charge."

"And punishable by death under Admiralty Law," Cork added with a note of grimness. "But it seems your troubles are over. Is John Knox still with you? I should like to meet him."

"To be sure. He is manning Tower One, while Secundus is in Tower Two. We have decided to hire keepers, but not for a while."

I smiled to myself at the Squire's penchant for naming things by number. A less precise man would have called the first tower the forward tower, and the second the aft, or rear, tower. But what could you expect from a man who had named his seven sons, Primus, Secundus, Tertius, and so on? He once told me that he originally had planned to use the names of the Apostles, but was forewarned by his wife that he was overreaching himself. The female Delaneys were being named for the nine Muses. The Squire is clearly a man of stern determination.

"So, my lads," he said, raising his mug, "I give you the Point Judith Pharos, long may it shine." As he said it, Delaney walked to a large bow window and threw back the drapes. "There are my beauties," he said and raised his glass anew.

Out in the distance, through a starless night, were the dark landslides of the towers, eerie halos of light radiating above their silhouettes as their fiery faces shone out to sea. As we watched the halos glistening, Cork explained that the halo was called a corona, and the rears of the lanterns were much like a view from the dark side of the moon. Then suddenly a toll of bells and the wail of handhorns sounded off in the distance.

"Why, it's like New Year's Eve," I said jokingly. Cork touched my arm and cocked his head into the sounds. He turned and looked at the Squire, who was white with fear.

"Oh, God," Delaney said, lips trembling, "a shipwreck!"

The ensuing hours of that horror-filled night will never be erased from my memory. Out in the darkness lay a sinking ship, its timbers grinding chillingly like the broken spine of a wounded and thrashing beast. Small boats with survivors bobbled in the surf as citizens from the surrounding countryside rushed to aid them. It was near dawn when the last of the longboats dispatched from shore returned from a sweep of the wreck area.

As the longboat was hauled onto the beach, the last survivors tumbled out. One was a young sailor of no more than 20. His hand was bleeding, and one of the countrymen came forward to help him. As he lifted the lad to carry him, he cried out in anger, "It's Primus Delaney, it is. The old devil Squire is at it again!"

By noon the Squire and Primus had been placed under arrest and locked in the brig of a Royal Frigate in Narragansett harbor. The charges were barratry, collusion to shipwreck, and murder, since three hands were lost in the tragedy. The towers were closed by Royal Navy order, and the Delaney household was in chaos.

Before the two Delaneys were clapped in irons, however, Cork was able to piece together the gist of what had happened at sea.

The doomed ship was the *Queen of Tortuga*, out of New York, bound for Narragansett. Her master, who was injured but alive, was Captain Amos Whittleby. At the time of the wreck he had been below deck, having left Primus as the watch officer, and helmsman Fergus Kirk at the wheel.

According to Primus, he had been given charts of his father's new enterprise and was anxious to use the navigation aid. On sighting the two beacons, he sounded the ship's bell and ordered Kirk into the channel-crossing maneuver.

"The lights were joined beautifully," he told us earlier that morning, while being fed hot broth by his mother. All the survivors had been taken to the Delaney home for care, but it was obvious that most of the crew were suspicious and angry. "I kept the lights in sight until they were one, and then told the helmsman to bring her into the west. All went well, and when the lights started to part again, I thought we were through the channel. In fact, I could see the fore and aft lights of a smaller craft still further west. I was about to order us back north, when the crunch of the bottom came, and—well, after that it was hell."

"And now, in broad daylight," Cork said at the time, "we can see that the wreck lies hundreds of feet from the entrance of the channel. So you were on a dead heading for the shoal all the time."

"Yet I couldn't have mistaken the lights' merge, Captain Cork. Fergus Kirk can tell you the same thing."

But it seemed the helmsman couldn't.

"Aye, the boy may be telling the truth," the Scotsman told us later. "I kept my eyes peeled to the compass, and could nae say what the lights done. This I do ken, sirs. No wee laddie should have say on the course of a bark under sail."

Cork interrogated the rest of the crew, but at the time of the wreck all were at meal or asleep in the fo'c'sle. A second hand on the night watch admitted to being asleep on the forward hatch. The others on the watch were lost in the disaster.

Captain Whittleby refused to answer any questions, and replaced cooperation with threats and castigation.

"You have one of two choices, Captain Cork," he snarled as his battered head was being bandaged by a crewman. "Either the light scheme is faulty, or the boy was derelict in his duty. In either case, one of the Delaneys will swing for it, and I want to be there to see the execution."

"We are assured the lights were operating properly, and the system has been tested time and again, Captain Whittleby," Cork had said with some annoyance. "But while we are speaking of dereliction, may I ask why the youngest mate in your crew was given command of the ship in a difficult passage? Surely you should have been on deck, or at the least your first mate."

"The setting of watches is my own business, Captain Cork, and I resent the accusation of dereliction. Why wouldn't I trust young Delaney? He was in home waters and following his father's charts. And I'm sure, if you are a mariner, you well know the youngest eyes and ears in the crew are called on when needed in a rough crossing."

"Then you admit to a rough crossing."

"He admits to nothing, sir." The speaker was the local man who had helped young Primus from the boat. His name was Myles Swaith, and he was truly no friend of the Delaneys. "I have heard of your reputation, Captain Cork—how you are able to twist and contort things to fit your own ends. But not this time. Delaney has lorded it over this vicinity for years, but now he's for it, and there's no help for him."

"There really isn't you know," I said to Cork when we left the room. "We ourselves are witness to the lighthouses working, and if Knox's calculations are correct, then it's error on Primus' part. But if the calculations are wrong, it's the Squire's neck."

"Yes," Cork said, stroking his barba in thought, "but when you have spent time at sea, Oaks, you learn not to trust the surface of the waves. It's what's below that counts. Let's talk to Knox and Secundus."

The lighthouse keepers were in a bedroom on the second floor. John Knox was in his mid-twenties, with flaxen blond hair and an aquiline nose. Secundus Delaney needed no description once you have seen the Squire or any of his offspring. The same red hair and round pixie face. It was as if they had all come from the same mold, which, when you thought about it, was precisely the case.

Knox sat in a chair with his head in his hands. Secundus, a lad of 18, lay despondently on the bed.

"I can't believe it, Captain," Knox said after we had introduced ourselves. "I am positive of my calculations. We tested them over and over again. If anyone should be blamed, it should be me."

"That's not true," Secundus said, getting up and patting his friend's shoulder. "My father and I have also used the system, and we know it works. And several ships' masters have done the same."

"All it proves is that your brother made an error," Knox said. "So what does that solve?"

"Mr. Knox," Cork broke in, "self-pity is a poor companion in dire straits. The Squire tells me that copies of the charts were sent to harbormasters of all major ports to the south. Did you draw those charts?"

"Why, yes, I did. Oh, I see what you mean. I must have made an error on one of them, and somehow it got to New York and on to the *Queen of Tortuga*. Then I *am* to blame!"

"Possibly. But there is another aspect. The New York chart could have been changed. How were they sent?"

"By coaster, sir," Secundus explained, "out of 'Gansett. It was the quickest way."

"And Primus' copy of the chart went down with the *Queen of Tortuga*. How fortunate." Cork smiled.

"Fortunate?" Knox looked perplexed.

"Fortunate for Primus' neck. I believe there will be a trial, and I plan to defend him. I have that right, as a ship's master and owner. Now we have a point of doubt in our favor. If the Court will accept the argument that the chart could have been changed—ever so slightly, for a jot on a chart is hundreds of yards at sea—then we introduce the possibility of collusion from a third party."

Knox's face took on brightness for the first time. "Why, I never thought of that. But wait, Captain, the harbormaster at New York— wouldn't he know?"

"I doubt that he would remember. Most seamen do not memorize charts they will never use."

Secundus smacked his hands together and let out a howl of glee. "Captain, sir, you're a marvel," he cried.

There was a commotion downstairs, and we all went down to find Primus and his father chained together and guarded by six towering Royal Marines. An English Captain named Cricker read formal charges and led the men away over the shrieks and wails of the Delaney women.

The rest of the day was spent within the legal machinery in preparation for a naval inquiry. Once in the town of Narragansett, we called on a local lawyer of some reputation. Giles Pomfret was an old eagle, trained in the Inns of Court, and regarded as a sound scholar. His offices were on the second floor of the Blue Whale, and after an explanation of the situation he sat back slowly touching the fingers of one hand to the other.

"I bow to you, Captain, in marine law, but this doubt-casting element about a chart being mysteriously changed—well, it is a thin line, sir. A very thin line, indeed, since the chart itself is fathoms down."

"That is only my first line, Mr. Pomfret, and I think you will agree that a good defense is the sum of many ramparts."

The old man nodded and then smiled. "To show you how ill equipped I am for the case, when you first said 'barratry,' my mind immediately went to the civil-law interpretation—the habitual maintenance of lawsuits or quarrels. Now in marine law, it means to sink a ship, does it not?"

"Technically, it is the use of fraud or gross or criminal negligence on the part of the master or mariners of a ship to the owner's prejudice."

"Yes. Yes, of course. And the Delaney boy being on the deck watch is the mariner in this case. But what of the charge of wrecking and murder?"

"The changed-chart theory, if proved, will obliterate all charges."

"Well, Captain"—Pomfret shook his head—"I wish you good fortune, but I'll also pray for the Delaneys at the same time. I will, however, prepare the necessary papers to allow you to represent them at the inquiry. If, however, this goes to a full Court, I suggest that you hire the finest marine lawyer money can buy."

We bid him goodbye on that sour note, and, when we were on the street, Cork walked in silence.

Finally he stopped for a moment and said, more to himself than to me, "Strange, a lawyer in a busy port, and he knows nothing of marine law."

"It could be his age. He seems in his dotage."

"That may be," he said, and then stopped a young boy. "Hey, my lad, who is the harbormaster in these waters?"

"That be old Peg and Patch, sir," the boy replied with a shudder.

"Old Peg and Patch, hey? And I suppose you address him so when you bid him good day?"

The lad lowered his head and then shot it up again. "When I sees him I brings myself about, sir. Beware churned waters, my old man says," he told us through a toothless grin.

"A fearsome fellow, then?"

"Like the devil himself, sir. Some says he was a pirate and lived with wild natives on a far-off isle where he was a cannyball."

"And where would his headquarters be, lad?"

"At the foot of Tillford's dock, sir, but you won't find 'im there. Best look in Sadie's, by the Front Street." Then he said, wide-eyed, "If ye have the heart, for you 'pear to be of quality."

"Mere clothes, my lad," Cork said, tossing a coin to him.

One of the outstanding aspects of New England life is the righteous piety of the population. Yet, in its port towns, there is usually one low place where evil flourishes and slakes the appetites of men home from long voyages. Sadie's was buried deep in the cellar of an old warehouse. Through the thick and acrid smoke I could see a stairway that led to the upper part of the building, and dared not think of the evil doings that must occur up there. A crone with tousled hair paid court to our obvious means, and directed us to the harbormaster at a table in a far corner.

From the boy's description I expected to see a demonic sot, racked with depravity. However, Captain Robert Tinker (for that was his true name) was a well kept man of 60. The appellation of Peg and Patch sprang from the spotless patch over his left eye and the ivory stump that served as his left leg from the knee down. To my further surprise he was a reasonably well-spoken Englishman of some education.

After we had taken seats, he must have noticed my own amazement, or sensed it.

"From the look on your face, Mr. Oaks, I take it you have been talking to the townspeople. I am no ogre, sirs. The eye and the limb were lost to gunfire in the service of King and Country. I guess I am resented because I was granted my post by Royal Appointment. Let me assure you, it is no sinecure."

An unbelievably buxom wench came to the table, and Captain Tinker ordered a bottle of Madeira. *His* Madeira.

"I take it you are here on the Delaney business, gentlemen. What service can I do for you?"

"I am told," Cork began, "that copies of the Point Judith charts were put aboard coasters and taken to southern ports."

"Aye. Four in all. Put them aboard myself, explaining in each case the Pharos to the ship's master."

"Do you recall the ships?"

"Ah, let me see, the *Tarrymae* was one."

"Excuse me, Captain," Cork interrupted, "to simplify it, which ship was New York bound?"

"The *Ice Cloud*, under Master Swaith."

"Miles Swaith?"

"Nay, his brother, Ishmael."

"Interesting. There were four wrecks in this area over the summer months, I gather."

"Aye. The Judith shoals were becoming a graveyard, until the Squire came along with this Pharos idea."

"Now I'm told that Delaney took salvage rights on the first bottom, but who took rights in the other wrecks?"

"The 'Gansett Corporation. After the rumors started when the *Bristol Girl* went down, Delaney wouldn't put an oar in the water. So Miles Swaith and a few local businessmen formed a group and took the jobs. Damned shame about young Delaney, though. Shouldn't put the deck under a youngster, I always say."

"Then you believe it to have been an accident?"

"What else, sir? I myself put the Pharos plan to the test and went through the channel like it was the Thames. Say now, don't go taking on this bilge that the Squire was a wrecker. He's as true as magnetic north."

"To be sure. You will be called as a witness if there is a trial, and I trust you will hold that position."

"You have my bond, sir."

When Cork offered to pay for the Madeira, which was excellent, Tinker refused. "First one's free, Captain," he said. "It's good for business. You see, I own this place."

That evening, on our return to the Delaney ranch, we took a meager supper in our rooms. The hearty familial spirit that had been drawn from the home had left only bleakness in its aftertide.

"It appears that the name Swaith abounds in this affair," I said, over the cold turkey and corn bread.

"Yes, the brother could have changed the charts, but we are on slanderous grounds. I want something with more meat to it."

"Your second rampart?"

"And a third, if we can find one."

With this, there was a tap at the window, which at first I thought was rain. Getting up, Cork opened the casement to admit Tunxis. Despite the fact that we were on the second floor, the Indian's sudden appearance was not in the least jarring to me. To come to the second floor like a normal person he would have to enter under a roof, so it was natural that he would scale the trellis to converse with Cork. The climb up must have winded him slightly, or set his mind a-bubble, for he spoke in English. Thrusting a sack through the window, he said, "Here, like you say, lower beach."

"Good fellow, Chawcua, and who was with you?"

"White man named Clint."

"Good. Wait below."

When Cork had closed the window again, he returned to the table with the sack and sat down.

"What's in that thing?" I asked, sniffing the air. "A skunk?"

"No. My second line of defense, Oaks."

I reached across, opened the sack, and quickly closed it. "Animal droppings. Dung is your second rampart?"

"Evidence is often as repulsive as the crime, Oaks. Now I'm off for the third."

"Not without me," I said, getting to my feet.

"You're a stout fellow, my lad, but not this time."

"And why not? Am I some slip of a girl, some piece of frippery? I may not have the woodsy wiles of that redskin, but I'm man enough to a given task."

There were few times in my long relationship with him that I experienced true camaraderie. He reached out, clapped my shoulder, looked at me with those cold blue eyes, and smiled. "I never doubted that, my friend. Come, we have some climbing of our own to do."

My moment of gallantry stuck in my throat as we approached the base of the forward tower on the Point. With the ground-level hatches of both structures sealed tight with Royal lead, Cork proposed to scale the side of the thirty-foot edifice fronting the sea.

"Not only is it dangerous, but pointless," I said, as Tunxis uncurled roping lines.

"Wrong on both counts, Oaks. The facing is of fine hammered sandstone with a wide bond, so, despite the mist, the footing is sure. As for examining the light room, it is crucial to the case. I will go first, Tunxis to follow. Once up, we will haul you up by rope."

"If you climb, I climb."

He looked at the Indian, and Tunxis nodded. A savage was giving his accord to my own valor. Perhaps, at last, I was accepted by him.

I will not embarrass myself by describing the toil and fear of the ascent. From one slippery stone to the next, never looking down into the blackness, I inched my way up into more blackness. Above me I heard the shatter of glass, as Cork broke one of the panes in the tower windows, and a sharp tug on the guy line around my waist alerted me that the end of the climb was near.

"Take care of the broken pane, Oaks," Cork whispered. "Reach above your head and you will find a rod running around the ceiling on the inside."

I swung into the window frame and got to my feet. Cork was examining the apparatus with a shielded candle. The now dark light was a wondrous machine. Twelve large candles were imbedded in a holding plate before a concave plate of polished brass. The candles, when lit, must have reflected a most powerful light out to sea.

"What are you doing, Captain?" I asked, as he tugged at the base of the holding plate.

"Solid as Gibraltar," he said. "Let's take the ladder below."

One by one we descended into a round room directly below the light chamber. It had been fitted out as living quarters for a permanent keeper, when he was eventually hired. A chair and a writing table were at one side of the room. Tunxis lit the lamp with his candle while Cork rummaged around. He found nothing in the table drawer, and obviously nothing of interest in the few books on the shelf.

"Looks like a wild goose," I said, sitting on the chair, still winded from the climb and the excitement.

"Perhaps," Cork muttered as he pulled back a curtain hanging on ring hoops to expose a bed.

"Are lighthouse keepers allowed to sleep?"

"We all must, eventually, Oaks. With the coal-fired beacons along the English coast, there is little chance of the light going out, so the keepers sleep. I'm sure that when Delaney hires a regular keeper, he will keep a night watch."

"Keepers, you mean," I corrected him. An opportunity I rarely have.

He looked at me from the shadows cast by the lamp and gave me that smirk-a-mouth again. "You! A man of ledgers and coin! My word, Oaks, that is astounding. One man can handle both towers. Stationed in this forward tower, he could see if the rear tower was lit at all times. What's below there, Tunxis?"

The Indian's head poked up the ladderway hatch from the deck below.

"Supplies, candles."

"Well," I said, "what next? I hope we are not going to climb the other tower."

"No need. Come, lads, there is nothing more here." Cork snuffed the lamp.

When we arrived back at the house, Tunxis went wherever he goes, and we entered to find a note from Lawyer Pomfret. Cork did not read it in front of Madame Delaney, but waited till we were in our rooms. He then tore open the sealed envelope and read quickly.

"They move with great haste in this matter." He tossed the paper to me and I read it with a sinking heart. Disregarding all the niceties and legal terms, its essence was that a Naval Court of Inquiry would convene two days hence to take advantage of the fact that Admiral Fenley-Blore, of his Majesty's fleet, was in the area, and had agreed to preside over the panel.

"My, my, a flag officer, no less. Is that good or bad, Captain?"

He shrugged. "All bad pennies have an obverse. If we lose, there is little chance for appeal in London. A Fleet Admiral's stamp will settle it forever."

"And if we win, that also ends it forever. But two days is so short a time to prepare."

"For us, yes. I feel other forces have been planning for weeks. But no use wailing over it. We must set some things to our advantage. Fetch me Secundus, will you, while I pen a note."

A note indeed. It was a missive of polite flattery and obeisance to Admiral Fenley-Blore. Cork expressed concern over the meager accommodations available in Narragansett to a naval hero of the Admiral's stature. He went on to describe the luxury of the Delaney home and extended its hospitality to further add to the Admiral's comfort, and suggested that the Court be convened in the main hall of the Delaney mansion in order that the Admiral's august presence have the proper dignified surroundings. The most amusing part was his signing it, "Your obedient servant." Cork has bowed to no man, and I am sure he has never been obedient.

Secundus was dressed for the night ride, and took the letter. "Mind, lad, for the Admiral's hands, and no other's. By the bye, before you go. Was anyone aware that your brother's ship was making for these waters?"

"Surely. It was posted in the harbormaster's office. Not the exact day, but on or about, you know."

"Estimated date of return, yes. Well, off you go."

The Admiral arrived the next afternoon with two aides. Fenley-Blore was an English sailor of the old line. In the days of Queen Bess he would surely have been one of the Sea Dogs. A shortish man, he tended toward portliness in his twilight years. But the weight of girth and age had not slowed his step or his agile mind. Cork, the sly fox, fawned over him like a lass to a fiddler.

It wasn't until the next morning that I saw through the reason for Cork's uncommon actions. We were at breakfast, and Fenley-Blore was saying, "Wild turkey, you say? Now that should be good sport, hunting from horseback. But I'm afraid we will have to get on with this inquiry business. I enjoy these sojourns ashore, but I must get back to sea."

"I understand, Admiral," Cork soothed him, "but why not have the best of all possible worlds? We can hunt today and hold the inquiry tonight. You have the power to convene at any hour, so why not at your leisure?"

"Well put. Tonight it is. Feel a bit sheepish at trying a man in his own home, though."

"Command is not always easy, Admiral."

He had hooked him. The inquest was to be held that night.

Before I describe that evening of surprises, dejections, and finally, of an uncanny solution, I must explain that I have simplified the text to avoid all the technical terms that fog understanding for the layman. I myself kept copious notes, and it took Cork three days to explain them to me. The air in the main hall that night was thick with such phrases as "points to the larboard," "keel lines," "true and magnetic course," and "lines of divination," as well as an hour's worth of talks and arguments about sails and winds and crosswinds.

The main point is that a ship was wrecked due either to negligence or to a faulty system—or so the Court claimed.

Cork went immediately to work on the changed-chart theory. He carefully laid the groundwork by describing how the copies of the chart sent to New York *could* have been changed. He was about to strengthen his question of doubt when one of the Admiral's aides leaned over and whispered into his superior's ear.

"Excuse me, Captain Cork," Fenley-Blore said, "but this line that the chart used aboard the *Queen of Tortuga* by young Delaney being missing is not correct."

I looked up at Cork, who was standing at our table facing the Court. His face showed surprise, and a chart was handed down the line of nine officers on the panel to the Admiral.

"Captain Cork," the Admiral continued, picking up the chart, "this was found with the flotsam of the *Tortuga*. It bears the inscription: *Delaney, Point Judith Pharos*. Would you kindly verify that it is the same as the original chart?"

Cork called John Knox, who was sworn in. The student looked at the chart carefully and said, "I'm afraid it's accurate, Captain," causing a murmur from the small group of townsmen who sat at the back of the long room. It appeared that Cork's first line of defense was breached, and I could see no rampart to fall back upon.

The Captain now went into skirmish maneuvers. He called the Delaneys, and Primus and his father both took an oath to their stories. He also put on the stand a Captain Jeggs, one of the mariners who had tested the system, and he too swore to Heaven that it was a genuine chart.

Next came Fergus Kirk, who would swear to nothing except that he was Fergus Kirk. He stuck to his story that he had been watching the compass. As Kirk stepped down, a voice from the back of the room said, "if it pleases the Admiral and the panel, sir, may I be recognized?"

I turned to see Lawyer Pomfret walking slowly forward. The Admiral recognized Pomfret, who stood facing Cork.

"Gentlemen, I am Giles Pomfret, counselor-at-law, representing the Virron Shipping concern of Maiden Lane, New York, owners of the *Queen of Tortuga*."

He shifted on his feet like a nervous bird, and faced the panel.

"We, of course, have an interest in this matter and its outcome, and it seems to me that the good Captain here has everyone in sight taking an oath. We can't believe both Delaneys and still have a logical explanation of the matter. Now I'm a local man and would like to see fairness tendered, but my clients demand justice."

"And, from justice, restitution?" Cork asked.

"Captain, you're a fine fellow and a superior host," the Admiral smiled, "but we will have to get more answers than we have so far."

Cork was about to resume, when Captain Jeggs motioned to him, and both men talked in low whispers for a few moments. "Admiral, I have no further need of Captain Jeggs. We have his testimony, and he has a tide to catch."

"Excused, and good weather, Captain," the Admiral said, tossing him a half salute.

"Now, gentlemen," Cork walked forward as a chair was brought up for Pomfret, who sat and crossed his spindly legs. "The crux of the matter is the Pharos system itself, and to fully understand it, the panel should see it in operation."

The Admiral pointed his finger at Cork. "Now see here, Captain, I have no intention of setting sail to watch lights."

"No need, Admiral. We can exhibit it right here, with your permission. It's very simple. All we will need is two candles and total darkness. I would use my friend Oaks to demonstrate, but that could be viewed as prejudice, so I will call on a man who has asked for Justice, Lawyer Pomfret."

The lawyer gladly accepted, and the room was set up much as we had it when I played the part of the ship. One major exception was that Cork had the panel table moved forward. That put us all facing the wall along which Pomfret would walk in darkness.

"Now, to truly imitate the conditions of the night in question," Cork said, before the tapers were extinguished, "I have fashioned a shield for the back of the candle holders. In that way, only Mr. Pomfret will be able to tell us what he sees. Now remember, Pomfret, when the lights are one, make your turn, not before or after, for those chairs could give you a nasty knock."

The lawyer left the room, and we waited, adjusting our eyes to the darkness. Cork lit the candles, for we could all see the halos above the shields. "Come ahead," he shouted, and a door opened and I could hear Pomfret slowly shuffling across the room ahead. Four, five seconds, and then he said, "I'm turning now," and then the crash of old bones and heavy mahogany chairs followed instantly.

It would have been a comic sight to see the old man lying on the floor rubbing his painful leg, had it not sunk the Squire once and for all. But then it occurred to me that Pomfret had deliberately turned too soon, in order to create a negative impression. I went forward in the low-lighted room and informed Cork in a low tone.

"Excuse me, gentlemen," Cork said to the Court, while he helped the snarling man to his feet. "It has been suggested to me that our legal friend here may have resorted to deceit to prejudice the case."

"That's a lie," Pomfret shouted, dusting himself off.

"You are correct, sir. I believe you did turn when the lights became one. Just as young Delaney did."

"Then you have proved the case against the Squire," the Admiral said.

"I have proved *a* case. Let us see who fits the mold."

He walked over to the window and drew back the drapes to the oh's and ah's of everyone. The Admiral came to his feet and hurried to the window. "What are those lights doing on?" he roared. The two towers had glowing halos above their tops. "They were ordered sealed, and by the gods, I'll hang any man who has broken them open."

"There are ways around seals, just as there are ways around systems, Admiral. Say, isn't that a ship out there? See the fore-and-aft running lights riding the waves?"

"You're right, Cork." The Admiral spoke with sudden anxiety.

An aide who had come to the Admiral's side muttered, "He'll have her on the beach in a moment."

The Admiral was now purple with rage. "Cork, I hold you responsible for the safety of that ship. It was lured into the area by those blasted lights."

"I take the responsibility, sir. May I produce the master of that 'ship'?"

"How? By magic?"

"No, by voice." Cork opened the window and called, "Ahoy!"

It *seemed* like magic, for the ship turned its prow into the beach and headed straight for the window. Then, as it got closer, we could see the trick.

"It's a donkey!" the Admiral cried. "A beast with lanterns hung over its head and tail."

"And the movement of a donkey walking on the beach would give an observer at sea the illusion that he was looking at a distant ship riding the waves."

"That's an old wrecker's trick, a damnable one," Fenley-Blore swore. "But what has this demonstration to do with the Pharos being faulty?"

"If we will all take our seats again, I will explain," Cork replied.

When the room was back to order, Cork addressed us. He now knew he was in safe water, and he played like a dolphin.

"Actually, I am presenting the evidence for acquittal in reverse. You will recall that Primus felt he was on a safe course when the beacons were joined, because he saw the running lights of a ship ahead. That disturbed me, because the overall plot was so well conceived, so wondrously scientific, that I couldn't believe such a shoddy element would be allowed to mar it. It was just too much sugar in the bun.

"The man out there with the animal is named Clint. On the morning after the wreck he and my Indian friend searched the beach area and found what my yeoman calls 'filthy evidence' that a beast of burden had traversed the ground. Now, Admiral, you are correct that this has nothing to do with the performance of the Pharos. I say it worked perfectly that night, and will continue to work perfectly."

"My shin seems to give that a sound argument," Pomfret put in.

"I am sorry about that, Mr. Pomfret. It was not done in malice, but perhaps with a touch—only a touch, mind you—of indignation at your performance in your office two days ago. I am sure you are skilled in marine law, and I do not like to be lied to. But leave it, sir. This conspiracy required a genius and a fool, and you are neither."

"Cork, get to the point," the Admiral admonished, irritably.

"I beg pardon. Would you be kind enough to walk the same course which was so painful to Mr. Pomfret? Oh, no, I will not have the lights out this time. Please, sir."

The Admiral got to his feet with a look of simmering anger and took a place at the far wall. Cork re-lit the candles and nodded for the old sailor to start. Fenley-Blore was a quarter of the way across when he stopped.

"What the devil are you doing, Cork? You're passing a screen over the forward candle."

"Yes, exactly as I did when Pomfret was our ship. Only in the lit room you can see the trick. Just as Primus Delaney could not see the trick out over the blackness of the sea. Seize him, Oaks."

John Knox was a slippery fellow, but I held him fast.

"You can't prove a thing, Cork," Knox said. "How could I hold a screen in front of the candles up there? It's too big for one man to do."

"When I said this conspiracy needed a genius and a fool, I should have added a dupe, but I didn't want to forewarn you, Mr. Knox. You have told us that you went to Yale College. Did you graduate?"

"No, I went only two years."

"That's strange. Yale is a fine school, but more regarded for its humanities and theology than for its science."

"My father was a master builder, and taught me his trade."

"Builder, yes. The construction of the towers is sound. But what of seamanship, navigation?"

"I've read books."

"Good sailors learn their trade before the mast, as soldiers learn their craft in battle." This last drew smiles from the entire panel.

"I suggest you are a dupe, Mr. Knox. To devise this plan would require years at sea, years of experience with difficult passages. And, I might add, an accurate mathematical ability.

"As for holding a screen in front of the lamp, I agree that it would be impossible for one man to do it alone, and if you blew out the candles, there would be no corona, or halo, to be seen from the back of the tower to gull us all into thinking that the light was in proper working order.

"Also, if you were simply to hold up a screen in front of the light, no purpose would be served. A ship running on a parallel line would see it one second and not the next. The abruptness of the change would make a mere cabin boy suspicious. No, Knox, the screen would have to move slowly between the lights from left to right to give the illusion that the lights were joining, long before that would really happen."

"That would be some trick," Knox said contemptuously. "What would I use? I took nothing from the tower that night, and it has been sealed since."

"You had no need to take anything away. The tools are still there in all their innocence. One thing I noted about your tower when I broke in the other night is that it is efficient. Yet the only purpose of a rod that runs around the ceiling of the front wall seems to be to give intruders a handhold. Another inefficiency is a bed that gives the sleeper privacy, when a lone keeper needs no privacy. Thus we have your screen, or curtain, which could be attached to the rod in the light chamber and used to slowly eclipse the light source from the front, while still providing a halo at the back."

"That's fanciful conjecture, Cork."

"No, I think the two gentlemen entering the room will back it up. Did it work, Captain Jeggs?"

Jeggs and a naval officer came forward and told of sailing out off the Point while Tunxis worked the curtain in Tower One.

"You are the dupe, Knox, and you have the privilege of going to the hanging string alone if you choose. Shall I produce the fool and the genius, or would you care to throw yourself on the Admiral's mercy?"

Knox looked at Fenley-Blore and back at Cork. He was frightened now, like an animal in a trap.

"Swaith! Miles Swaith is the culprit!" he screamed. "When I came here to build only one tower, he offered me money to advise the Squire against it, because he had been wrecking the ships with that donkey trick and spreading rumors about the Delaneys. When the Squire insisted on going ahead, Miles Swaith brought me the Pharos scheme, plans, charts, and all. Believe me, Squire, I didn't know Primus was aboard that ship. When I saw the running lights through the long glass, I didn't know it was the *Queen of Tortuga*."

Miles Swaith was on his feet frothing at the mouth. "He can't bring me into this, he can't! I deny everything he says, and it's his word against mine."

"And your donkey against whose, Swaith? When I sent Tunxis to scour the neighborhood with Mr. Clint, he learned that you are the only one in the immediate vicinity who keeps such a beast. Oxen are used hereabouts, which, as any wrecker knows, are too slow and too even-footed to give the illusion of a cruising ship. Admiral, I give you Miles Swaith, the fool in the plot. If he had followed his master's plan, and trusted the light system alone, without using the donkey trick, we would have never uncovered the plot."

"By the Duke's guns!" The Admiral thumped the table. "When I first laid eyes on you I said, 'There is a remarkable fellow.' Now I double it, sir. You are a genius."

"I thank you, sir, but there is only one genius abounding, and we must pin him before we have the lot."

"If you can do that, my boy, I'll give you a man-of-war for a toy. I don't know when I've enjoyed myself more. Well, go on, go on." The Admiral was as gleeful as a small lad on Christmas morning.

"I have given profound thought to his identity. Swaith is discounted, for he is merely a rude and greedy bumpkin. Our student is too limited in skill. So who have we? Let me see. We need a master mariner, to be sure, and a scientist of some prowess. Forgive me, Admiral, if this description seems to fit you."

For a moment the old boy looked concerned, and then he broke into laughter. "Very remarkable fellow," he said to the aide at his side.

"But, combined with these laudable attributes, we need also a man with a smidgen of evil, with an attraction to the low life. The criminal mind operates that way. A cut-purse or a highwayman will risk his life for a bag of gold, and then squander it on wine and whores. Another forgiveness, Admiral, but when I asked your naval lieutenant to accompany Captain Jeggs on tonight's cruise, I also requested that he have your Captain of Marines arrest a suspect—the only one who qualifies as a master mariner and a scientist with a touch of evil. May I produce him?"

The commotion at the back of the room turned all our heads. There, between two Marines, was Captain Robert Tinker, the harbormaster, old Peg and Patch, as the street urchin had so aptly named him. . . .

Well, nothing is more jubilant than an Irishman who has just escaped the noose, and since both Delaneys were free, it was merriment in double time at the ranch. Fiddlers were called, punch-bowls filled, and great sides of meat were put to the spits. The celebration lasted until past dawn, when the Admiral and his party took their leave.

"Technically, he owes you a ship of the line," I said as we repaired to our rooms. "He made you that promise before witnesses."

"What would we do with it, Oaks? Start a navy? You know, this idea of closing off the Pharos light with a screen is intriguing when properly done. If a clock mechanism could be devised to shield the beacon for a specific amount of time—say, seconds or minutes—ships could recognize the seamark by the frequency of the light flashes."

"Excellent idea, and possibly profitable. Put it to paper tomorrow."

"It *is* tomorrow, and I'm for sleep."

So, I fear, it is to be with all his tomorrows. Sleep. Drink. Carouse. And, of course, solve. I shall persevere in spite of him.

Fredric Brown (1906–1972) expanded the limits of the mystery story by writing totally unique novels and stories featuring multiple points of view, unstable narrators, and ingenious plots and crimes to drive his work. Whether it was short stories or novels, the reader was never exactly sure what was going to happen next. His best short fiction was collected in the anthology Carnival of Crime. *"The Jabberwocky Murders" shows him running true to form.*

The Jabberwocky Murders

Fredric Brown

Chapter 1
Looking-Glass Shadow

'Twas brillig, and the slithy toves
Did gyre and gimble in the wabe:
All mimsy were the borogoves,
And the mome raths outgrabe.

I took another drink out of the bottle on my desk and then typed the last take and handed it to Jerry Klosterman to take over to his linotype. He looked it over.

"About one sentence strong, Doc," he said. "There were fourteen lines to fill."

"Then cut out the part about sullying the fair name of Carmel City," I told him.

He nodded and went over to the machine. I took the last drink and dropped the bottle into the wastebasket. Then I walked over to the window and looked out into the dusk while the mats clicked down the channels of the linotype. Smoothly and evenly. Jerry rarely poked a wrong key.

The lights of Oak Street flashed on while I stood there. Across on the other sidewalk Miles Harrison hesitated in front of Smiley's Inn, as though the thought of a cool glass of beer tempted him. I could almost see his mind work.

"No, I'm a deputy sheriff of Carmel County and I have a job to do yet tonight. The beer can wait."

His conscience won. He walked on. I wonder now whether, if he had known he'd be dead before midnight, he wouldn't have taken that beer. I think he would have. I'd have done it, but that doesn't prove anything, because I'd have taken it anyway. I never had a New England conscience like Miles Harrison.

But of course I wasn't thinking that then, because I didn't know any more than Miles did what was going to happen. I found mild amusement in his hesitation, and that was all.

Jerry called to me from the stone, where he had just dropped in the newly set lines at the bottom of the column.

"She's a line short now, Doc. But I can card it out."

"Lock it up and pull a stone proof," I said. "I'll be in Smiley's. I'll buy you a drink when you bring it over."

I put on my hat and went out.

That's the way it always was on Thursday evenings. The Carmel City Courier is a weekly, and we put it to bed all ready to run on Thursday night. Friday morning the presses roll—or to be more accurate the press, singular, which is a Miehle Vertical, shuttles up and down. And about Friday noon we start to distribute.

Big Smiley Wessen grinned when I came in.

"How's the editing business, Doc?" he said, and laughed as though he'd said something excruciating. Smiley has as much sense of humor as a horse.

"Smiley, you give me a pain," I said. It's safe to tell Smiley the truth. He always thinks you're joking anyway.

He grinned appreciatively. "Old Henderson?"

"Old Henderson it is," I said, and he poured it and I drank it.

He went down to the other end of the bar and I stood there, not thinking about anything. This time Thursday evening always was a letdown. So I just stood there and tried not to see myself in the mirror and didn't succeed.

I could see myself, Doc Bagden, a small man getting gray around the temples and thin on top. Editor of a small-town weekly and, thank goodness, not much chance of ever getting any higher than that. Another twenty—thirty years of that is bleak to look forward to, but anything else is bleaker. Nor a harp at the end of it. I envy some of my fellow townsmen their confidence in harps, for it might be something to wait around for.

I heard a car swing in to the curb out front and, for no reason, blow its klaxon.

"Al Carey," I told myself.

He came in, which was a treat for Smiley's Inn, for Alvin Carey usually went to swankier places in the nearby larger towns. Not that I blamed him for that. He had a spot to fill as the nephew of the town's richest man and naturally he spent as much of his uncle's money as he could get his hands on. Which was pretty much for Carmel City, although it wouldn't have made a splash in New York.

Of course I'd called him a wastrel—not by name—in editorials, because people expected me to. But I liked him, and had a hunch I'd make a worse scion of wealth than Alvin did.

Besides, he read a lot of the right things and had more of an idea of what it was all about than the rest of town.

"Hi, Doc," he said. "Have a drink, and when are we going to have another game of chess?"

"Old Henderson," I told Smiley. "Alvin, my son, I am playing chess now, and so are you. The White Knight is sliding down the poker. He balances very badly."

He grinned. "Then you're still in the second square. Have another drink."

"And there," I said, "it takes all the drinking I can do to stay in the same place. But that won't be for long. From the second square to the fourth, I travel by train, remember?"

"Then don't keep it waiting, Doc. The smoke alone is worth a thousand pounds a puff."

"Old Henderson," I said to Smiley.

Then Al left—he'd just come in for a short snort.

"What the devil were you guys talking about?" asked Smiley.

There wasn't any use trying to explain. "Crawling at your feet you may observe a bread-and-butter-fly," I said. "Its wings are thin slices of bread-and-butter, its body a crust, and its head is a lump of sugar."

"Where?" said Smiley. I don't think he was kidding.

Then Jerry Klosterman appeared with the rolled-up stone proof of the final page. I don't think I ever did get around to telling Smiley what Al and I had been talking about.

It was getting too much trouble to keep track of individual drinks, so I bought the rest of the bottle from Smiley, and got another glass for Jerry.

Then we took the page proof over to a table and spread it out, and I gave it a rapid reading. I marked a few minor errors and one major one—a line in an ad upside down. The ads, if you don't know, are the most important part of a newspaper. And I circled, for my own convenience, all the filler items that could be pulled out in case anything worth mentioning happened in Carmel City during the night. Not that it ever did or that it would tonight. Or so I thought.

"We can catch these in the morning," I told Jerry. "Won't have to go back tonight. Did you lock up?"

He nodded and poured himself another drink.

"There was a phone call for you just after you left," he said.

"Who?"

"Wouldn't give a name. Said it wasn't important."

"That," I said firmly, "is the fallacy of civilized life, so-called, Jerry. Why should things be arbitrarily divided into things that are important and that aren't? How can anyone tell? What is important and what is unimportant?"

Jerry is a printer. "Well, Doc, it's important that we get the paper up, isn't it?" he said. "And unimportant what we do afterward."

"Not at all," I told him. "Just the opposite, in fact. We get the blamed paper out of the way solely so we can do what we please afterward. That's what's important—if anything is."

Jerry shook his head slowly. "You're really not sure anything is, are you, Doc?" He picked up his drink and stared at it. "How's about death? Isn't that?"

"Somebody you like," I said. "His death can be important to you. But not your own. Jerry, there's one thing sure. If you were to die right now, you'd never live to regret it."

"Poor Doc," he said, downed his drink and stood up. "Well, I'm going home. I suppose you'll get tight, as usual."

"Unless I think of a better idea," I agreed. "And I haven't yet. So long, Jerry."

"So long, Doc."

I stared for a while at the calendar over the bar. It had the kind of picture on it that you usually see on calendars over bars. It was just a bit of bother to keep my eyes focused properly, although I hadn't had enough to drink to affect my mind at all.

One corner of my mind persisted in wondering if I could get Beal Brothers Store to continue running a half-column ad instead of going back to six inches. I tried to squelch the thought by telling myself I didn't care whether anybody advertised in the Courier or not. Or whether the Courier kept on being published. I didn't, much.

The picture on the calendar got on my nerves. "Smiley, there aren't any women like that," I said. "It's a lie. You ought to take it down."

"Women like what? Take what down?"

"Never mind, Smiley," I said. After all, the picture was a dream. Somebody's dream of what something ought to be like.

The air was hot and close, and Smiley was rattling glasses, washing them, back of the bar.

I turned around and looked out the window, and a car with two dead men in it went by. But I didn't know that, although I had a feeling of wide-awareness that should have told me, if there's anything in prescience.

"There goes Barnaby Jones to the bank," I told Smiley. That was all it meant to me.

"The bank?" Smiley answered. "Ain't it closed?"

I looked at him to see whether he was kidding, and then remembered he hadn't any sense of humor. But I thought everyone in town knew about the Barnaby Jones Company payroll. Old man Barnaby's shoe factory was in the next town, but he banked in Carmel City, where he lived, and every first and fifteenth he took the payroll over himself. Two trips, one for the day shift and one for the night shift. Miles Harrison had to strap on a gun and go with Barnaby over to the bank for the money and then guard him on the way.

"The bank opens up any time Barnaby Jones wants it to, Smiley," I explained. "Tonight's payroll."

"Oh," Smiley said, and laughed. I wanted to choke him.

Maybe there was something important, after all, I decided—a sense of humor. That was why I never stayed at Smiley's on Thursday evenings. I always bought a bottle and went home where my bookcase gives me the best company there is.

I bought a bottle and started home with it. It was still fairly early evening, but the streets were dark.

Darker than I thought.

Chapter 2
Smell of Blood

Beware of Jabberwock, my son!
The jaws that bite, the claws that catch!
Beware the Jubjub bird, and shun
The frumious Bandersnatch!

Maybe I weaved just a little along the sidewalk, for at this stage I'm never quite as sober as I am later on. But the mind—ah, it was a combination of crystal clarity with fuzziness around the edges. It's hard to explain or define, but that's a state of mind which makes even Carmel City tolerable.

Down Oak Street past the corner drugstore, Pop Hinkle's place, where I used to drink Cokes as a youngster, past Gorham's Feed Store, where I'd worked summers while I was going to college, past the bank, with Barnaby Jones' Packard still standing in front of it, past the Bijou, past Hank Greeber's undertaking parlor—beg pardon—H. Greeber, Mortician, past Bing Crosby-Dorothy Lamour at the Alhambra, with a lot of cars parked in front, and I recognized Alvin Carey's even with the klaxon silent—a big contrast from the sedate black Packard his uncle used, back at the bank—past Deek's music store, where I'd once bought a violin, past the courthouse, with a light still burning in the room I knew was the office of Pete Lane, the sheriff.

I almost turned in there, from force of habit, to see if there was any news. Then I remembered it was Thursday night, and kept on walking.

Out of the store district now, past the house Elsie had lived in and died in, while we were engaged, past the house Elmer Conlin had lived in when I bought the Courier from him—past my whole blasted life, on the way home.

But with a bottle in my pocket and good company waiting for me there, my old tried-and-true friends in the bookcase. Reading a book is almost like listening to the man who wrote it talk. Except that you don't have to be polite. You can take your shoes off and put your feet up on the table and drink and forget who you are.

And forget the newspaper that hung around your neck like a millstone every day and night of the week except this one.

So to the corner of Campbell Street and my turning.

My house ahead, with no lights waiting. But on the porch a shadow moved.

And came forward as I mounted the steps. The dim light from the street lamp back on the corner showed me a strange, pudgy little man. My own height, perhaps, but seeming shorter because of his girth. Light, insufficient to show his features clearly, nevertheless reflected glowing pin-points in his eyes, a cat-like gleam. Yet there was nothing sinister about him. A small, pudgy man is never sinister, no matter where nor when, nor how his eyes look.

"You are Doctor Bagden?" he inquired.

"Doc Bagden," I corrected him. "But not a doctor—of medicine. If you are looking for a doctor, you've got the wrong place."

"No I am aware that you are not a medico, Doctor. Ph.D., Harvard, 1913, I believe. Author of 'Lewis Carroll Through the Looking-Glass,' and 'Red Queen and White Queen.'"

It almost sobered me. Not that he had the right year of my magna cum laude, but the rest of it. The Lewis Carroll thing had been a brochure of a dozen pages, printed eighteen years ago, and not over five hundred copies run off. If one existed anywhere outside my own library, it was a surprise to me. And the "Red Queen and White Queen" article had appeared at least ten years ago in an obscure magazine long discontinued and forgotten.

"Why, yes," I said. "What can I do for you, Mr.—?"

"Smith," he said gravely, and then chuckled. "And the first name is Yehudi."

"No!" I said.

"Yes. You see, Doctor Bagden, I was named forty years ago when the name Yehudi, although uncommon, did not connote what it connotes today. My parents were not psychic, you see. Had they guessed the difficulty I might have in convincing people that I am not spoofing them when I tell them my given name—" He laughed ruefully. "I always carry cards."

He handed me one. It read:

Yehudi Smith

There was no address. Absently, I stuck it in my pocket.

"There's Yehudi Menuhin, the violist, you know," he said. "And there's—"

"Stop, please," I said, "you're making it plausible. I liked it better the other way."

He smiled. "I have not misjudged you then. Have you ever heard of the Vorpal Blades?"

"Plural? No. Of course in Jabberwocky—in 'Alice Through the Looking-Glass,' there's a line about a—Great Scott! Why are we talking about vorpal blades on my front porch? Come on in. I have a bottle, and I presume it would be superfluous to ask a man who talks about vorpal blades whether he drinks."

I unlocked the front door and stepped in first to light the hall light. Then I ushered him back to my den. I swept the litter off the table—it's the one room my housekeeper, who comes in for a few hours every day—is forbidden to clean, and I brought glasses and filled them.

"Take that chair," I said. "This is the one I drink in. And now, Mr. Smith—to Lewis Carroll."

He raised his glass.

"To Charles Lutwidge Dodgson, known as Lewis Carroll when in Wonderland," he said.

We put down our glasses empty, and I filled them. I was more than glad I'd brought home a quart. There was a warm glow in my body—the glow I'd lost on the long walk home.

"And now," I said, "what of vorpal blades?"

"It's an organization, Doctor. A very small one, but just possibly a very important one. The Vorpal Blades."

"Admirers of Lewis Carroll, I take it?"

"Well, yes, but—" His voice became cautious. "—much more than that. I feel that I should tell you something. It's dangerous. I mean, really dangerous."

"That," I said, "is marvelous. Wonderful. Go on."

He didn't. He sat there and toyed with his glass a while and didn't look at me. I studied his face. It was an interesting face, and there were deep laughter-lines around his eyes and his mouth. He wasn't quite as young as I thought he was. One would have to laugh a long time to etch lines like those.

But he wasn't laughing now. He looked dead serious, and if he was faking, he was good. He looked serious, and he didn't look crazy. But he said something strange.

"You've studied Dodgson's fantasies thoroughly, Doctor. I've read your articles on them. Has it ever occurred to you that—that maybe they aren't fantasies?"

I nodded. "You mean symbolically, of course. Yes, fantasy is often closer to fundamental truth than fact."

"I don't mean that, Doctor. I mean—we think that Charles Dodgson had knowledge of another world and creatures of that world, and had entry into it, somehow. We think—"

The phone rang. Impatiently, I went out into the hall and answered it.

"Bagden speaking," I said.

"This is Evers, Doc. You sober?"

"Why?" I asked.

"You offered to sell me the Courier last week. I've been thinking it over. Seriously."

"I'll talk it over with you tomorrow, Evers," I told him. "Tonight I'm busy. I have a guest, and anyway if I talked to you tonight, I'd be tempted to sell the Courier for fifteen cents."

"And tomorrow?"

"At least twenty cents. Providing you take over the debts. But I can't talk now, honestly. I got to see a man about a Jabberwock."

"You are drunk, Doc."

"Not yet, and you're keeping me from it, 'Night."

I put the receiver back on the hook and went back to the den. I poured two more drinks before I sat down.

"Let's get one thing straight," I said. "Is this a roundabout way of selling me an insurance policy or something?"

"I assure you I have nothing to sell. Nor am I crazy, I hope. If I am, I have company. There are several of us, and we have checked our findings very thoroughly. One of us—" He paused with dramatic effect. "—checked them too thoroughly, without taking proper precautions. That is why there is a vacancy in our small group."

"You mean—what?"

He pulled a wallet from his pocket and from an inner compartment took a newspaper clipping, a short one of about four paragraphs. He handed it to me. I read it, and I recognized the type and the set-up, a clipping from the Bridgeport Argus. And I remembered now having read it, a few days ago. I'd considered clipping it as an exchange item, and then decided not to. The heading read as follows:

Man Slain by Unknown Beast

It had caught my eye and interest. The rest of the article brought matters down to prosaic facts.

A man named Colin Hawks, a recluse, had been found dead along a path through the woods. The man's throat had been torn, and police opinion was that a large and vicious dog had attacked him. But the reporter who wrote the article suggested the possibility that only a wolf or possibly even a lion or panther, escaped from a circus, could have caused the wounds.

I folded the article up again and handed it back to Smith. It didn't mean or prove anything, of course. Anybody could have clipped that article from a newspaper and used it to help substantiate a wild yarn. Undoubtedly somebody's vicious police dog, on the loose, had done the killing.

But something prickled at the back of my neck.

Funny what the word "unknown" and the thought back of it can do to you. If that story had told of a man killed by a dog or by a lion, either one, there's nothing more than ordinarily frightening about it. But if the man who writes the article doesn't know what it was did the killing and calls it an "unknown beast"—well, if you've got imagination, you'll see what I mean.

"You mean this man who was killed was one of your members?" I said.

"Yes. Are you willing to take his place?"

Silly, but there was that darned chill down my spine again. Was I alone here in the house with a madman?

He didn't look mad.

Funny, I thought, here I don't like life particularly. But now suddenly pops up danger, and I'm afraid. Afraid of what? A madman—or a Jabberwock?

And the absurdity of that brought me back to sanity and I wanted to laugh. I didn't, of course. I was host and even if fear of his slitting my throat wouldn't keep me from laughing at a possible madman, then politeness would.

Besides, hadn't I been bored stiff for years? With Carmel City and with myself and with everything in it? Now something screwball was happening and was I going to funk out before I got to first base?

I picked up my glass.

"If I say yes?" I asked.

"There is a meeting tonight, later. We will go to it. There you will learn what we are doing. The results, thus far, of our research."

"Where is the meeting to be held?"

"Near here. I came up from New York to attend it. I have directions to guide me to a house on a road called the Dartown Pike. About six miles out from Carmel City. My car will get us there, or get me there alone, if you do not care to come."

The Dartown Pike, I thought, about six miles out from here.

"You wouldn't by any chance be referring to the Wentworth Place?"

"That's the name. Wentworth. You know it?"

Right then and there, if it hadn't been for the drinks I'd taken, I should have seen that this was all too good to be true. I should have smelled blood.

"We'll have to take candles," I said. "Or flashlights. That house has been empty since I was a kid. We used to call it a haunted house. Would that be why you chose it?"

"Of course, Doctor. You are not afraid to go?"

Afraid to go? Gosh, yes, I was afraid to go.

"Gosh, no," I said.

Chapter 3
Appointment with Death

He took his vorpal sword in hand:
Long time the manxome foe he sought—
So rested he by the Tumtum tree,
And stood awhile in thought.

Perhaps I was a bit more drunk than I thought. I remember how utterly crystal clear my mind was, and that's always a sign. There's nothing more crystal clear than a prism that makes you see around corners.

It was three drinks later. I was interested particularly in the way Smith took those drinks. A little tilt to the glass and it was gone. Like a conjuring trick. He could take a drink of whisky neat with hardly a pause in his talking.

I can't do that, myself. Maybe because I don't really like the taste of whisky.

"Look at the dates," he was saying. "Charles Dodgson published 'Alice in Wonderland' in eighteen sixty-five and 'Through the Looking-Glass' in Seventy-one, six years later. He was only thirty-two or thereabouts when he wrote the Wonderland book, but he was already on the trail of something. You know what he had published previously?"

"I'm afraid I don't remember," I told him.

"In Eighteen Sixty, five years before, he'd written and published 'A Syllabus of Plane Algebraic Geometry' and only a year later his 'Formulae of Plane Trigonometry.' I don't suppose you have ever read them?"

I shook my head. "Math has always been beyond me."

"Then you haven't read his 'Elementary Treatise on Determinants,' either, I suppose. Nor his 'Curiosa Mathematica'? Well, you shall read the latter. It's nontechnical, and most of the clues to the fantasies are contained in it. There are further references in his 'Symbolic Logic,' published in Eighteen Ninety-six, just two years before his death, but they are less direct."

"Now, wait a minute," I said, "if I understand you correctly, your thesis is that Lewis Caroll—I can't seem to think of him as Dodgson—worked out through mathematics and symbolic logic the fact that there is another—uh—plane of existence. A through-the-looking-glass plane of fantasy, a dream plane—is that it?"

"Exactly, Doctor. A dream plane. That is about as near as it can be expressed in our language. Consider dreams. Aren't they the almost-perfect parallel of the Alice adventures? The wool-and-water sequence where everything Alice looks at changes. Remember in the shop, with the sheep knitting, how whenever Alice looked hard at any shelf to make sure what was on it, that shelf was always empty although the others around it were crowded full?"

"'Things flow about so here,' was her comment," I said. "And the sheep asks if she can row and hands her a pair of knitting needles, and they turn into oars in her hands, and she's in a boat."

"Exactly, Doctor. A perfect dream sequence. And the poem Jabberwocky, the high point of the second book in my estimation, is in the very language of dreams. 'Frumious,' 'manxome,' 'tulgey'—words that give you a vague picture, in context, but that you can't put your finger on. Like something you hear in a dream, and understand, but which is meaningless when you awaken."

Between "manxome" and "tulgey" he'd downed his latest drink. I replenished his glass and mine.

"But why postulate the reality of such a world?" I asked him. "I see the parallel, of course. The Jabberwock itself is the epitome of dream-creatures, of nightmare. With eyes of flame, jaws that bite and claws that catch, it whiffles and burbles—Freud and James Joyce, in tandem, couldn't do any better than that. But why isn't a dream a dream? Why talk of getting through to it, except in the sense that we invade that world nightly in our dreams? Why assume it's more real than that?"

"You'll hear evidence of that tonight, Doctor. Mathematical evidence—and, I hope, further actual proof. The calculations are there, the methods, in Curiosa Mathematica. Dodgson was a century ahead of his time, Dr. Bagden. Have you read of the recent experiments with the subconscious of Liebnitz and Winton? They're putting forth feelers in the right direction—the mathematical approach.

"You see, only recently, aside from a rare exception like Dodgson, has science realized the possibility of parallel planes of existence, existences like nested Chinese boxes, one inside the other. With gaps between that consciousness, the mind can bridge in sleep under the influence of drugs. Why do the Chinese use opium except to bridge that gap? If the mind can bridge it, why not the body?"

"Down a rabbit-hole," I suggested. "Or through a looking-glass."

He waved a pudgy hand. "Both symbolic. But both suggestive of formulae you'll find in his Syllabus, formulae that have puzzled mathematicians."

I won't try to repeat the rest of what he told me. Partly, if not mainly, because I don't remember it. It was over my head and sounded like Einstein on a binge.

This must have been partly because I was getting drunker. At times there was a mistiness about the room and the man across the table from me seemed to come closer and then recede, his face to become clear and then to blur. And at times his voice was a blur of sines and cosines.

I gave up trying to follow.

He was a screwball, and so was I, and we were going to a haunted house to meet other screwballs and to try something crazy. I'm not certain whether we were going to try to fish a Bandersnatch out of limbo or to break through a looking-glass veil ourselves and go hunting one in its native element. Among the slithy toves in the wabe.

I didn't care which. It was crazy, of course, but I was having the best time I'd had since the Halloween almost forty years ago when we—but never mind that. It's a sign of old age to reminisce about one's youth, and I'm not old yet.

But part of the mistiness in the room was smoke. I hadn't opened the window and I looked across at it now and wondered if I wanted it opened badly enough to get up and cross the room.

A black square, that window, in the wall of this lighted room. A square of glass against which pressed murder and the monstrous night.

As I watched it, I heard the town clock strike ten times. I reached for my glass and then pulled back my hand. I'd had enough, or too much, already for ten o'clock in the evening.

The window. A black square!

We are not clairvoyant.

Out there in the night a man, a man I knew, lay dead with his skull bashed in and blood and brains mixing with his matted hair. The pistol butt was raised to strike the other man's head.

A third murder was planned, already committed in a warped brain.

Ten o'clock, the hour they would ask an alibi.

"I was with Yehudi," I would say.

Who's Yehudi?

Oh, if murder was ever funny, this set-up was funny. Some day when I'm as drunk again as I was at ten o'clock that evening, I'll be able to laugh at it.

Murder and the monstrous night.

But I merely decided that the smoke was too thick after all, and I got up and opened the window. I could still walk straight.

Men were being murdered, and Smith spoke. "We'll have to leave soon," he said.

"Have another drink," I asked him. "I'm ahead of you. I drank at Smiley's."

He shook his head. "I've got to drive."

I stood at the window and the cool air made me feel a bit less fuzzy. I took in deep draughts of it. Then, because if I left it wide open the room would be too cool when I returned, I pushed it down again to within an inch or two of the sill.

And there was my reflection again. An insignificant little man with graying hair, and glasses, and a necktie badly askew.

I grinned at my reflection. "You blasted fool, you," I thought to myself. "Going out with a madman to hunt Jabberwocks. At your age."

The reflection straightened its necktie, and grinned back. It was probably thinking:

> *"You are old, Father William," the young man said.*
> *"And your hair has become very white.*
> *And yet you incessantly stand on your head.*
> *Do you think, at your age, it is right?"*

Well, maybe it wasn't, but I hadn't stood on my head for a long time and maybe this was the last chance I'd ever have.

Over my shoulder, in the mirror of the window glass, I could see Smith getting to his feet. "Ready to go?" he asked.

I turned around and looked at him, at his bland, round face, at the laughter tracks in the corners of his eyes, at the rotund absurdity of his body.

And an impulse made me walk over and hold out my hand to him and shake his hand when he put it in mine rather wonderingly. We hadn't shaken hands when we'd introduced ourselves on the porch, and something made me do it now.

Just an impulse, but one I'm very glad I followed.

"Mr. Smith, frankly I don't follow or swallow your theory about Lewis Carroll," I said. "I'm going with you, although I don't expect any Jabberwocks. But even so, you've given me the most enjoyable evening I've had in a good many years. I want to thank you for it, in case I forget later. I'm taking the bottle along."

Yes, I'm glad I said that. Often after people are dead, you think of things you'd like to have said to them while you had the chance. For once, I said it in time.

He looked pleased as could be.

"Thanks, Doc," he said, shortening the title into a nickname for the first time. But also, for the first time, his eyes didn't quite meet mine.

We went out to his car, and got in.

It's odd how clearly you remember some things and how vague other things are. I remember that there was a green bulb on the speedometer on the dashboard of that car, and that the gear-shift knob was brightly polished onyx. But I don't remember what make of car it was, nor even whether it was a coupe or a sedan.

I remember directing him across town to the Dartown Pike, but I can't for the life of me recall which of several possible routes we took.

But then we were out of town on the pike, purring along through the night with the yellow headlight beams cutting long spreading swaths through the black dark.

"We've clocked five and a half miles from the town limits," Smith said. "You know the place? Must be almost there."

"Next driveway on your right," I told him.

Gosh, but the place must be old, I thought. It was an old house forty years ago when I was a boy of twelve. It had been empty then. My dad's farm had been a mile closer to town, and Johnny Haskins, who lived on the next farm, and I had explored it several times. In daylight. Johnny had been killed in France in 1917. In daytime, I hope, because he'd always been afraid of the dark. I'd picked up a little of that fear from him, and had kept it for quite a few years after I grew up.

But not any more. Older people never stay afraid. By the time you pass the fifty mark, you've known so many people who are now dead that ghosts, if there were such things, aren't such strangers. You'd find too many friends among them.

"This it?" Smith asked.

"Yes," I said.

Chapter 4
Bottle from Wonderland

And as in uffish thought he stood,
The Jabberwock, with eyes of flame,
Came whiffling through the tulgey wood
And burbled as it came!

We stood in front of the house that had been the bugaboo of my childhood, and it looked just about as it had looked then.

I ran the beam of my flashlight up on the porch, and it seemed that not a board had changed.

Just imagination, of course. It had been lived in for twenty years since then. Colonel Wentworth had bought it in about 1915 and had lived there until he died eight years ago. But during those eight years it had stood empty and again it had gone to rack and ruin.

"The others aren't here yet," Smith said. "But let's go in."

We went up on the creaking porch and found the door was not locked. The beams of our flashlights danced ahead of us down the long dimness of the hallway.

Was someone else really coming here tonight? I wondered. Again that prickle of danger roughed the hair on the back of my neck. Undoubtedly I was a fool to have come here with a man I didn't know. But there was nothing dangerous about Smith, I felt sure. Crackpot he might be, but not a homicidal one.

We turned into a huge living room on the left of the hallway. There was furniture there, white-sheeted. But the sheets were not too dirty nor was there much dust anywhere. Apparently the inside of the place, at least, was being cared for.

Furniture under white muslin has a ghostly look.

I took the bottle out of my pocket and held it out to Smith, but he shook his head silently.

But I took a drink from it. The warm feeling began to drive the cold one from the pit of my stomach.

I didn't dare get sober now, I told myself, or I'd start wondering what I was doing there.

I heard the sound of a car turning in the driveway.

Or so it seemed. For we stood quiet a long time and nothing happened. No footsteps on the porch, no more car-sound. I began to wonder if I'd been mistaken.

Maybe a minute passed, maybe an hour. I took another drink.

Smith had laid his flashlight on top of the bureau, with the switch turned on, pointed diagonally across the room. The furniture made huge black shadows on the wall. He stood in the middle of the room and when he turned to face me the flashlight was full in his face.

He looked a bit scared himself, until he smiled.

"They'll be here soon, I'm sure," he said.

"How many are coming?" For some reason we were both talking softly, almost in whispers.

I was finding it hard, deucedly hard, to keep my eyes in focus on his face. It was an effort to stand up straight, and I took a step backward so I could lean against the wall. Somehow, I didn't want to sit down in one of those sheeted chairs.

I didn't feel any too good, now. I wished I was back home, so I could lie down for a while and let the bed go around in soothing circles.

Smith didn't seem to hear my question about how many were coming. Again I thought the engine of a car was running, but Smith turned and walked to the window, and the sound of his footsteps drowned the noise, if there was any noise.

When he reached the window, he stopped and I heard it again, distinctly. A car, if my ears told me aright, was driving away from the house. Had someone come, and gone? Finally the sound died away.

It didn't make sense, but then what did?

I was tired of listening to nothing and looking at Smith's back. He kept staring at the blank, black pane of window as though he could see out of it. I was sure he couldn't.

For no particular reason, I took another look around the room.

In the shadows of one corner there was a single article of furniture that was not covered by a dust sheet. It was a glass-topped table. A small, round three-legged affair, like a magician's table. There was something on it that I couldn't make out.

I looked away, and then, because something about it haunted me, I looked back. Where had I seen a table like that before? Somewhere.

No, a picture of one. I remembered now.

In the John Tenniel illustrations of Alice in Wonderland, of course. The glass-topped table Alice had found in the hall at the bottom of the rabbit hole. The table on which stood a little bottle with a label tied around the neck.

I walked over and, yes, there were two things on the table, as there should have been. A bottle and a key. The key was a small Yale key, and the bottle was really a vial, about two inches high, just as in the Tenniel picture.

The label, of course, said "DRINK ME." I picked the bottle up and looked at it unbelievingly, and I became aware that Smith was standing at my elbow. He must have heard me walking across the room and left the window.

He reached out, took the bottle from my hand and looked at it. He nodded.

"They've been here, then," he said.

"Who? You mean this—the table and the key and all—is part of—uh—what we came here for?"

He nodded again. "They brought this, and left it."

He loosened the cork in the bottle as he spoke.

"I'm sorry, Doc," he said. "I can't let you have the honor. But you're not really a member yet and—well—I am!"

He put the bottle to his lips and drank it off with the same quick motion he'd used in polishing off the whiskeys I'd given him back in my room.

Don't ask me what I expected to happen. Whether I expected him to shut up like a telescope and shrink to about ten inches high, just the right height to go through the little door into the garden, I can't say. Only, like Alice, he'd neglected to take the key off the table first.

I don't know what I expected to happen. But nothing happened. He put the bottle back down on the table and went right on with what he'd been saying.

"When you have met the others and have been accepted, you may, if you wish, try out our—"

And then he died.

What the poison was, I don't know, but its action was sudden despite the fact that it had not paralyzed his lips or mouth. He died before he even started to fall. I could tell it by the sudden utter blankness of his face.

The thud of his fall actually shook the floor.

I bent over and shoved my hand inside his coat and shirt and his heart wasn't beating. I waited a while to be sure.

I stood up again, and my knees were wobbly.

If he'd tried to poison me! But he hadn't. He drunk it himself, and his death had been murder and not suicide. Nobody, no matter how mad he might be, would ever commit suicide in the offhand manner in which he'd tossed off the contents of that bottle.

The empty bottle had jarred off the table and was lying on the floor beside him and my eyes went from it back to the glass table and the key. I picked the key up and looked at it.

It was a false note, that key. It should have been a gold key, and small as it was, it should have been smaller. And not a Yale key. But maybe it opened something. What good is a key without a lock? I stuck it absently into my pocket and looked down again at Smith.

He was still dead.

And it was then that I got scared and ran. I'd seen dead men before, plenty of them, and it wasn't Smith I was afraid of.

It was the utter complete screwiness of everything that had been happening this mad night.

That, and the fact that I was alone. In a haunted house, too! Like all cynics who don't believe in haunted houses, I have a good deal of respect for them.

I stumbled and fell in the darkness of the hallway, and then remembered the flashlight in my hip pocket, and put it into action. I got out the door and off the porch before I even wondered where I was going, or why.

The police, of course. I'd have to get word to Sheriff Pete Lane as soon as I possibly could. I considered knocking someone awake in a nearby farmhouse and telephoning, but it would be quicker, in the long run, to take Smith's car and drive the six miles back to town. I could do that in fifteen minutes and it might take twice that long to find a telephone.

Beyond this, beyond notifying the sheriff, I wasn't thinking yet.

I had a hunch that if I thought about what had happened and tried to figure out what it all meant and why that "DRINK ME" bottle had been poison, I'd have gone off my rocker.

The less thinking I did before I talked to Pete Lane, the better off I'd be.

So I flashlighted my way around the corner of the house to where we'd left the car, and I got another jolt.

The car was there, or a car was there. But it was my own car, not the one Smith had driven me out in. My own Plymouth coupe, which up to that afternoon, had been out in my garage on blocks, with the air let out of the tires. There'd been only a few miles left in those tires anyway and I'd decided to save those few miles for something important, if anything important ever came up.

Well, something important had come up, and here was my car. There was air in the tires, too. And gas in the tank, probably, unless somebody had towed it there.

I walked around it warily, almost expecting to see it vanish in a puff of smoke or to find the March Hare or the Mock Turtle seated behind the steering wheel. Those drinks were still with me.

But there wasn't anyone behind the steering wheel, and I got in. I flicked on the dashboard lights and looked at the gas gauge, and there were three gallons in the tank.

Could I have been driven here in my own car without realizing it? No, I remembered that onyx gear-shift knob, and the green light on the dashboard of the other car. And the instrument panel had been different. I was sure of that.

I took a deep breath and started the engine. It purred smoothly, and I eased the coupe out to the road and aimed it south for town.

I think I might have driven wide open if it hadn't been my own car. But the familiar feel of it sobered me a little more and that was just enough to realize how drunk I still was. The road ahead seemed like a weaving ribbon at times. And one of those tires might give way any minute.

I parked in front of the courthouse, and there was still a light on in the sheriff's office.

I started in, but stopped in the doorway long enough to take another drink. This wasn't going to be easy.

Pete Lane was talking on the telephone when I went into his office.

"You're blamed right, we're trying," he said into the mouthpiece. "I got two of my own men on it, and I've just notified the state police. Huh? No, we ain't told anybody else yet. No use doing that till we find 'em."

He hung up the receiver and looked at me. He looked angry and harassed. "What the devil do you want, Doc?" he said.

"I got to report a murder," I said. I closed the door and leaned against it. Then I was catapulted nearly off my feet and onto the sheriff's desk as the door opened violently from the outside. Harry Bates came in. He had his clothes on over his pajamas, for the bottoms of them showed below his trouser cuffs. His shoes weren't tied.

"Walter just phoned from Burlington," Bates said. "Your line was busy so I took it on the switchboard. He didn't find much."

Pete interrupted him. "Just a minute, Harry. What's this about a murder, Doc?"

"Out at the old Wentworth place on the road to Burlington. There's a man dead there."

"Is it Jones?"

"Jones?" The name didn't register with me. "No. His name was Smith, not Jones. Or that's what he told me. His first name was a funny one."

I didn't quite dare. There was the card Smith had given me, in my pocket. I handed it to Pete.

He looked at it and let out a howl.

"Yehudi?" he yelled. "Doc, if this is a rib, I'm going to smack you."

I sat down on the corner of the desk because I felt safer sitting down.

"It's no rib, darn it," I told him. "He got me out there with him, and then he took poison out of a bottle that we found."

Pete wasn't even listening to me. He was staring at the card I'd handed him. Suddenly he looked up.

"Doc, what's your bug number?" he asked me.

"My bug number?" For an awful instant I thought he was crazy too. Then I remembered that some people call the union label—that tiny device which, with the number of the shop, must appear on every job printed in a union print shop—the "bug."

"Seventeen," I told him, and he cursed.

"Doc, you printed this yourself," he said. He cursed again. "Yehudi! Doc, if you weren't drunk, I'd ram your teeth down your throat for barging in here like this. We got trouble, and I mean trouble.

Barnaby Jones started for Burlington with his payroll, taking Miles Harrison along, three hours ago, and didn't show up there. Three hours, and it's only twenty miles. Get the devil out of here."

I didn't move.

"Pete, sure I'm drunk," I said. "But blast your hide, you've known me all your life, and would I pull a gag about something like this? I tell you there's a dead man at the Wentworth place. I went there with him. I'd never seen him before tonight."

"What'd you go there for?"

Although the incredulity had left his voice, I knew it wasn't the time to say why we went there. I could imagine his face if I told him a tenth of it.

"That's not important, now," I said. "Man, this is a murder. Come out there with me and I'll show you the body."

"Just a minute, Doc. Harry, is Walter still on the line?"

"He's waiting for us to call him back with instructions. Here's the number." He put a slip of paper on Pete's desk.

"Walter's got to drive past the Wentworth house anyway. I'll have him look in. What room?"

"Living room," I said. "Middle room on the north side, downstairs. He'll find a body on the floor, and he'll find a glass table, and a bottle lying by the body, with a label."

But I stopped just in time. Whew! Pete Lane picked up the phone and asked for Burlington.

Chapter 5
Head on a Platter

> *One, two! One, two! And through and through*
> *The vorpal blade went snicker-snack!*
> *He left it dead, and with its head*
> *He went galumphing back.*

No, I didn't feel good. In fact, I felt goofy.

But I sat in a chair back in the corner of Pete's office, with Pete barking orders to half a dozen people, in person and over the phone, and I felt glad that he was paying no attention to me.

He was holding my case in abeyance as being less important than the disappearance of Barnaby Jones and Miles Harrison. Maybe he had it down as a figment of my drunken imagination.

I kept wishing that he was right, but I knew better.

As soon as he got the report from Walter that the body was really there, he'd swarm all over me with questions. But I was only too glad to wait because then—with a body in hand, so to speak—the answers I'd have to give him would sound a lot more plausible.

The office was taking on a fuzzy look, and my tongue was starting to feel like an angora kitten. It was easier to keep my eyes shut than try to make them see straight. All I really wanted was to get this over with, go home and slide into bed.

But I heard Pete walking out of the office and opened my eyes and stood up. There was one thing I felt curious about and now was the time to find out. I walked over to his desk and picked up the Yehudi Smith calling card. I held it close to my eyes, and—yes, there was the little union label in the corner and the number seventeen under it. Either it had been printed in my own shop, or someone had gone to a little trouble to make it seem that it had. The type was ten-point Garamond. I had Garamond in stock.

I was putting the card down thoughtfully when Pete came back and saw me.

"What's the idea of that card?" he asked.

"I was just wondering," I told him. "I didn't print it, and Jerry Klosterman didn't either, or I'd have seen the order for it. I'd remember a name like that."

He laughed without humor. "Who wouldn't. Listen, Doc. I've done everything I can do at the moment about the Jones and Harrison business. The search is organized, and we'll find them. But until then— well, let's get back to this Wentworth place business. You say a man you don't know took you out there?"

I nodded.

"Anyone see him with you? What I mean is—can you prove it?"

"No, Pete. You'll have to take my word for it. That and the fact that he's still out there, dead."

"We'll skip that till I get the report. This card?" He looked at it and scowled. "Any other souvenirs?"

I shook my head, and then remembered.

"This," I said, and took the key from my pocket and handed it to him. Again, somehow, it looked familiar. But all Yale keys look alike. Still, the minute I'd given it to him, I wished I hadn't. It would probably turn out to open something at the Courier office. It might be as phony as that calling card.

"He gave you this key?" Pete asked.

"No, not exactly. I found it at the Wentworth house, but it may not be important."

Walter Hanswert came in without knocking. Walter is the man who does most of the work for the sheriff's office, but Pete Lane has the job and draws the pay. You'll find some hardworking horse like Walter back of every politically-elected sheriff, or else the mechanism of law and order goes to pot.

"Anything?" Pete said.

"Not a lead, Pete. I drove slow all the way back from Burlington, looking for any place a car might have skidded off the road or any sign of something to help us. No dice."

"How about the Wentworth house, Walter?"

"I stopped there. Not a thing. I went through it fast, from attic to cellar."

Maybe you stop being surprised after a while. This didn't really jar me.

"Walter, were you in the living room?" I said. "Didn't you find a glass table and a bottle on the floor?"

"Nope. That's the room Pete said to search. I even looked under all the dust covers. Couple of tables there, cloth-covered, but neither of them glass, and no bottle. Front door of the house was open."

"I left it open, I guess," I said.

My knees were getting that way again. I didn't want to argue, but I had to.

"Cuss it, Pete!" I cried. "There was a body there. Somebody took it away. Heaven knows why. Heaven knows what any of this is all about, but I didn't imagine they'd clean up things so quick."

He put a gentle hand on my shoulder. "Doc, Walter will drive you home. Sleep it off."

The word "sleep" got me. Oh, I knew quite well that I wasn't going to sleep off what had happened. But I could, and wanted to, sleep off this fuzziness. Tomorrow, in the clear light of day, maybe I could add things up and make sense out of them.

A few hours' sleep, I told myself, just two or three hours, and everything might look different.

"Okay, Pete," I said. "Perhaps you're right."

"Got your car here?"

"In front." I should have left it go at that, but my tongue was loose. "We took Smith's car out to the Wentworth's place, but mine was out there after he was killed. I don't know how that happened."

"Just a minute," said Pete. His face looked different. "Your car's really downstairs? I thought you had it blocked up? You had it out tonight?"

"Yes and no, Pete. I didn't take it out of the garage but it's out just the same."

"It's in front," Walter said. "I saw it."

Pete Lane looked at his assistant, and then back at me. "And you had it out on the Dartown Pike tonight, Doc?"

"I told you that," I said impatiently. I didn't know what he was getting at, but I didn't like the way he was doing it.

"Doc, you never liked Barnaby Jones, did you?"

"Barnaby?" I was surprised. "He's a stuffed shirt and a miser and a prig. No, I don't like him. Why?"

He didn't answer. He leaned back against the desk and stared into the far corner of the room, with his lips pursed as though he was whistling, but no sound coming out of them.

When he spoke, he didn't look at me this time. And his voice was soft. Almost soothing.

"Doc, we're going to take a look at that car of yours," he said. "You can wait up. No, you come along with us, and then I'll drive you home."

I didn't get the idea, but I didn't care particularly. Just so I got home, and the sooner the better.

We went outside, Pete, Walter and I, and I noticed that they worked it so I walked between them.

My car was parked right outside the door, and the sheriff's car, which Walter had used to drive to Burlington and back, was in front of it. An open roadster with the top down.

Pete opened the door of my coupe and looked in. He pulled a flashlight out of his pocket and flashed it around inside, and looked carefully at the seat cushions and the floorboards. He looked carefully, but didn't seem to find anything.

He fished through an assortment of junk in the glove compartment, and then reached into the door pocket. His face changed and he pulled his hand out slowly with a revolver in it. He held it by the cylinder, between his thumb and forefinger, just the way he'd first got hold of it.

"This yours, Doc?"

"No," I said.

He looked at me, hard, for a second or two and then sniffed at the end of the muzzle.

"Either hasn't been fired," he said, "or it's been cleaned." He was talking to Walter, not to me. "Let's look further."

He turned the gun over and held the lens of his flashlight close to the end of the butt. Even from where I stood back on the sidewalk I could see there was a smear there. A smear that might have been blood.

Pete Lane took a clean handkerchief from his pocket. It was folded and he shook it open and put it down on the running board of the coupe and laid the pistol gently on top of it.

"Where's the key to the rumble, Doc?" Pete asked me. "I'm afraid we'll have to look in there."

I shook my head. "Haven't got it. With me, I mean. When I blocked up the car, I took the keys off my ring and left them in the drawer of my desk. The one at home."

He turned and looked back in the car, aiming his flashlight at the instrument panel. The ignition key was in the lock there, but there were no other keys with it.

"That one isn't in your desk at home," said Pete. He walked around to the back of the car and stared at the lock in the handle of the rumble seat.

He looked at it a minute, then reached into his pocket and took out a key. The key I'd handed him. The key that had been on the glass table beside the "DRINK ME" bottle. The key that should have been the key to the little door into the garden where Alice had found the Two, Seven and Five of Hearts painting white roses red so the Queen wouldn't order their heads chopped off.

Pete put the key into the lock of the rumble seat and it fitted, and turned. He lifted the lid.

From where I stood, all I could see was a small brown leather grip, but I recognized it. It was the grip that Barnaby Jones used to carry the payroll money in, from Carmel City to Burlington.

But the grip wasn't resting on the seat. It was resting on something that was lying on the seat or it wouldn't have stuck up that way. I heard the hissing sound of Pete Lane sucking in his breath, and Walter Han-swert took a quick step to look down into the rumble seat, too.

I didn't. I didn't have to be sober to guess what was in there, and I'd already seen one murdered man tonight.

Somebody had done a beautiful job of something. I'd come galumphing back from my date with a Jabberwock carrying, not its head, but my own, on a silver platter to the police.

And shades of Old Henderson, what a story I had to go with the bodies of Barnaby Jones and Miles Harrison! A story based on a little man named Yehudi—the little man who wasn't there! Yehudi whom no one but myself had ever seen. I'd given the sheriff my two souvenirs of the evening and one had been printed in my own shop and the other was the key to my own car and the incriminating evidence in it.

I don't know whether I was suddenly very drunk or very sober to do what I did. But like a flash of lightning I had a picture of myself in court or an alienist's office telling him about a glass-topped table and a bottle labeled "DRINK ME" and the death of Yehudi the vanishing corpse.

I lunged for the running board of my coupe and got the pistol Pete had left there and forgotten for the moment in the excitement of his find in the rumble seat.

Pete yelled at Walter and Walter dived for me, but too late. I had straightened up with the pistol in my hand before he got within grabbing distance and he stepped back.

"Now, Doc," said Pete, in a wheedling voice, as one would use to a child. But there was fear in his eyes, plenty of it, although Walter's a brave man. He thought he was facing a homicidal maniac.

I didn't try to disillusion him. I didn't even have my finger inside the trigger guard. If he'd reached out and grasped the gun, I'd have let him take it.

"Step out from behind there, Pete," I said. "Both of you back into the courthouse."

I groped behind me and took the ignition key out of my own car and pocketed it. I wasn't going to take that car, with its ghastly burden. But I didn't want them to use it either.

I moved toward the sheriff's car while they sidled cautiously across the sidewalk toward the courthouse. I was gambling that Walter hadn't bothered to take the keys out when he'd come upstairs to report. And I was right.

They stepped through the doorway and the instant they were out of sight I heard running footsteps. Pete was sprinting for his office for his own gun, if I guessed correctly, and Walter would be taking the switchboard to block all the roads out of town.

That was all right by me. I wasn't going out of town. I put the murder gun down on the curb—I didn't want it any more than I wanted my own car—and got in Pete's car and drove off.

Chapter 6
Hidden Foe

"And hast thou slain the Jabberwock?
Come to my arms, my beamish boy!
O frabjous day! Callooh! Callay!"
He chortled in his joy.

Swinging around the corner, I gunned the engine to get up speed, and then shut it off. On momentum, I swung it into the alley back of the courthouse and let it coast to a stop.

Looking up, I could see the lighted window of Pete's room, and could imagine the frantic telephoning going on right now to stop and hold a car that would stand, probably unnoticed, for the rest of the night, right under his window.

I got out quietly by stepping over the door instead of opening it, and walked up the alley, going on tiptoe until I was out of earshot of the courthouse.

They'd be looking for me, I knew, at the outskirts of town, not in the middle of it. The place I had in mind ought to be safe for a couple of hours, at least. And I didn't care, beyond that. I wasn't making a get-away. I just wanted a chance to do a few chores and think out a few things before I gave myself up. Gave myself up, that is, unless I could work out my plans.

I went along the alley two blocks and turned in at the back door of Smiley's. Pete and his men, I felt sure, would be too busy to do any drinking for a while.

"Hi, Doc," Smiley said. "Thought you'd be asleep long ago." He laughed his meaningless laugh.

"Old Henderson, double," I said. "I've been asleep ever since I left here, Smiley. Maybe I can wake up. Leave that bottle on the bar."

There was a pinochle game in the back corner. Outside of that I had the place to myself.

I downed the double Henderson and felt a little better. I gave it time to get home and took another. There's a second-wind stage of inebriation, and hitting that was my only chance to get my mind hitting on six cylinders. Sobriety's good for thinking, too, but I hadn't a chance of getting sober for hours yet. The other way was quicker.

I looked at the calendar a while, but that didn't help. Things went in dizzying circles inside my head. Who's Yehudi? Where is what's left of him? Why did he drink the "DRINK ME"? Was he really expecting other members of some nitwit organization to show up there?

Had he been kidding me, or was he being kidded?

Jabberwocks. Glass tables with "DRINK ME" bottles and keys that should have been gold and led into a garden, but which were Yale and led into the nuthouse by way of a rumble seat. And of all names, Yehudi Smith!

Oh, it would have been funny, it would have been a wow of a practical joke, if there hadn't been three corpses cluttering up the scenery, and the fact that this meant the end of my freedom, whether I ended up in a bughouse or a hoosegow. Or at the end of a rope.

No, looking at the calendar didn't help.

"Give me a deck, Smiley," I said.

I took another drink while he got it, and deliberately I didn't think at all while I counted out the stacks for solitaire. Then, as I started the game, I let go. I mean, I didn't try to think, but I didn't try not to. I just relaxed.

Red queen on a black king. Wasn't the Red Queen the one who met Alice in the second square, and told her about the six squares she'd have to go through before she could be a queen herself?

And a black jack for the red queen.

But that was a red chess queen, not a card queen. The one who ran so fast. "A slow sort of country," she'd told Alice. "Now here, you see, it takes all the running you can do to keep in the same place."

An ace up on top, and then I took another drink before I put the red six on the black seven. The cards looked different now—sharp of outline, crystal clear.

Like my mind felt. Ten on the jack.

Yehudi had been a pawn. A sucker, like me. Somebody had moved him. Somebody had hired him to come there and pull a razzle-dazzle on me. To give me a story that nobody'd believe in ten lifetimes, a story whose only proof was a card some friend of mine had printed in my own shop. Yehudi had been made as incredible as possible, from Christian name to "DRINK ME."

There was only one answer to Yehudi. A character actor at liberty, probably hired in New York and brought here for the purpose of framing me. And he framed himself. Given a set of instructions for the evening that included the planted drink-me bottle, and went beyond it, because he hadn't been told what was in that bottle.

So Yehudi wasn't in on the real play. Somebody had hired Yehudi to play what he thought was an elaborate practical joke.

Nine on the ten, and bring up a deuce for my ace on top.

Somebody who knew me intimately, and who knew how I felt Thursday evenings and my predilection for Lewis Carroll and nonsense in general, and that I'd be sure to fall for a gag like Yehudi's. Someone who came to see me at the print shop and at home, once in a while, at least. Maybe to play chess with me?

Anyway, there was the other red queen.

"How you coming?" Smiley asked.

"I'm in the fifth square," I told him. "I crossed the third by railroad, with the Gnat. And I think I just crossed the brook into the fifth."

"Squares? There ain't any squares in solitaire."

"Cards are rectangles," I said. "And what's a square but a rectangle somebody sat on? You're a swell guy, Smiley, but shut up."

He laughed and moved off down the bar.

I took another drink, but just a short one. The edges of the cards and the outlines of the pips on them were very sharp and clear now. No fuzziness, no mussiness.

Another ace for the top row.

Because, if the money was still in that bag that was planted in my car, there was only one person who benefited by what had happened tonight. The man who'd inherit Barnaby Jones' factory and his fortune. The one man who'd need a scapegoat, because of his a priori motive.

That was the sixth brook. I had a hunch I was entering the seventh square now. But I took a look back to be sure.

Alvin Carey would inherit his uncle's fortune. Al knew me pretty well. We played chess, and somebody who played chess had engineered the set-up tonight. Al Carey knew my screwy literary tastes, and my Thursday night habits. He'd dropped in here, in Smiley's, early. And that would have been to check up that I was running true to form.

Al Carey had enough money to have hired a character actor to lead me to the slaughter. Al Carey was smart enough to have made a dupe of the actor instead of an accomplice who could blackmail him afterwards.

Al Carey had everything.

Al Carey had me in a cleft stick. He'd finagled me into a situation so utterly preposterous that the more of the truth I told, the crazier I'd look. Nuttier than peanut brittle I'd look.

"Smiley," I said. "Come here. I want to ask you something."

He moved along the bar toward me, and grinned. He always acted that way when he was puzzled.

"One more brook to cross," I told him. "But it's wider than the Mississippi. What good does it do to know something if you can't prove it?"

"Well," he said, "what good does it do you if you can prove it?"

"Smiley," I said, "I reach the king-row, and I'm crowned. But this side of that last brook, I'm still a pawn, in pawn. What do you know about Alvin Carey?"

"Huh? He's a crackpot like you, Doc, but I don't like him. I think he's a sneak. But he's smart."

"Smiley," I said, "you surprise me. And for once I mean what I say. Some day I'll write an editorial about you, if I ever get a chance to write another editorial. What else do you know about Alvin, to his detriment? To his disadvantage, I mean."

"Well, he's yellow."

"I'm not sure of that," I said. "The draft board turned him down, if that's what you mean. Something about a trick knee. And—well, I know one stunt he pulled recently that took a lot of cool nerve."

"But don't you remember the time last year when a little chimney fire broke out at his place?" said Smiley, quickly. "A little smoke, that's all. But he ran out in his pajamas without waking anybody else up to tell 'em. He didn't stop till he reached the fire station, because he was too excited and scared to think there was a thing as a telephone."

"Smiley," I answered, "I bow before you. It's an outside chance. Pete's got his hands full right now, and is working like a Trojan to find somebody. Probably he hasn't called Alvin Carey yet. Shut up, sage, and let me think fast."

I closed my eyes and opened them again.

"I need three things, and I need them quick," I said. "I need a gun, and I need a candle stub, and I need a bottle of some kind of a cleaning fluid that smells like gasoline but is non-inflammable."

"Carbozol. I got a bottle of it, sure. And a candle, because once in a while the lights here go on the blink. But no gun."

"Smiley, this is in a desperate hurry, and I can't explain," I said. "But take a plain pint bottle, no label, and fill it with Carbozol for me. And get me a candle. Cut it off short, to half an inch or so. A quarter of an inch, if you can cut it that fine. And have you got anything that looks like a gun?"

For a moment Smiley rubbed his chin thoughtfully. Then he grinned.

"I got an old thirty-two pistol I took away from a drunk in here one night when he got waving it around. But there ain't no bullets. I had the firing pin filed off so I could give it to my kid."

"That's the gun I want," I told him. "Quick, Smiley, get it and the other things for me. And I'll let you finish this game of solitaire for me. And it's going to play out, too."

I sat back in the chair and waited for him to return.

And then, with the stuff he gave me safely stowed in my pockets, I went out the back door and cut through alleys as fast as I could travel without getting out of breath. Pretty soon I got there.

There wasn't any lights on, which was a good sign. It meant that maybe Pete Lane hadn't got around yet to notifying the nearest of kin. If I knew Pete, he'd try to get me first, so he'd have crime and criminal all in the same report and make a good impression on Carey. For, as Barnaby's heir, Al was going to be the richest guy in town. Unless my wild idea worked.

It was a warm evening and some of the downstairs windows were open, and that was good, too. The screens were put on with turnbolts from the outside and I took one off without making any noise.

I got inside, and I was quiet about it. I didn't kid myself that Al Carey might be asleep after the night's work he'd done. But he'd be in bed, playing possum, waiting for a telephone call.

Inside the window, I took off my shoes and left them. I sneaked into the hallway and up the stairs. Outside Al's door, which was an inch ajar, I took a deep breath.

Then I stepped inside and flicked on the light switch. I had the gun ready in my hand and I pointed it at Al Carey.

"Be quiet," I warned him.

The flick of the light switch had brought him bolt upright in bed. He was in pajamas, all right, and his hair was tousled. But his eyes showed he hadn't been asleep.

I didn't give him a chance to think it over. I walked right up to the edge of the bed, keeping that broken pistol aimed smack between his eyes, and then before he could guess what I was going to do, I raised it and brought the butt down on top of his head.

Chapter 7
Test by Fire

Twas brillig, and the slithy toves
Did gyre and gimble in the wabe:
All mimsy were the borogoves,
And the mome raths outgrabe.

That was the trickiest thing I had to do—to gauge that blow just right. I'd never hit a man over the head before.

And if this stunt I had in mind was going to work, it all depended on conking him out, not for too long, and without killing him. Just long enough for me to tie him up, because I couldn't have done that and held the gun on him at the same time.

If the blow killed him it wouldn't have hurt my conscience too much. Miles Harrison had been a nice guy. So had Yehudi Smith, whatever his real name was. But if the blow killed Carey, well, there'd be one more evidence of my homicidal mania for the police.

Al went out like a light, but his heart was still beating. And I worked fast at tying him. I used everything I could find, bathrobe cords, belts, neckties—he had almost a hundred of them—and I tore one sheet into strips.

He was swathed like a mummy when I got through, tied with his head and shoulders braced up against the head of the bed so he could see the bed itself. And a handkerchief inside his mouth held in by a scarf around the outside made a good gag. I used the strips of sheeting to tie him so he couldn't roll off the bed.

But I left his right arm free from the elbow down.

Then I slapped his face until his eyes opened. They looked groggy, at first, so I wet a washrag in the bathroom and sloshed him a few times with that. When he tried to get loose, I knew he knew what was going on.

I grinned at him. "Hello, Al," I said.

I took the pint bottle of non-inflammable cleaning fluid out of my pocket and took out the cork. Smiley had given me the right stuff.

It smelled like gasoline, all right.

I poured it over Al and over the bed, all around him.

Then, down by his knees, on a spot where the mattress was pretty wet with it, I put the half-inch stub of candle. I struck a match and held it to the wick.

"Better stop struggling, Al," I said. "You'll knock this over."

He stopped, all right. He lay as still as though he were dead, and his horrified eyes stared at that burning wick. Stared at it with the terrible fear of a pyrophobiac. For that's what Smiley's story of Al Carey and the chimney fire had reminded me of. Al had an abnormal, psychopathic fear of fire.

I took out of my pocket the notebook I always carry, and a stub of pencil, and put them down within reach of his free right hand.

"Any time you want to write, Al," I told him. Turning my back on him, I walked over to the window. I waited a minute and then looked back. I had to avoid looking at his eyes.

"It'll burn down in ten minutes," I said. "You'll just about have time if you start writing. I want it in full, the main details, anyway, addressed to Pete Lane. And tell him where to find the body you hid or buried. The actor. Tell him where to look for the glass-topped table, and the bottle that had the poison in it. You'll have to write fast. If you finish in time, I'll pick up the candle."

I said it calmly, as though it didn't matter.

Then I turned away again. Only seconds later, I heard the scratch of the pencil. . . .

It was nine o'clock when Jerry and I finished remaking the paper. We'd had to rip it wide open to make room. For three murders in one evening was the biggest thing that had ever happened in Carmel City.

It rushed us more than we had been rushed in years, but we didn't mind that. Nor the extra trouble. Hot news never seems like work.

The phone rang, and I answered it, and it was Jay Evers.

Jerry was staring at me in utter amazement when I put the receiver back after I finished talking.

"Who the devil were you talking to like that?" he asked me.

"Evers," I told him. "He wanted to buy the Courier, and I said no."

"But couldn't you have said no without that embroidery on it? Why insult him like you did? He'll never speak to you again."

"That was the idea," I told him. I grinned cheerfully. "Look, Jerry, if I didn't insult him, he might ask me again tomorrow."

"But what's that got to do with what you're telling me?"

"And tomorrow, Jerry, I'm going to have the ancestor of all hangovers, and I'd sell the paper to him, and I don't want to sell it. I like the Courier, I like Carmel City. And I enjoy being free and not in the booby-hatch and the hoosegow. So let the presses roll!"

"Doc, you better sit down before you fall down!"

But he was too late. Seconds too late.

Donald Olson can take ordinary people in an ordinary situation and turn it into a nightmare that will forever change the characters' lives. A frequent contributor to Ellery Queen's Mystery Magazine, *he displays his skill at ratcheting tension to almost unbearable levels in "The Stone House."*

The Stone House

Donald Olson

We've decided on a trial separation," Robert would tell their friends, and then laugh at their astonishment. "No, no, not *us*. A separation *of* us—from the city." A move designed, as he put it, to restore him to sanity—which of course no one took seriously, Robert being a socially well-adjusted and perfectly sane young man, so far as one can apply such terms to any dedicated artist deeply committed to his work.

What he really meant was that by escaping from the city he hoped to achieve a freshness of vision, to rediscover the indefinable something he'd lost. Although his last two shows had not been flops exactly, neither had they done anything to advance his reputation; he began to fear his powers were waning.

His wife Nicole, on the other hand, remained at first openly dubious, feeling that Robert might be using the city and its climate of violence as a scapegoat for his own personal misgivings. For years the city had been the source and subject of his inspiration, and she failed to see how moving to the country could restore his faith in himself as an artist.

Gauguin, she argued, might have been an even greater artist if he'd never gone to the South Seas; Van Gogh might have lived to a productive old age had he not fled Paris for the sunny fields of Arles. "How can a change of scene make you a better painter?" she asked Robert.

"All I know, darling, is that the very atmosphere of the city is starting to cloud the way I *see* things. It's distorting my vision."

A specious argument, thought Nicole, while being forced to admit that Robert's increasingly dark moods of cynicism were starting to erode what at least on the surface had been a life of domestic harmony.

She'd begun to fear that their marriage itself was revealing tears in its fabric which she'd hoped time alone together could mend.

For Robert, the rape and murder of a young coed by a gang of hooligans in the alley below their apartment was the deciding factor.

"That does it," he declared. "I'm going to tell Ernie we're accepting his offer."

The offer was for a summer's loan of a small country place upstate which would be vacant while their friend was in Europe for three months.

"Darling, it's not as if we're buying the place," Robert said. "If it turns out to be a mistake, I'll be the first to admit it."

"What about the shop?" Nicole was the co-owner of a small antiques shop in the City.

"We've been through all that. Summers are slow. Pauline can handle the shop. Think what fun you can have nosing out treasures in the country."

The farmhouse outside the village of Scandia came as a delightful surprise to Nicole, who hadn't trusted friend Ernie's description of its charms. The living room had a fieldstone fireplace and windows offering a superb view of the foothills; kitchen and bath had been updated, and most of the furniture was of that vintage oak recently much sought after by the antiques trade. Robert turned the north-facing sun porch into a studio and in only a few days Nicole was pleased to observe a change, a lightness and buoyancy, in his mood. The peaceful solitude seemed to produce an effect like that of a powerful antidote upon a chronic infection of the spirits.

They made love for the first time in weeks.

"I knew it would be like this," Robert declared happily, holding Nicole in his arms. "Didn't I tell you, darling? Isn't it wonderful being able to go to bed without even locking the doors?"

"And waking up to the sound of birds instead of sirens?"

"The way I feel now I don't ever want to go back," he said. "I think if I went back . . . I don't even *want* to think about it."

"You won't get bored with only me for company?"

"Don't be silly. And we can have our friends up for weekends, but not yet. Not till I've begun doing some really good work."

"Blissfully peaceful, isn't it? As if nothing bad could ever happen out here."

"It's because people out here know how to live in peace, with themselves and each other."

They'd been there a week when Robert burst into the house from one of his sketching trips about the countryside. "Darling, you must come with me tomorrow. I've found the ideal subject for my first canvas. There's this old stone house—it has to be eighteenth century—set in a grove of cedar trees at the foot of a long slope. Pure Wyeth. You'd love it."

"Great. I'll bring a picnic lunch."

"And pick wildflowers. That's how I see it, with this field full of buttercups in the foreground and the pale blue hills beyond."

Such enthusiasm reminded Nicole of the old Robert, and with a light heart she packed their lunch next morning. Robert hummed joyfully beside her as they drove along the dusty road that wound to the top of a high ridge where they parked. The sun was already halfway up the sky and a gentle breeze tempered the heat of the day. They walked through the trees to the edge of the slope, where Robert set up his easel in the shade of a massive oak behind a low screen of hawthorn.

"Look down there," he said. "Lovely, isn't it?"

The house at the foot of the slope was quite as charming as Robert had promised, weathered brick and a slate roof, with a white-painted clapboard extension obviously of later date. Nor did the somewhat dilapidated outbuildings detract from its appeal.

"But Robert, you said it was abandoned. It can't be, there's washing on the line."

"It looked abandoned yesterday. I didn't see a soul. Check out that old Ford. There's an antique for you."

"No one can see us, can they?"

"Not way up here in the shade. No matter if they did."

"I doubt country folk welcome trespassers any more than us city critturs."

"Look at that old well in the yard. Must be as old as the house."

"I wonder what the house is like inside. I'd love to see it."

"Maybe we could drop in later."

Nicole settled down on the grass. It was cool under the oak tree and the scent of grass and flowers delighted her. It was a scene, on that warm summer day, to gladden the heart of any refugee from the stress and clamor of the city and she loved Robert for wanting to share it with her. It seemed ages since they'd really shared anything.

Robert had worked for only a few minutes when the first sign of life appeared in the scene below them. The door of the house opened and a man came out, stood for a moment looking around him, and then moved off toward the somewhat tipsy barn. Even from atop the slope Nicole could see that he was tall and broadly built, with thick dark hair; in fact, from this distance he looked a lot like Robert, even to the jeans and plaid shirt he wore.

"A man of the soil," Robert murmured. "I envy him. I envy the life he must enjoy down there. I'll bet he doesn't know the meaning of the word stress."

Nicole teased him with a laugh. "Sounds like we're recapturing our romantic vision of life."

Presently the man came out of the barn with a coiled length of rope over his shoulder. Dropping it near the well, he disappeared back inside the barn. Moments later a woman came out of the house carrying a wicker laundry basket. Nicole sat up to watch her as she began taking the washing off the line, folding each sheet and garment and placing it in the basket. She too wore jeans and what might have been a man's white shirt. The sun shone on her long blond hair. Suddenly a big ginger cat streaked across the yard and jumped into the basket. The woman plucked him out, nuzzling him against her cheek.

Nicole was touched for an instant by that same sense of envy Robert had voiced. There was something idyllic about the scene, a glimpse into another world, a simpler, cleaner, gentler world, immune from the anxieties and endless harassing complexities of city life. A line of poetry drifted across her mind: *For thus I live remote from evil-speaking; rancor, never sought, comes to me not. . . .*

Now the man came out of the barn carrying a large can by its handle.

"Darby and Joan," said Robert, busily sketching.

"Too young. Dick and Jane."

"A toddler or two and the cast is complete."

Nicole sighed. "What a great place to bring up kids. Oh, Robert, how I envy them that house. I can almost picture the rooms, the antiques I'd fill them with."

"And the toddlers?"

"Why not?" Robert had always sidetracked the issue of starting a family. The city was no place to raise children. Whereas here . . .

The man stood watching as the woman picked up the basket and returned to the house. He must have said something to her, for she paused at the door, looked across at him, and appeared to shake her head before vanishing into the house. The cat curled up on the doorstep. The sun rose higher in the cloudless sky. The day grew warmer.

Nicole stood up and peered over Robert's shoulder. The picture was already taking shape in an underpainting of the gray tones.

Down below, the man stripped off his shirt and flung it down, sunlight gleaming on his broad shoulders and deep chest.

"Try doing that in the city," said Nicole. "You'd be arrested for indecent exposure."

"Not really," he laughed. "But that's what I mean. These people still enjoy a kind of primitive freedom we're denied. Look at that guy. Adam before the Fall. I'd like to paint him."

"He wouldn't let you. He'd be too shy."

At that point something happened to shock them out of their enchantment with this tapestry of pastoral beauty. The man strode across the yard to the house, picked up the cat by the scruff of its neck, walked slowly to the old stone well, lifted his arm, and dropped the cat into the well. Nicole uttered a gasp of disbelief.

"Good God," said Robert. "Did he really do that?"

"I can't believe it. How horrible."

"Maybe the well's filled in. Maybe it's a game they play and the cat'll come crawling out."

They watched, neither believing it would happen. The man returned to the barn and soon reappeared holding some unidentifiable object which he carried across the yard and placed close against the foundation of the white-painted annex.

"What the *hell* is he doing now?" asked Robert.

Morning light still bathed the house, yet Nicole felt a creeping uneasiness, as if the sun had turned its face away, leaving the scene as colorless as Robert's canvas.

Robert had moved away from the easel and now crouched beside Nicole behind the screen of hawthorn.

Presently the man, moving with an air of calm deliberation, picked up the can, returned to the annex, and began pouring something along the foundation all the way to the corner, where he vanished from sight for a few minutes before reappearing without the can.

"Somehow I don't think he was watering the flowers," said Robert.

"There are no flowers."

The man crossed to a wooden bench built to encircle the trunk of the tallest cedar tree, where he sat down, hunched forward with his hands resting on his knees, remaining there motionless, as unmoving as Robert and Nicole high on the slope above him. Presently—perhaps ten minutes had passed—they saw the man lift his head as the door of the house opened and the woman came out, now wearing a dress, pale blue in the sunlight. She was carrying a suitcase, obviously heavy from the way her arm and shoulder sagged. She set it down, stood erect, and appeared to be staring across the yard at the man on the bench. Then she picked up the suitcase and started walking slowly away down the drive leading from the house to the dirt road just visible through the trees.

At that point the man leaped up and swiftly followed her, reaching out and seizing her by the arm. She dropped the suitcase and tore free. They faced each other, seemingly engaged in a heated dispute. Then once more, with what looked like a violent gesture of rejection or despair, the woman picked up the bag and got as far as the mailbox at the foot of the drive before the man came running after her, this time seizing her from behind in a tight embrace, then all but dragging her back up the drive. At one point she broke free and started running, only to be dragged back, this time all the way into the house.

Nicole grabbed Robert's arm, turning her face away from the scene below. "Darling, I don't want to watch anymore. I don't want to stay here. I don't like it."

Robert didn't move or look at her, his face pale, his eyes fixed on the stone house. Nicole gave his arm a shake. "Robert, come away. This has nothing to do with us. We shouldn't even be watching."

Still he said nothing; she felt his body tense as the man came out of the house moments later, strode purposefully to the barn, and this time came back into view carrying a shotgun.

"Robert . . . please." Nicole's voice was a whisper of entreaty and dismay.

The man, holding the shotgun in the crook of his arm, moved back across the yard and entered the house. Seconds later the sound of a shot, surprisingly loud, seemed to echo and fade away. Robert sprang to his feet and stepped forward into the sun's glare. Just then, the man came through the door and moved to whatever he'd placed below the annex wall, dropped to his knees, and engaged in some action hidden from the watchers' view. Quickly thereafter he crossed to the well, picked up the coil of rope, and returned to the house.

Before Nicole could stop him, Robert started down the slope. She ran after him, seized him as violently as the man had seized the fleeing woman, and tugged frantically at his arm.

"Robert, no! Don't go down there. We mustn't."

"You stay here," he ordered, but she refused to release his arm.

"No! It's got nothing to do with us."

His eyes blazed at her with a look of angry rebuttal. "That's just what you said the night we heard the screams in the alley. The very words."

With that he broke free and moved swiftly down the slope, Nicole trailing behind him at a clumsy trot. Had the sun been less bright, they might have spotted it sooner; as it was, they were halfway down the slope before the flames, licking the lower boards of the annex, outshone the sun's brilliance.

"My God," cried Robert, "he rigged something to start a fire. He must be nuts."

They were both running now, their legs whipping through the tall grass and buttercups. Breathless at the foot of the slope, they both paused momentarily as Robert, looking around, spotted a tarpaulin covering a small tractor. He raced forward, snatched it up, and ran toward the house, proceeding to smother the flames by stamping on the tarpaulin.

Only when they were out did he move, panting and sweaty toward the fanlighted front door of the house. Again, Nicole tried to restrain him. "Don't, Robert, please. Don't go in there."

The door was ajar. Robert pushed it open just far enough to peer inside, and then more boldly thrust it wide open and stepped across the threshold. Nicole, trembling and uncertain, followed.

At first they saw nothing but a wide entrance hall with an oval braided rug on the highly polished floorboards, a pine settle, and a plain oak staircase. The stone walls of the house seemed to enclose and thicken the heavy silence that greeted them.

Robert moved to the door on the left and stopped abruptly, his hand gripping the frame. Looking past him, Nicole gasped as she spotted the dripping stains of blood on the white-painted wall.

"Jesus," Robert whispered hoarsely.

The woman's blood-soaked body lay at the base of the pine-paneled fireplace, the shotgun beside her. Robert shoved Nicole back into the hall before moving to kneel beside the body, feeling for signs of life. There were none.

In a pantry or storage room beyond the kitchen, they found the man's body hanging from what might have been a meat hook in the ceiling.

Nicole rushed outside to be sick, arms wrapped tightly around her chest as if to still the wild beating of her heart. Moments later Robert stumbled through the door and leaned heavily against the stone wall, feeling its warmth soak into his cold flesh.

"Go back up the hill," he said. "I'll see what name is on the mail-box."

Without a backward glance, Nicole trudged up the long grassy slope and waited, shivering, for Robert to join her.

Without speaking, he gathered up his equipment, folded his easel, and with Nicole beside him carrying the picnic basket, made his way back to the car.

At the farmhouse Robert called the sheriff's office, said only: "You'd better get out to the Dorset place. Something awful's happened," and quickly hung up. Then he kindled a fire in the stone fireplace, and when it was ablaze thrust the picture of the stone house into the flames.

That night Nicole woke from a restless sleep to find Robert standing at the window gazing out into the night. She rose and went to him, putting her arm around his naked waist.

"Try not to think about it," she pleaded. "There was nothing you could do."

"We knew something was happening down there. Something bad. When we saw the gun in his hands we could have shouted, waved, made him see us. We might have stopped it."

"We might have got ourselves killed."

"We'll never know what it was all about," he said. "We'll never know *why.*"

"She was leaving him, that much seems clear."

With a tremor in his voice, and as if he were trying to penetrate some mystery too deep for human understanding, he said, "God, it was so beautiful down there. So peaceful. So perfect."

"Come back to bed, darling. We want to get an early start in the morning."

Nicole tidied the house while Robert packed, and midmorning found them ready to leave.

We'll go back to the city, Nicole thought. We'll pick up where we left off. Our lives will be the same as before. Nothing will have changed.

Yet she knew in her heart this was not true, any more than was Robert's vision of the country and of life in the stone house. Perhaps it was the miles of silence that lengthened his unsmiling eyes or perhaps something more subtle and complex, as unfathomable as the mystery they were leaving behind, something, at any rate, created in Nicole's mind an unsettling awareness that with every mile they drove, Robert was somehow drifting further and further away from her, and that when they reached the city from which he'd so desperately wanted to escape, she would be arriving home with a stranger.